TEC

THE OTHER SIDE OF THE ISLAND

THE OTHER SIDE OF THE ISLAND

ALLEGRA GOODMAN

RAZORBILL

The Other Side of the Island
RAZORBILL
Published by the Penguin Group
Penguin Young Readers Group
345 Hudson Street, New York, New York 10014, U.S.A.
Penguin Group (USA) Inc., 375 Hudson Street, New York, New York 10014, U.S.A.
Penguin Group (Canada), 90 Eglinton Avenue East, Suite 700, Toronto, Ontario, Canada
M4P 2Y3 (a division of Pearson Penguin Canada Inc.)
Penguin Books Ltd, 80 Strand, London WC2R 0RL, England
Penguin Ireland, 25 St Stephen's Green, Dublin 2, Ireland
(a division of Penguin Books Ltd)
Penguin Group (Australia), 250 Camberwell Road, Camberwell, Victoria 3124, Australia
(a division of Pearson Australia Group Pty Ltd)
Penguin Books India Pvt Ltd, 11 Community Centre,
Panchsheel Park, New Delhi – 110 017, India
Penguin Group (NZ), 67 Apollo Drive, Rosedale, North Shore 0632, New Zealand
(a division of Pearson New Zealand Ltd.)
Penguin Books (South Africa) (Pty) Ltd, 24 Sturdee Avenue,
Rosebank, Johannesburg 2196, South Africa
Penguin Books Ltd, Registered Offices: 80 Strand, London WC2R 0RL, England

10 9 8 7 6 5 4 3 2 1
Copyright © 2008 Allegra Goodman
All rights reserved

Library of Congress Cataloging-in-Publication Data

Goodman, Allegra.
The other side of the island / by Allegra Goodman.
p. cm.
Summary: Born in the eighth year of Enclosure, ten-year-old Honor lives in
a highly regulated colony with her defiant parents, but when they have an
illegal second child and are taken away, it is up to Honor and her friend
Helix, another "Unpredictable," to uncover a terrible secret about their
Island and the Corporation that runs everything.
ISBN 978-1-59514-195-8
[1. Science fiction.] I. Title.
PZ7.G61353Ot 2008
[Fic]—dc22
2007050915

For my children:
Ezra, Gabriel, Elijah, and Miranda

PART ONE

ONE

ALL THIS HAPPENED MANY YEARS AGO, BEFORE THE STREETS were air-conditioned. Children played outside then, and in many places the sky was naturally blue. A girl moved to a town house in the Colonies on Island 365 in the Tranquil Sea.

The girl was ten years old, small for her age but strong. Her eyes were gray. Her hair was curly to begin with, and it curled up even more in the humid island air. She had been born after the Flood in the eighth glorious year of Enclosure, and like everyone born that year, her name began with the letter *H*. Her name was rare, and in later cycles it was discontinued, but at that time it was still on the lists. She was called Honor.

The town house stood almost at the barriers near the beach. There was a downstairs with a living room and a tiny kitchen, and upstairs, a bathroom and two bedrooms, one big and one small. If you stood at the window in the smaller front bedroom, the ocean was frighteningly close, but there were protective bars on the windows.

Honor's parents were young and clever, and they loved to laugh. Will and Pamela Greenspoon did not wear brown or tan like most people, but old-fashioned clothes in strange colors: peach and gray and even black. They were both engineers. They had nothing to put in their house because their trunks had not arrived yet from the North. Honor's parents had no coupon books for the Central Store, because they had not yet started their new jobs. They had never been to the Colonies, and they didn't know anyone on the island, but they told their daughter that was part of the adventure.

"That's what you said last time," Honor pointed out as she lay down to sleep on the bare floor with her father's raincoat balled up for a pillow.

"We won't move again for a while," said Pamela.

"How long is a while?" Honor asked.

"We'll see," said Will.

"A year?"

"We'll see."

"Three years?"

"It's late," Pamela cut in. "You need to get your sleep. You've got the school interview tomorrow."

Even though the Greenspoons had no furniture, they had taken Honor for testing at the famous Old Colony School.

The admissions tests for the Old Colony School took an entire day. There were tests in reading, copying, mathematics, science, and geography. If students did well enough on those tests, they were invited to interview. But interviews were not held at school. The interviewer came to the house to examine the whole family.

Before breakfast, Honor heard the knock on the door. Her parents were nervous because the house was so empty. They had borrowed folding chairs from the neighbors, but they worried that the interviewer would mark them down for lacking a proper couch.

Honor opened the door and saw a blue-eyed woman with soft curly hair under her sun hat. Her eyes were clear blue as marbles, her skin pale powdery white.

"Good morning. My name is Miss Blessing," said the woman.

"Please come in," said Pamela. "Come sit down."

"Would you like something to drink?" asked Will when they were all seated. "We have cold guava juice."

"No thank you," said Miss Blessing. She didn't look at Will and Pamela at all. She was looking straight at Honor. "Your test scores are excellent," she told Honor. "I have a few simple questions for you today."

Honor glanced at her father. He smiled at her encouragingly.

"Tell me the name of your old school," Miss Blessing said.

"I didn't go to school," Honor said.

"Why don't you tell me some of your favorite activities," Miss Blessing said in a friendly way. Honor didn't answer immediately, so Miss Blessing said, "Pottery, for example. Music, gardening, sewing . . ."

"Climbing trees," Honor said.

"Oh, you're interested in forests?" asked Miss Blessing, smiling. "Do you like to study trees?"

"No, I just like climbing them," Honor said. At that time she still remembered the great trees in the Northern Islands, the oaks and pines, the white birches, the carpet of pine needles underfoot. She remembered weeping willows. She remembered lying for hours in the branches of the willow trees.

"Do you love the earth?"

Honor nodded.

"Who leads us and guides us?"

"Earth Mother," Honor said.

"What are Her watchwords?"

"Peace, love, and joy."

"And who guards the earth?"

"The Corporation."

"Very good," said Miss Blessing. Honor was happy because she thought she was done. "Please recite the Corporate Creed for me."

"*Our Councilors who are seven,*" Honor began softly.

"A little louder," said Miss Blessing. "Please speak clearly."

"*Our Councilors who are seven. Corporation is your name. Your plan to come, Enclosure done—on earth as it is in heaven. Give us this day . . .*" She hesitated. Her family was not religious. She did not recite her prayers every night. "*Give us this day our daily bread. And correct all our trespasses. As you correct those who trespass against us.*" She was stuck again. Anxiously she looked at her mother.

"*And lead,*" Pamela whispered.

"And lead us not into Inaccuracy, but deliver us from lies." Honor recited fast, racing to get to the end. *"For ours is the planet and the power and the glory. Amen."*

Miss Blessing said nothing. Then she said to Honor's parents, "We ask our students to work without any hints or help."

"I think Honor is a little nervous," said Will.

"I'm afraid she is deficient," murmured Miss Blessing. "What was Earth Mother's Five-Year Plan?"

Honor hesitated. Miss Blessing was looking at the bare living room walls. "Where is your picture of Earth Mother?" she asked Will and Pamela.

"Our things haven't arrived yet," Will said.

"What did She achieve in the first Five-Year Plan?" Miss Blessing asked Honor.

Honor panicked. She tried to think, but she had no idea.

"She is enclosing the Earth," Miss Blessing said quietly. Her face was gentle and pitying, as if she were saddened that a big girl of ten did not know. "She is making the world Safe and Secure. Isn't that right?"

Honor nodded.

"May I speak with you alone for a moment?" Miss Blessing asked Honor's parents.

"Go ahead upstairs," Will told Honor.

Slowly, Honor climbed the staircase to the second floor. Then, when she was out of sight, she sat down on the top step to listen.

"She was terribly nervous," Pamela was saying.

"She is terribly deficient," said Miss Blessing. "She does not know what every little child should know. She would have catching up to do in her Earth and Weather classes."

"If you gave us a book, then perhaps we could tutor her at home," said Pamela.

"I think you've been tutoring her enough," said Miss Blessing. "I'm afraid that's the problem. Now, about her name."

"It's on the list," said Pamela.

"Yes, I've brought the list with me," said Miss Blessing.

Honor heard papers rustling as Miss Blessing took out the Approved List of Girls' Names.

"The trouble is—and I'm sure you realize this—the *H* in Honor is silent. If she walks around with a name like that, people will think she belongs in year O. She won't fit in with her peers."

"But here it is on the list," said Pamela. "Right between Honey and Hope."

"Hope is a lovely name," said Miss Blessing. Her voice was sweet and gentle. "Hope is simple. You can hear the *H*. Honey is also pretty."

"But her name is Honor," said Will.

"It sticks out," said Miss Blessing.

"We don't mind," said Pamela.

"Yes, I'm sure you don't," said Miss Blessing, "but you should consider your daughter's feelings—and her future."

"Are you suggesting she can't go to school because you don't like her name?" Honor's father asked.

"Will," said Pamela in a soft, warning voice.

"Her math score was perfect," said Miss Blessing. "Reading, excellent; copying, fair. I am sorry to say she failed geography. Her map skills are poor."

"It's our fault," Will said quickly.

"I realize that. It's clear to us, however, that with support, Honor could succeed. She is a bright child. We are selecting her for Old Colony."

"Thank you," said Pamela.

"She's a quick study," said Will.

Honor could hear the relief in her parents' voices.

"We think she will do very well with us," said Miss Blessing, "and in time, she'll change her name. We've seen it in the past."

Honor peeked over the banister. Her parents were not smiling.

"You'd force her?" Pamela asked.

"No, no, of course not," said Miss Blessing. "She'll decide on her own. One day, she'll become, for example, Henrietta."

"Why do you say that?" Will demanded.

"Because," said Miss Blessing, "we will educate her. We will train your daughter properly. She will know instinctively that her name isn't right. Our mission is overcoming difference, and a Colony education is comprehensive. We teach the whole child."

TWO

SCHOOL WAS FREE OF CHARGE, AS WERE LUNCHES, uniforms, and transportation. This was fortunate. While Honor's father had begun his new job, her mother had not. Honor's parents bought her a cot to sleep on, but they could not afford beds for themselves. Will and Pamela were tired and stiff from trying to sleep on the bare floor.

Will rubbed Pamela's shoulders as the family stood together at the bus stop on Honor's first day of school.

There were no other families at their stop, only a couple of workers in white jumpsuits collecting recycling bins. The workers looked strange, like grown-up living dolls. They all looked alike, with blank faces and bald heads. They didn't make a sound. "Who are they?" Honor asked.

"Orderlies," Honor's mother told her. "Don't stare. It's not polite."

"Where are the other kids?" Honor asked.

"The other children come from different neighborhoods," said Pamela.

"They'll be getting on later," said Will. "You'll be alone at first, because you're the first stop."

"Are you sure the bus will come here?" Honor asked. Their neighborhood was desolate. Do Not Enter signs and barbed-wire fences marked the barriers near the shore, where ancient hotels stood submerged in water. A stench of rotting kelp and mildew filled the air. The only clean new thing in the neighborhood was the Corporation watchtower, which stood tall and slender on stilts. Honor could just make out a man with binoculars inside.

"Look," said Honor.

"Never point at a Watcher."

Honor was startled by the fear in her mother's voice. She had never lived in a city and had never seen a Watcher before. "He could probably see the bus from up there," she ventured.

"He sees everything," her mother said, as she touched up Honor's sunscreen.

Honor looked down at her new sandals and book bag. These were part of her uniform, as were her broad-brimmed sun hat, her khaki skirt, and her white shirt with the letter *H* embroidered in green on the pocket. She felt strange in the uniform.

"Don't worry," Pamela said, but her voice trembled.

"There's the bus," said her father.

A blue school bus pulled up to the curb. The doors opened with a whoosh of cool air.

Honor looked up at the open doors, and for a moment she

was overcome with dread. She felt suddenly that once she got on the bus she would be leaving her parents for good.

"We'll be waiting for you right here at the end of the day," Will said.

"What if I don't know the answers?"

"Let's go," ordered the bus driver.

Honor ducked her head down and ran up the stairs.

"If you don't know, don't say," said Will.

"Be careful, sweetie," Pamela called after her.

Honor sank down into a seat and clutched her book bag to her chest.

"Buckle up," said the driver.

As the bus lurched to the next stop and then the next, students of all ages crowded on. The big kids from years *F* or *E* boarded cheerfully, but some of the little children were crying. The embroidered letters on their shirts were *N* and *M* and *L* and even *O*. The youngest were just three years old and didn't want to leave their parents. Some even tried to run back down the aisle of the bus and escape, but the bus driver was a strong, burly man, and he scooped up the littlest children and strapped them in with special locking seat belts. The windows were unbreakable as well. Children could pound with their fists, but they soon discovered that the glass was stronger than they were. Then all the little ones could do was scream. The bus driver didn't mind. He wore earplugs.

Honor covered her ears and gazed out the window as the bus drove up a steep road through great iron gates wrought in the shape of long trumpet flowers. She began to see a whole fleet of buses entering terraced school grounds. A great field spread before them, framed by whitewashed buildings, ocean view, and sky. Teachers stood on the grass holding white pennants painted with class letters.

"Everybody off," announced the driver. He marched down the aisle unsnapping the seat belts of the littlest children. "Go find your flag. No pushing."

The sun was hot now. Honor was sweating as she made her way to the middle of the field, where the other ten-year-olds were gathered around a flag painted with the letter *H*.

"Boys on this side, girls on that," said the teacher's kindly voice. "Are you the new girl? Over here, dear, for the head count. Twelve?" the teacher asked another adult.

"Yes, twelve," the other teacher replied.

"Line up nicely, boys and girls." The two teachers spent some time straightening the lines and straightening the students as well, adjusting hats and patting down shirt collars.

"Off we go inside," said the teacher at the head of Honor's line. "Follow me."

After the sweltering sunshine on the field, the classroom was deliciously cool. The room was large. Twelve desks stood ready, with a microscope on each. There were twelve easels and twelve armchairs in a circle for reading time. Twelve standing looms and twelve glossy black upright pianos. On one wall, gardening tools hung from hooks. A giant saltwater aquarium sparkled with tropical fish, lacy coral, sea anemones, and even a class octopus called Octavio. At the front of the classroom above the blackboard hung a framed portrait of Earth Mother. Honor could not remember ever seeing such a big picture of

Earth Mother. Her eyes were blue and twinkling, her hair silver, tucked up in a bun. She wore a red cardigan sweater and reading glasses on a chain around her neck.

At the blackboard, the teacher wrote, *Mrs. Whyte.* She was an elegant-looking woman with long cool fingers and white hair to match her name. She took attendance.

"Hagar," Mrs. Whyte called out. "Harriet, and—why, yes, here's another Harriet. You shall be Harriet K. and Harriet V. Haven . . . Hedwig . . . Helena . . . Hester . . . Hilary . . . Hildegard . . . Hiroko . . ." She paused for a moment and stared at the attendance sheet with a puzzled look on her face. "Honor," she said at last, and then went on. "Hortense."

Because Honor had never been to school before, she watched the other girls to learn what to do. Everyone in the classroom had a job, and no one else could do that job. The book monitor distributed books for reading. The snack monitor wheeled in a cart with cups of juice and plates of cheese and crackers and lychees. The fish monitor fed the fish. There were many rules at school and many classes: painting, math, copying, science, gymnastics, music, weaving, and, of course, geography, Earth and Weather.

For geography, Mrs. Whyte rolled down a great map over the blackboard. This was a map of the world. The map was entirely blue, except for the tiny dots of green representing the world's islands. "Who can find the Colonies on the map?" asked Mrs. Whyte, offering her pointer to any student who could find the islands in the deep blue Tranquil Sea. "Who can find our island on the map?"

The girls strained their eyes, but there were so many islands it was hard to find their own. Mrs. Whyte had to point to the correct island herself. "And what sort of island is this?" Mrs. Whyte asked.

"Big," suggested Hagar.

"It is relatively big," said Mrs. Whyte. "But what sort of island is this?"

"Tropical," said Harriet K.

Mrs. Whyte nodded.

"Important," said Hortense.

Mrs. Whyte looked pleased. "Yes, Hortense, this is an important island for several reasons. But that's not the answer I was looking for. This is a volcanic island. We are living on the tip of a great volcano that rises from the ocean. And you will all enjoy learning about volcanoes this year. Who can find the Northern Islands?"

"Me!" Honor called out, but Mrs. Whyte called on Hester because she was raising her hand.

"Who can find the Polar Seas?" asked Mrs. Whyte. "And who would like to tell us what they were like before Enclosure?"

"They were cold," said Hiroko, standing at the map and pointing to the oceans near the North and South poles.

"Stormy," said Hilary.

"The blizzards could kill you," added Harriet K.

"Very good," said Mrs. Whyte. "Who will show us what they are like now?"

Honor's hand shot up, and this time Mrs. Whyte called on her. Honor got to stand on a special footstool and roll down a transparency over the map of the world. The transparency was tinted over both Polar Seas and the Northern Islands as well, so that those parts of the earth now looked rosy pink and warm.

"Honor," said Mrs. Whyte, "you come from the North. What's the North like now? Are there polar bears up there in the Northern Islands?"

Some of the girls giggled.

"I saw one," Honor said from her place up on the stepladder. The giggling stopped. Mrs. Whyte looked so severe that Honor's heart began pounding.

"We do not lie in this classroom," said Mrs. Whyte. "We do not exaggerate or tell untruths, *ever.*"

Honor flinched.

"Do you know what happens to children who lie?"

"I didn't lie . . . I really . . . It was swimming," Honor spluttered. She remembered her mother calling after her, *Be careful, sweetie!* "I think it was another kind of bear."

Mrs. Whyte's face softened. She helped Honor off the ladder. "Oh, now I see what you meant," she said kindly. "That's absolutely right." And as Honor took her seat, Mrs. Whyte told the children, "The Polar Seas and Northern Islands are Enclosed. What does that mean?"

"They're Safe," said Hiroko.

"Secure," said Hildegard.

"They have a ceiling," said Hortense, tossing her blond hair with some importance.

"Yes, they are ceiled," said Mrs. Whyte, smiling, "and because of that, they are enjoying what we call . . ."

"New Weather," chimed the girls.

"Are the Northern Islands cold?"

Sometimes, thought Honor.

"No," answered the girls.

"Are the Northern Islands hot?"

Sometimes, thought Honor.

"No."

"What is the New Weather there?"

"Sunny!" said Hilary.

"Gorgeous!" said Hedwig.

"Perfect!" said Hortense.

"Good," said Mrs. Whyte.

Honor shook her head. She wanted to say, "No, the North isn't perfect. Some days are sunny and some days are cold. The Northern Islands are muddy and icy. Sometimes you can see to the next island and sometimes there are only marshes as far as the eye can see." She wanted to ask the other girls, "How can you know a place you haven't been?" but she kept quiet until the lesson was over and Mrs. Whyte told the girls to line up for target practice. It was time for archery.

At hour five, when school ended, Honor was exhausted. Slowly, she gathered her books and made her way to the door. Something caught her eye just as she was about to leave. Something or someone was watching her. She pivoted slowly, searching the room. The other girls were hurrying out the door. None of them so much as glanced in her direction, and yet, she felt watched. She searched again. Then she saw that the octopus was staring at her. He was bunched up against the glass of the saltwater tank, and he was watching her with one great bulbous eye.

She walked to the aquarium. Octavio was looking deeply at her. She reached out to touch the glass.

"Stop! You'll be late," called Mrs. Whyte. "Hurry to the door. Run."

Honor raced outside. By the time she reached her bus, she was out of breath. She squeezed into the last seat and sank down with her head against the window. What happened if you missed the bus? She didn't want to know. The bus rumbled down the hill and Honor closed her eyes. Maps and weather filled her mind, uniforms and rules and Mrs. Whyte and the dark-eyed octopus.

One by one, the other children got off the bus. Round and round the island the blue school bus drove. Honor drifted off to sleep.

"Last stop. Your parents are waiting." The bus driver shook Honor roughly by the shoulder, and she stumbled down the stairs into the arms of Pamela and Will.

"How was it?"

Honor shrugged.

"Did you make any new friends?"

"No."

"What did you learn on your first day?"

"Nothing."

"Oh, I can't believe that," Will said stoutly as they walked home. The air reeked with rotting mangoes and mushy bread-fruit. Only a few people lived in bungalows along the way to the Greenspoons' development. Chain-link fences and ferocious lunging dogs defended those houses that were inhabited. A brown rat darted into the deserted street. And then, in an instant, the silent flash of a taser stunned the animal. Honor shrank back close to her parents.

"Don't worry," said Pamela, "the Watcher got him."

"Our Corporation at work," said Will.

Honor shuddered. The rat wasn't dead yet but crazed, limping off into the open mouth of a compost bin by the side of the road. Any creature hit by a taser turned instantly to find a compost bin. That way no festering bodies littered the road.

"Do we have to be the last stop?" Honor asked.

"Yes, we have to be the last stop." Pamela sighed.

Honor looked up at her mother. In all the times they'd moved, she had never heard her sigh like that before. It was hour six by the time the family arrived home. The sky was the color of orange sherbet.

"Look at the clouds." Honor was puzzled. The clouds were not white, as they had been back home. They were tinted the same color as the sky. "Why are the clouds orange too?"

"Shh," said Pamela as Will unlocked the front door.

Will tensed as he raised his hand to turn on the lights. A hulking form stood before them in the living room and another in the hall. But with a flick of the switch, fear turned to joy. The Greenspoons saw that the hulks were their own belongings. Their trunks had finally arrived from the North.

THREE

THERE WERE THREE OLD STEAMER TRUNKS STANDING IN THE house, and each had been unlocked and unpacked by the neighborhood Postal Officer. Clothes and bedding were piled neatly on the floor.

"My bear," said Honor, scooping up her old worn teddy.

"My coffeepot!" her mother cried, and rushed with it to the galley kitchen.

"Oh, he's torn," Honor said. Her bear was badly injured, lumpy from lost stuffing.

"He's been searched," her father murmured, examining the ripped seam in the bear's back. "Look at this, Pamela."

"What were they searching for?" asked Honor.

But her parents didn't answer.

There were sheets and blankets, pillows, clothes, dishes for the kitchen, pots and pans. There were no electronics, no computers, televisions, or books allowed in private homes, because of Safety Measures. Children could read and study books from school, and when they were old enough, they could borrow books from the school library, but there were no new books printed. There were no authors, except for Earth Mother herself. She wrote all the history books and songs and sayings. She and her Corporation Councilors wrote the laws and established Safety Stations on each block, with call buttons for emergencies. At that time in the Colonies there were no telephones in houses. This was part of building a Safe and Secure community.

Unpacking further, Will found that an old-fashioned windup alarm clock had been disassembled by the Postal Service, but it wasn't broken too badly. There had been some family treasures: a pair of silver candlesticks and a fine silver goblet wrapped in old scratchy wool blankets. These had been taken, and only the blankets, one blue mohair and the other black and green plaid, remained.

Will and Pamela dragged two of the trunks upstairs, one for each bedroom. Standing up, the trunks were designed to serve as armoires on long ocean voyages. They were fitted out with cedar drawers on the bottom and hangers on top. One of the trunks even had its original hangers.

Will turned the third trunk on its side and made a table for the living room. As the family ate a dinner of baked beans and sausages, Honor ran her hands over the brass-studded surface of that trunk and read the strange names stuck onto it: Istanbul, Cordova. Will had found the trunks in the Port of the North, packed, and mailed the family's possessions in them.

"It's a mother of a mother, or the mother of a father," said Will.

> *Over the river and through the wood*
> *Oh, how the wind does blow!*
> *It stings the toes*
> *And bites the nose*
> *As over the . . .*

"Shh! Listen." Pamela heard the sharp rapping.

Will threw the blanket off and hurried to the door. "Who is it?"

"Neighborhood Watch."

Will opened the door and they saw a tall white-haired man in a bathrobe and slippers.

"Michael Pratt," the watchman said. "Your neighbor right next door. Just wanted to make sure everything was all right." He held an official, government-strength flashlight and sent the beam dancing into every corner. Honor cried out in pain when the light shone in her eyes.

"Everything is absolutely fine," said Pamela.

"I thought I heard singing," said Pratt.

"Oh, that," said Will. "We were singing lullabies to our daughter."

Pratt's eyes narrowed as he looked at Honor. She could see him thinking—*She's too old for lullabies*. "It's a school night," he said. "Don't you know it's past hour nine?"

"Clock's broken," said Pamela, holding up the disassembled alarm clock.

"That's the Postal Service these days," Pratt said in a friendlier voice. "I've sent in a couple of complaints myself."

"Really? How would we go about that?" Will asked. "We've got some—"

But Pratt cut him off. "You can go ahead and contact the Postal Service in the morning. For now, let's settle down and get some sleep."

Pratt shut the door, and in the darkness and the heat, the ocean seemed to surge louder and louder. Honor trudged upstairs to bed. Her mother followed her.

"Do you want your bear?"

"Not really," Honor said.

Pamela propped the torn bear next to Honor on the floor.

"We never had a Neighborhood Watch before," said Honor.

"We didn't live in a neighborhood," Pamela reminded her.

"Did I have a grandmother?"

Pamela looked puzzled for a moment. "Yes, I think so," she said.

"Was she your mother?"

"She must have been," said Pamela.

"What was her name?"

Pamela searched her memory. She closed her eyes to think, but at last she shook her head. "I wish I could remember," she told Honor.

"Why did you forget?"

"Everyone does," Pamela said sadly. "It's the water we drink, the food we eat."

"What do you mean?"

"It's late," said Pamela, "and you have to wake up for school tomorrow."

"Couldn't we go back to the—"

"No," said Pamela.

Honor did not think she could sleep with the Tranquil Sea raging right outside the window, but she was so tired her eyes closed anyway. Within five minutes she was dreaming.

She dreamed she was with her parents in the North. They were dragging their boat onto a beach covered with little pebbles. The water was clear and cold. Honor saw something move. "What's that animal?" she asked.

"A polar bear," her father murmured.

"No, it can't be," said her mother, terrified, disbelieving. "There are no polar bears anymore."

"Don't move." Honor's father held her tight as the great bear approached. His fur looked like it had once been white but now had yellowed. His body was gaunt, and he moved up on them fast.

Honor's father threw a rock, and then another. He hit the bear with a stone. The animal was weak. Frightened, it limped toward the water.

"Go on," said Honor's father. "I don't want to hurt you."

But he'd wounded the bear. "Oh no!" Honor cried. "His stuffing is coming out!"

Sure enough, the great animal's fur was torn, and gobs of white fluff trailed behind him in the water.

FOUR

AS THE DAYS GREW HOTTER, HONOR AND HER PARENTS SLEPT downstairs, because the upstairs bedrooms felt like ovens. A cooling unit cost four hundred points at the Central Store, and the Greenspoons could not afford one. Will had a job now in the City, but Pamela still had not been chosen for employment.

Every morning Honor woke up drenched with sweat. Even the cold water in the bath was warm. Honor stopped dragging her feet on the way to the bus stop. She stepped up into the cool bus, eager to escape the stifling salty air.

School took all of Honor's time. Her parents were pleased that she was learning so much. She was studying geometry and graphing and statistics. She was weaving a long narrow cloth of deepest purple and lavender. She observed tiny organisms under a microscope and drew their pictures in her lab book. In archery she learned to shoot and string her bow. Her map skills were improving, although the maps she copied looked nothing like the world she used to know.

School maps showed the North shaded deep pink by Enclosure. In geography class, the Northern Islands were entirely Safe and Secure, with perfect New Weather. Mrs. Whyte showed the class pictures of emerald trees and lawns and cloudless skies. She showed films of flowers blossoming again and again in perfect sunlight.

At first Honor had trouble staying quiet when the class learned about the North, but as time went on, Honor's memories of rain and cold and sleet began to fade. The waterways and the great pine trees slipped from her mind. Her activities at school pushed the old days from her memory, and the films she saw of the North began to replace the pictures in her mind. Only in dreams, fragments of her old home came back to her. In her dreams the trees in the North were gold, the leaves tinged copper, burnt orange, scarlet.

One day Mrs. Whyte said, "Honor, you lived in the North; tell us about the leaves there."

Then Honor thought Mrs. Whyte was asking her to tell the class about how leaves change color. "Every year they turn red, yellow, brown," Honor told the class.

Mrs. Whyte shook her head and said, "Not anymore. Not anymore. Not by any means. Do trees change color, class?"

"No," the class chorused. Some of the girls were covering their mouths with their hands. They were laughing at Honor for saying otherwise.

"But you've never even been to the Northern Islands,"

sputtered Honor. "How do you know the trees are always green?"

"How do you know, class?" asked Mrs. Whyte.

For a long moment no one spoke. The girls seemed almost puzzled.

Then Hildegard raised her hand and held up the climatology textbook. "It says in the book: trees in the Northern Islands are green all year round."

Now Mrs. Whyte smiled. She was not angry anymore. All the sunshine seemed to return to the room. "That is exactly right," she said. "We know what trees look like in the North from our book. This is known as doing the reading," she told Honor. "Those who do the reading need not exaggerate."

"But I did see the—" Honor began.

"Search your memory," said Mrs. Whyte.

How strange. As soon as Mrs. Whyte told Honor to search her memory, Honor's memory failed her. There stood Mrs. Whyte, absolutely certain in front of her, and there sat the other girls, giggling and scoffing behind her. She could no longer remember seeing colorful leaves with her own eyes. She could only remember dreaming them.

"Do you remember when the leaves changed?" Honor asked her parents that night as she lay down to sleep.

"I think so," said her mother.

"Do you remember the colors?"

"I remember the leaves fell from the trees," said her father.

"But before they fell. Didn't they turn colors?"

Her parents tried to remember, but they could not.

"They turned brown and died," her father said. "I remember that."

All three of them had trouble remembering the old life in the North. It was like forgetting a language they had once known. A few words remained, but they lost more and more each day.

History lessons were difficult. Honor had to memorize the events of the Peaceful Revolution from her textbook.

"After the Flood, disease, warfare, and famine decimated the human population. Then Earth Mother, the Provider, rose up. She was a simple schoolteacher, a cookie baker. She loved flowers and children and sunshine and song. She believed in Safety First. Her Peaceful Revolution was to protect and defend the islands that remained. Her program: to build seawalls and Safe cities, to Enclose the Polar Seas and establish New Weather in the North with regulated temperatures all year round. The First Glorious Year of Enclosure marked the securing of the Arctic Circle, the establishment of the new calendar, the new clock . . ." Honor recited the words to herself in the bathtub as she soaked in tepid water. *"A new compact of—"*

"Are you all right in there?" asked Pamela outside the door.

"Oh, you made me lose my place." Honor sat up with a splash.

"I'm sorry, what did you say?"

Honor pulled the plug. She dried herself with a scratchy white towel and changed into her nightgown.

"I have to recite in history tomorrow," she told her mother when she opened the door. "I need to practice."

"It's late," said Pamela. "You need to go to bed."

"Please. I need to get this right," Honor begged, "or I'll miss recess again."

"Is that what they do? They punish you for forgetting your recitation?" Pamela looked shocked.

"They don't call it punishment; they call it thinking time," said Honor.

"What are you supposed to think?" asked Will, who was pinning up laundry to dry on a rack in the bedroom.

"You're supposed to think about correcting your Inaccuracies," said Honor. "Obviously."

"Don't take that tone of voice with me," said Will.

Honor stayed up late and practiced her recitation. She sat up in her nightgown in the living room and she stared at the ceiling lamp above her head as she recited, *"A new compact of nations, a new generation without . . ."*

In the glass globe of the ceiling lamp, she saw a dead black spider with stiff, folded legs. Next to it, a living spider tried to climb up inside the slippery globe to escape. The spider inched upward only to fall back again, shrinking from the scorching heat of the lightbulb. Again and again, the spider tried to climb, but each time, he failed. Honor wanted to look away, but she could not. She needed to keep practicing, but she couldn't think about the recitation with that spider struggling above her head.

"Could you get him out? Could you unscrew the globe?" she begged her father.

He stood on a chair and he could reach, but the globe was hot and screwed in tight. "I'm afraid I'll break the glass if I try to force it loose," Will said.

"He's going to die in there," said Honor.

"Maybe if we turn off the light, he'll have a better chance," said Pamela.

"That's right. He'll make his escape in the dark," Will said.

"No, he won't. You're just saying that," said Honor. "You just want me to go to bed."

In the morning, Honor dressed for school and trudged downstairs, imagining the humiliation to come.

"It's not so bad," said Pamela encouragingly. "Just remember: 'a new compact of nations, a generation without fear, a world of Safety and Order.'"

"Why don't you recite it yourself, then?" Honor grumbled. She hated the hot morning. She hated the soggy cereal in her bowl. She tried to keep her head down and avoid looking at the light fixture. She didn't want to know, and yet she had to see.

Just as she left the house, she looked. She saw that she and her father had both guessed wrong. The spider wasn't dead, and he had not escaped either. He was still struggling against the glass.

All day Honor sat at her desk and wished she were home. Not home in the hot town house, home in the North, in the strange wild places. Home where her parents paddled boats through marshy fields and the ruins of old buildings. Home where ducks nested in drowned fairgrounds. In her homesickness a memory returned to her. She was sitting in a boat and trailing her hand in the water. Beneath the surface she saw something glint and shine. She saw the head of a horse adorned with gold and jewels.

"This was called a carousel," Will told Honor.

"Look at the mirrors," said Pamela, pointing at the spotted silver gleaming underwater.

"Children rode on these painted animals. See the lion? And the white swan? I'm not sure what this one is called. What's this orange one?" Will asked Pamela.

Honor reached through the water to caress the mysterious painted creature with black and orange stripes. Water rippled over his long, sinewy body. She tried to touch his sparkling eye.

Honor rarely dreamed now of the cool mornings in the North and scarlet trees. She could no longer picture the wild sky with its Unpredictable colors, changeable and always new. The sky she saw now was only one color at a time, and those colors changed each hour, according to the clock. In the City, a golden yellow sky was pure yellow without any other hue mixed in. When the sky was blue, it was Sky Blue, exactly like the crayon in the box.

As the clock on the wall ticked away, Honor sensed her classmates waiting too. They loved to hear Honor lose her place in recitations. The other girls lived on high ground in the City, in tall apartment buildings waves could never touch. They lived in villas in the mountains with flowering gardens and turquoise sprinkler pools. Honor saw these places as she rode the bus. The other girls visited each other after school, but they would never visit her. "Did you know?" they whispered to one another. "She lives by the shore." The girls were always polite to her in class when Mrs. Whyte was looking, because politeness was the rule, but they taunted Honor the minute the teacher's back was turned.

"Shorebird, shorebird," they chanted softly.

The moment came. The whole class waited as Honor stood trembling by the board.

"Take your time," said Mrs. Whyte.

"After the Flood, disease, warfare, and famine . . ."

"Use your whole voice," said Mrs. Whyte.

". . . decimated the human population. Then Earth Mother, the Provider, rose up. She was a simple schoolteacher, a cookie baker. She loved flowers and children and sunshine and song. She believed in . . ."

Honor looked out at her classmates in their identical school uniforms. Everyone sat perfectly, heads up, backs straight. Everyone held still, except that in the second row, Hester was slowly, slowly crossing her eyes. Honor looked away quickly, but she'd lost her place. *"She believed in . . ."* All she could think was that Hester's dark eyes were drawing closer and closer together.

"Believed in what?" Mrs. Whyte asked.

Honor had no idea.

"Search your memory," said Mrs. Whyte.

Honor hung her head. When she looked up, Hester was smiling at her again. Her eyes were in the right places.

"Honor," said Mrs. Whyte. "Once again, you are unprepared."

"But I—"

"Are you contradicting me?" asked Mrs. Whyte.

"No," said Honor.

"You need a simpler text," said Mrs. Whyte. "Can you read this?" She handed Honor a card with just a few lines printed on it. "Can you remember this?"

Honor nodded.

"Recite it with your whole voice."

No, Honor thought when she saw the nursery rhyme. *Please don't make me.*

"Let's hear it," snapped Mrs. Whyte.

"Ladybug, ladybug, fly away home," Honor recited. *"The earth is on fire. Your children will burn."*

"And the next one." Mrs. Whyte handed Honor another card.

Honor took a breath. *"Atmosphere is falling down, falling down, falling down . . ."*

"I believe this is a song," Mrs. Whyte reminded her.

"Atmosphere is falling down. My fair lady," Honor sang haltingly.

Then her classmates could not cover their giggles any longer. Their laughter rang through the classroom.

"Take the sky and close it up, close it up, close it up. Take the sky and close it up. My fair lady," sang Honor. The other girls put their heads down on their desks and laughed until they cried.

Mrs. Whyte let them laugh. She did not say a word, but let the laughter come until Honor's cheeks burned.

• • •

At recess Honor wandered alone. The whole Lower School had recess together on the Lower Playground while the teachers sat and talked at picnic tables in the shade. Honor's classmates gossiped, whispering to each other as they walked in pairs. She stayed as far away from them as possible.

She stood by the playground fence and stared at the orderlies pruning bushes on the other side. The orderlies wore white jumpsuits and hats on their bald heads. They looked neither happy nor sad, because they had no eyebrows.

"Hello," she said through the fence. The orderlies didn't even glance at her.

"My name is Honor," she said, and then asked the nearer orderly, "What's your name?"

Out of nowhere, Mrs. Whyte was upon her, taking her by the hand and hurrying her away. "Too close. Too close!"

"Why?" Honor asked.

Mrs. Whyte was fuming, muttering, "Ten years old and speaking to the . . . Haven't your parents told you never to talk to orderlies?"

Honor shook her head. "We didn't have orderlies where we lived."

"It's as if you've been raised by wolves," exclaimed Mrs. Whyte.

"I just wanted to know their names," said Honor.

Mrs. Whyte turned on her. "They don't have names. Run along. Find an activity."

Honor stood at the edge of the field and watched the boys running and kicking an orange ball. Her parents had never told her to stay away from orderlies, only not to stare.

She wandered over to a dusty place under the trees. Two girls swung a rope and the rest took turns jumping in. The first chanted as she jumped:

"A my name is Alice, and I am an engineer. My husband's name is Abner, and we bring back aluminum."

Then she jumped out and the next girl jumped in, chanting:

"B my name is Brodie, and I am an engineer. My husband's name is Berthold, and we bring back beryllium."

They kept going as far as they could through the alphabet. Honor didn't ask to play. If you forgot an element, the game had to start all over again and the girls got annoyed.

She walked to the empty sandbox. The girls never went there. They were all afraid of sand because they thought it came from the shore. Honor had seen her classmates shudder as they walked past, especially if some sand had drifted onto the grass. "Ooh, don't go near the sand. It's filthy! It's got bugs! It's got fleas! You'll get sand in your pants!"

Honor sat on the wooden edge of the sandbox. She began to trail her fingers in the smooth white sand. She scooped the sand up in her hands and let it fall away again.

"There's no bottom," said a boy standing at the edge. It was Helix Thompson, a kid with long blond hair that always fell in his eyes. His eyes were either dark brown or black. His hair was always falling over his face, so it was hard to tell. Helix stepped into the sandbox. He dangled a magnet from a string over the surface of the sand. "This is a metal detector," Helix said.

"What are you detecting?" Honor asked wearily.

"Anything with iron. Screws, nails, ancient tools," said Helix. "I scan the surface with my magnet. Then I sift the sand through my fingers."

"Let me see."

They bent over the magnet together. "If you had a magnet like this, you could make a metal detector," Helix said.

"How many points are they?" Honor asked.

"I don't know. Why? Are you poor?" Helix asked with sudden interest.

Honor hesitated. Then she said, "Yes, I'm poor and I live by the shore."

"Are you a refugee?" asked Helix.

Honor wasn't sure what a refugee was, but she was too proud to let on. "Maybe," she said. "I hate school," she whispered.

"You don't have to be a refugee to hate school," said Helix.

The next day at recess Helix was looking for Honor. He dug into his pocket and took out a big magnet tied to a piece of string. "This one's for you," he said. Together they walked across the playground, trying to detect scrap metal. Honor found a rusty nail.

"Beginner's luck," said Helix, and they kept walking.

"Your father works for my father," Helix said. "They work in the same building."

"The Central Computer Building?"

Helix nodded. "What island are you from?"

"I don't think it had a number."

"You came from a numberless island?" Helix was fascinated.

Honor nodded. "In the North."

"But nobody can live on a numberless island. You were evacuated, weren't you?"

"Yes," said Honor.

"What was it like? How did they find you? Did Retrievers come for you?"

Honor didn't answer.

"Why were your parents sent here?"

"The same reason everyone else was," snapped Honor. The Colonies were the only islands with official numbers. They were the only islands where the Corporation permitted people to live.

"But why to this island?"

"For work," Honor said.

Helix looked at her skeptically. They were standing under a tree, but even in the shade the sun beat down on their shoulders. Their hair was wet with sweat under their sun hats. "If they were sent for work," Helix said, "then why hasn't your mother been chosen for employment?"

"When are you going to get a job?" Honor asked her mother that night. She was sitting on the kitchen counter, and her parents were cooking chicken and rice in a pot.

Pamela didn't answer.

"Everyone else has a job," said Honor.

Pamela looked at Will. Then she said, "Sometimes the Corporation has too many engineers in one place."

"They wouldn't send you here if there were too many engineers on the island already," Honor pointed out. "Don't you want to find work?"

"Of course I do," Pamela said.

"If you get a job, we could move. We could afford to live on higher ground."

"Yes, I realize that," said Pamela. "I want a job very much. I have gone to the City every day and applied at every office."

"Then why won't they give you one?"

"Well, in my case," Pamela said, "it's because we're going to have a baby."

Honor stared at her parents in horror.

"You're going to have a brother or a sister," said Will. Honor gasped. Brother and sister were swear words.

"We're having the baby in month seven," said Pamela.

"*How?*" Honor demanded. She was dumbfounded. A mother, a father, and a child made a family. Families came in threes. She had never heard of a family of four.

"The baby will be interesting," said her mother, "and it will grow and go to school like you."

"No one at school has babies at home," Honor said.

For just a second her father looked angry. "What do you care?"

"We aren't like other people," said her mother.

"Who are we like, then?" Honor asked.

Her parents laughed.

Then Honor ran out the back door to the rocky place where her father had planted bananas, and she crouched down under their broad green leaves and cried.

Her father came out after her, but she pushed him away. She kept crying until her mother bent down and whispered that she had to come inside. If she kept making so much noise, the Neighborhood Watch was sure to hear. She went inside and dried her tears. She sat silently at dinner.

"I'm sorry we laughed," her father said.

"A baby is wonderful," said Pamela. "You'll see."

"We'll find a better house. We aren't going to live here forever, you know," her father said.

Her parents didn't understand. After the baby, her family would never fit in. Other families were three, and hers would be four. Other families were the right number, and hers would be too big.

Honor decided she wouldn't tell anyone at school about the baby. Not even Helix. But he surprised her. They were standing on a picnic table and taking turns jumping off. They laid sticks down on the ground to measure how far they jumped.

Honor was poised to jump off the table when Helix said, "I heard my father say your mother is going to have a baby."

Honor had been so close to jumping that she lost her balance and fell in a heap in the dirt. "Now look what you made me do."

"Sorry," said Helix, and he climbed onto the table for his turn.

She scrambled back up. "No, it's still my turn. That doesn't count."

"Is it true?"

"Shh."

"It's a secret?"

"Don't tell anybody."

"Why?"

From her perch on the table Honor watched as Helena, Hortense, and Hiroko strolled past. "Because I have enough trouble already! I live by the shore. No one will come to my house."

"You can come to our house," said Helix.

Honor thought he was just feeling sorry for her. "I don't want to," she said.

"Yes, you do."

"No, I don't."

"We have a sprinkler pool."

"I'll ask my parents," Honor said.

Honor could keep the baby a secret at school, but at the town houses, everyone noticed that Pamela was getting bigger. Honor was glad that none of the neighbor children went to the Old Colony School.

Sometimes before dinner she played with the girls from the other town houses. They were children of the island's First People, girls with tanned skin and brown eyes. Their names were Felicia, Gina, and Hattie. Honor envied their smooth black hair.

There were basketball hoops in the paved lot in front of the town houses. Honor and the other girls played basketball, and a group of boys kicked a soccer ball. They played a wild game called Forecaster where one boy pelted the others with a ball. The game was Not Allowed, because the word Forecaster was Unacceptable. Whenever the boys got caught by the

Neighborhood Watch, they had to rake and sweep and break down boxes for recycling.

"Do you know what you are saying when you use the word *Forecaster?*" Mr. Pratt demanded once. "The Forecaster is a madman. He'd drown you as soon as look at you. He worships Old Weather. He thinks the world was better off before. And all he wants is for you to disobey. Take these brooms and sweep the steps." He gestured to the cement stairs from the empty lot to the town houses.

The boys hung their heads and accepted their punishment, but after some weeks had passed, they played Forecaster again. The girls could hear them using the F-word as they slammed the ball into each other. "I'm gonna forecast you!" At a safe distance, a cluster of little girls jumped rope. If the little girls found a bit of chalk, they'd draw hopscotch squares on the asphalt. They'd play clapping games, chanting:

> *Miss Mary Mack, Mack, Mack*
> *All dressed in black, black, black*
> *With silver buttons, buttons, buttons*
> *All down her back, back, back*
> *She asked her mother, mother, mother*
> *For fifty cents, cents, cents*
> *To see an elephant, elephant, elephant*
> *Jump the fence, fence, fence*
> *He jumped so high, high, high*
> *He reached the sky, sky, sky*
> *And didn't come back, back, back*
> *Till the Fourth of July, ly, ly.*

The girls had seen pictures of the elephants that had once roamed the wild grasslands, but no one knew exactly what July had been on the old calendar. The older girls argued about it. Hattie thought July had been a summer month at the end of the year, but Honor was sure July had been a winter month. Why else would Miss Mary be buttoned up in back? She must have been cold. Honor imagined cool breezes way up in the July sky. What a beautiful word. She wished the impossible: that her parents could name the baby July.

FIVE

THE AFTERNOON THEY WENT TO HELIX'S HOUSE, HONOR'S family took the bus high up the slope of the volcano. Helix had the loveliest house Honor had ever seen. The outside was white, and the roof was tiled with blue-green tiles like the scales of a dragon. When Helix's mother opened the door, Honor felt the breeze of cooling units. She could see right through the living room to a white courtyard blooming lavender and pale pink with flowering trees. There was the tiled sprinkler pool shining in the center of the courtyard.

All afternoon she and Helix played in the sprinkler pool. The water was knee-deep and the fountain in the center pelted them with droplets. Helix's parents, the Thompsons, sat with Honor's parents in chairs outside and sipped drinks in little glasses. As usual, the grown-ups talked about the weather and the Corporation and the New Five-Year Plan for extending Enclosure into the Tranquil Sea.

When Honor and Helix got hungry, they wrapped themselves in big white towels and padded into the kitchen. Helix opened the refrigerator and Honor saw apples and oranges and packages of cheese and every kind of juice, even blueberry juice. When Helix opened the cupboard, there were chocolate cookies and date bars and dried apricots and pretzels and animal crackers. Helix took a fistful of animal crackers for himself and a fistful for Honor.

"Are you High Level?" she asked Helix.

"Yup," said Helix with his mouth full. "My parents are members of the Corporation."

"Oh," said Honor. Her parents were not members of the Corporation. There were never animal crackers at her house.

"My father is working in Future Planning," Helix boasted. "He's designing future weather in the Tranquil Sea. And my mother—"

"It's starting to rain," interrupted Honor.

The two of them looked through the kitchen window. The sky was dark. Leaves and napkins whipped around in the wind outside. The adults raced inside with their drinks.

"They weren't predicting a storm," Honor's mother said.

"They're usually very good here. Usually you get at least a day's warning," said Mr. Thompson. "But every once in a while . . ."

"Yes, every once in a while the weather is Unpredictable," said Will.

The windows in the airy house began to rattle. Honor felt a prickle of fear.

Mrs. Thompson reassured them, "We have a safe room."

"I wish we did," Pamela said.

"Wouldn't make much of a difference," Will pointed out. "We're too close to the shore."

"Why don't you all follow me." Mr. Thompson opened a door in the living room and showed them a stairway. "It's just a few steps down."

Then the lights went out.

In the dim light of the windows, they descended the stairs into a dark room. Mrs. Thompson fumbled and found a flashlight, which she turned on. Then Honor saw that the room was lined with shelves, and on the shelves were neatly stacked boxes of crackers and cookies and cans of tuna fish and vegetables and juice. There was a whole shelf full of flashlights and packages of batteries. There were shelves of games and puzzles. Lower shelves held rolled-up sleeping bags and even pillows. Through an open door, Honor saw that the safe room had its own bathroom with a toilet and a bathtub and stacks of white towels.

"You have *everything*," whispered Honor, and her parents and the Thompsons laughed.

"I've even got my old fiddle down here," said Mr. Thompson.

"Will you play for us?" asked Pamela.

"If I had my harmonica, I'd play with you," said Will. "The Postal Service got that when we moved here."

"Won't you play us a song?" Pamela asked again.

"Oh, I can't play for you," said Mr. Thompson. "I'm so out of practice. I haven't played in years. If I did, I'd have to play new music in the Colony Orchestra. I just couldn't . . ." He glanced at Honor and Helix where they sat on the floor drinking apple juice from cans. "I just don't have the time."

The apple juice tasted like metal, but Honor liked it.

"How long do they last, in general?" her father asked Mr. Thompson.

"We've only had one bad storm, and that was years ago," Mr. Thompson said.

"At least three years ago," Mrs. Thompson said. "The last one went on about two days. We had some broken windows. Broken tiles on the roof. A lot of trees came down."

"The trees blocked the roads," said Mr. Thompson. "Most of the shore was underwater."

Honor tensed.

"That was before they built the seawall," Mr. Thompson added quickly.

"Our house is going to be underwater, isn't it?" Honor asked.

"It'll be fun," her father told her. "We'll see what we can fish out."

"Let's not borrow trouble, Will," said Pamela.

No one spoke for a moment. Then Mrs. Thompson said, "You can stay with us as long as you need to."

They couldn't see the storm, but they could hear it. They heard a noise like the rattling of dishes, and they heard the wind howling, and the wail of the Storm Warning sirens that meant everyone should move to high ground.

"What do you do if you're outside?" Honor asked her father.

"Run for it," Will said grimly.

Honor shuddered. She could feel the house shaking above them.

"What will happen if the wind gets too strong for the walls?" she asked.

"Then the house could blow off the mountainside," said Mr. Thompson. "Or if there's a mud slide, it could slide down. We could end up in our neighbor's garden."

"Look at her face, Daniel," Mrs. Thompson chided her husband. "Can't you see you're frightening her? Even if the walls go," she told Honor, "we'd be safe underground."

"Unless there's an earthquake," said Helix.

"Why don't you get out your cards," said Mrs. Thompson.

"Then the whole house would crumble. . . ."

"Helix Hephaestus Thompson."

Honor and Helix and the four parents played Cooperation, and they played Truce.

Mrs. Thompson opened tins of oily sardines. Honor had never eaten sardines before. They were silvery and delicious. The adults laid them neatly on crackers and ate them with small bites. Helix and Honor held them by the tails and dangled them into their mouths. Dessert was chocolate-covered caramels dusted in smoky salt. The caramels were so good and so sticky that Honor and Helix begged for seconds and thirds, but they only got two each.

"No fair," said Helix.

"It's fair enough," said Mr. Thompson.

"It's a special occasion," said Helix.

"Time for bed," said Mrs. Thompson, and she spread out puffy down sleeping bags for the children.

"Close your eyes and pretend you're sleeping," Helix whispered to Honor. "Then you'll find out secrets and dangerous stuff."

It was hard for Honor only to pretend she was sleeping when the sleeping bag was so soft and warm. Even so, she tried to listen for secrets.

"Look at the New Directives, for example," she heard Mr. Thompson say.

". . . we'll all be taken by next year if you believe those," said Honor's father.

"So you don't believe them," said Mrs. Thompson.

"Is that a question?"

"No."

"You're suggesting that we're Unpredictable."

"Aren't we all Unpredictable here?" asked Mrs. Thompson.

Will and Pamela laughed softly. Honor had been drifting off, but the laughter and the word *Unpredictable* woke her. She looked over at Helix. He was lying on his stomach with his arms folded under his head. His eyes were wide open.

"The New Directives are a sham," said Honor's father. "Everybody knows that."

"Shh, not in front of the children," said Honor's mother.

Honor and Helix lay still as could be in the dark.

"No pens and paper in private homes? How could they enforce that?"

"There used to be computers in private homes," Mr. Thompson pointed out.

"That was fifty years ago," said Honor's father. "Before the Flood."

A smashing noise silenced them for a moment. Something— a window or a tree—had crashed upstairs.

"The Corporation banned telephones and televisions and radios. The Internet. Why not pens and paper, then?"

"No maps, no binoculars." Honor's father was reading from a piece of paper. "No telescopes. No sextants. No compasses. No materials for mapmaking, surveying, orienteering, amateur astronomy . . . Ridiculous."

"If we can't make our own maps, we have to accept Hers," said Pamela.

"And follow Her Directives," said Mr. Thompson.

"Was there ever a time before Her?" Mrs. Thompson murmured.

"Will there be a time *after* Her? That's more to the point," said Will.

"If you believe the Forecaster . . ."

Honor turned her head in the dark toward Helix, but he kept still.

"I don't believe there is a Forecaster," said Pamela. "I think those messages come straight from Earth Mother. I think the Counter-Directives are a trap for Partisans."

"You think they come from the Communication Bureau?"

"Absolutely," said Pamela. "I think they've got a special office to write those up."

"It's an elaborate trap, then," said Mr. Thompson.

"No single person could print all those leaflets and drop them in the City."

"That's why they call him the Prophet," said Will.

"No," said Pamela. "No one could do that without getting caught. The leaflets come from the Communication Bureau."

"Eat fruit from trees, not processed food. Learn to swim. Find dark places and study the unregulated sky. Exercise your memory each day," Will recited. "Patience. Silence. Begin the revolution in yourself."

"You can't begin a revolution in yourself," said Pamela. "It doesn't work that way."

The storm raged all night and through the morning. Late in the afternoon they heard the All Clear siren. Helix and Honor rolled up their sleeping bags. Mr. Thompson climbed the stairs and called down, "Not so bad."

Mrs. Thompson collected the wrappers and boxes and empty cans from the safe room and brought them upstairs to recycle. Together the two families looked out at what was left of the courtyard. The white walls of the house were cracked. All the windows were blown out, and the courtyard was full of shattered glass. The Thompsons' flowering trees were gone, drowned in the sprinkler pool. Beyond the house, the lush green neighborhood was almost bare; scarcely a leaf remained on the trees or other plants.

The Thompsons asked Honor's parents to stay, but Will and Pamela were anxious to get home and see what had happened there. Mrs. Thompson asked if they wanted to leave Honor while they went to check.

"No, no, I don't think that's a good idea," said Honor's mother.

"I don't know if the buses are running," Honor's father pointed out. "It might be hard for us to get her back."

Slowly, the three of them made their way down a road now choked with mud and branches. Orderlies were clearing away piles of twisted metal, shattered glass. Rain fell softly as the family waited for their bus home. "We should put buckets out to collect the rain," Honor's father told Pamela. "I don't know if we'll have running water."

"Then we should have stayed with Daniel and Clara," Honor's mother said.

"No, we might need to make repairs," said Will.

"If the house is still above water," Pamela said.

SIX

"IT'S STILL HERE!" HONOR SHOUTED.

The town house was still there, barely. Water coursed down the terraced hillside, and the lower town houses were submerged in soupy muck. Palm trees lay flat, with their fronds splayed out on the ground. Shattered glass and bits of furniture littered the hillside. Honor saw the leg of a baby doll in the mud.

The Greenspoons were lucky. Their row of houses stood intact. The roofs had not blown off. All the walls were standing. Some of the neighbors had lost their front doors, but the Greenspoons' door was still shut tight. When Will opened the door, a small rivulet of water rushed out, but the water was only ankle deep on the first floor.

All around them the neighbors were dragging rugs out of their houses. They draped the sopping rugs over metal fences in hopes that they would dry when it stopped drizzling. They carried wet pillows from their houses and wrung them out. There was no electricity. The garbage orderlies had not come, and flies were gathering at the community garbage bins. First the flies were ordinary and black, then bigger flies came, heavy flies the size of bees. And finally strange flies with iridescent eyes swarmed the garbage. Their eyes glowed green and blue and red. The stench of spoiling food filled the air. Rats feasted, tugging and clawing, fighting over scraps. The neighborhood watchtower had fallen, and orderlies were busy building it up again. Without the Watcher, the neighborhood felt wild and lost. A dog swam in the empty lot where Honor used to play with the neighborhood girls. School was closed.

Honor and her parents took brooms and pushed water out the front and back door. They mopped their soaking tiled floor.

"You see, it's a good thing we never got a carpet," Will pointed out.

"Neighborhood Watch," announced Mr. Pratt at the door. Mr. Pratt was wearing rubber boots and a rubber raincoat too. He held his flashlight as usual, even though it was broad daylight. "Everyone accounted for?"

"Yes, sir," said Will.

"We didn't see you in the shelter," said Mr. Pratt.

"We were visiting friends on the hillside," said Pamela, "and we couldn't get home."

"We'll need names, times, dates." Mr. Pratt took a white form out of his raincoat pocket. "And you'll initial here"—he pointed to a line on the form—"and here"—he pointed to another place. "And you'll sign here."

"All that just for the night?"

"Yes, unless you want an unexcused absence," said Mr. Pratt. He added, "Three of our neighbors have returned to the earth."

"Shh." Pamela stuck her mop in a bucket and drew closer to Honor.

"Five are still missing," Mr. Pratt said. "We are volunteering this afternoon to search."

"Is there still a chance?" Will asked.

"We'd like to find the bodies," said Mr. Pratt bluntly. "No one wants a watery grave."

A watery grave. Honor couldn't stop thinking about those words. If water swept you off, then you were no place. If water sucked you under, then how could anyone ever find you? The ocean would erase your name.

At night Honor listened to the wind and couldn't sleep. The wind sounded different now that all the trees were down. The wind howled, no longer rustling gently in the palms.

After three days, school opened again. Big striped tents stood as temporary classrooms on the Upper Field. For many weeks Honor went to school in a tent. Orderlies were working night and day to repair the school buildings.

"There is something I must tell you," Mrs. Whyte announced to the class the first day back. "During the storm there was a great deal of damage. Our pianos were flooded."

Honor could not help smiling at this. She did not like playing the piano in music class. She would get distracted and forget to count, so that when all the girls were playing together, she came in at the wrong time and stuck out.

"Miss Blessing has ordered new pianos for us," said Mrs. Whyte, glaring at Honor. "We will have extra music time when they arrive. There is something else I must tell you. Something we must all Accept."

The girls bowed their heads and tried to look accepting, as they had been taught.

"The storm smashed our aquarium. Our octopus is gone, but he is probably Safe. He is a tree octopus from the forest and he can breathe outside the water. However, I am sorry to tell you that all of our beautiful classroom fish have returned to the earth."

The girls gasped. Helena and Harriet V. began to cry. They were still sniffling when the class lined up to go outside for archery.

"I can't believe it," said Helena.

"Returned to the earth," said Harriet V.

Honor shook her head at the two of them. "Don't be ridiculous. Fish come from the water," she told them. "Fish can't return to the earth. They go to a watery grave."

The other girls stared at her in horror. Helena and Harriet V. cried harder.

At the head of the line Mrs. Whyte folded her arms and gazed at Honor. "Are you making light of what we must Accept?" she asked at last.

Honor shook her head.

"No?" demanded Mrs. Whyte.

"No," said Honor.

After Honor and her class returned to their regular room,

they practiced storm drills every week. Mrs. Whyte blew her whistle once to practice for regular storms, and all the children crouched down under their desks. The teacher blew the whistle twice for hurricanes, and the children lined up and hustled to the storm shelter underground. They walked quickly, but they didn't run, and Mrs. Whyte timed them with her stopwatch. Honor's class learned the science of lightning, floods, earthquakes, forest fires, and especially tsunamis. On the first day of each month an air raid siren sounded, a wail everyone could hear all over the island. That siren tested the tsunami warning system. If there were a real tsunami, the siren would warn everyone on the island to run for high ground.

Honor's class watched films of what tsunamis had done to islands in the past. The films were old, but they were terrifying. Palm trees flailed like grass; waves of water rose so high they smashed all the houses before them. Dead bodies lay puffed up on the beaches.

Something changed in Honor when she saw those films. For the first time she began to understand why New Weather was important. For the first time she understood what Earth Mother was up against. If people did not join hands to secure the world against the storms and seas, then there was no hope. If Enclosure failed, then the last islands would go under. Now history and geography began to mean something to Honor. Now, strangely, she had no trouble reciting from her history text.

"The Flood destroyed the ancient world," Honor recited to the class. *"Where there were continents, only islands are left. Where there were archipelagos, only mountainous islands remain. After the Flood, and the wars that followed, Earth*

Mother organized the Great Evacuation to the remaining islands in the Tranquil Sea. Then the Earth Mother rose up and spoke. 'What is freedom? What is choice? Words and only words. We need Safety. We need shelter from the elements. Without shelter all other words are meaningless.' Earth Mother pledged to Enclose the Polar Seas. She pledged to establish New Weather in the North and reclaim the islands there, one by one. Finally, she pledged to make a new world in the islands of the Tranquil Sea, islands She numbered and named the Colonies."

Honor stood before the class and recited these words perfectly. Mrs. Whyte beamed at her and applauded. Seeing that, all the girls in their seats clapped their hands as well.

"I'm proud of you," said Mrs. Whyte.

Honor flushed with happiness.

"Today you've come prepared."

This was true. Honor had studied diligently. But the real reason she recited so well was that the passage was not just words to her. After the storm, she understood her schoolbooks as she had never understood before. She believed them.

When Honor saw films in school, she had nightmares. She dreamed of those dead bodies with white puffy skin and bulging eyes. She dreamed of a wave so tall it rose as high as her own house. She struggled, but she couldn't run. She couldn't breathe. There was no escape.

"I don't want to drown," she cried to her father in the night.

"You aren't going to drown," he said.

"I want to move," she sobbed.

Her mother held her. "We will. We will," Pamela said. "We'll move as soon as we can."

"There's a warning system on every watchtower," her father reassured her. "Sirens would sound and then buses would come and drive us to the mountains."

Honor gazed out the window into the great black night. "But what if the wave is Unpredictable?"

"Come with me," Will said. He took her by the hand and led her downstairs in her nightgown.

"No, Will," Pamela whispered. There was a curfew in the Colonies for Safety Measures. No one was allowed outside past hour eight. "It's after nine," she said.

"I don't care," he told her.

"She's too young."

"She's ten years old, Pamela."

"She isn't ready." Pamela stood near the door, almost blocking Will.

"She needs to know," he said.

"Will!"

But he took Honor and brushed right past Pamela into the night.

Honor was afraid. Her father's mood frightened her. She had never seen him oppose her mother like that. "Where are we going?"

"Shh." Will rushed her through the unlit gravel lot in front of the town houses and gestured for her to follow him.

Since they'd moved to the island, Honor had never been outside after dark. The night was warm and sticky but mild, as if the sun had stopped to take a breath. The air was gentle on her face and shoulders. She wanted to look everywhere at once—at the stray cats scampering in their path, at the shining stars, the round moon so much brighter than she remembered. She'd heard from the neighbor kids what a bad place the moon was; that was where the worst people went, the crazy ones who didn't fit. They had to live on the cold dusty moon in the lunatic asylum. "How can the moon be so pretty?" she asked her father. She had never expected it to shine so bright.

"It's an overlay," her father said.

"What's an overlay?"

"A light show," whispered her father. "The Corporation projects a moon and stars onto the sky above each city. They aren't natural."

"They're perfect," Honor protested. The stars sparkled. She wanted to touch all seven of them where they shone in a circle around the silver moon. "Can I look at them? Please?"

But Will was in a rush and didn't answer. He glanced often at the tall watchtower, almost rebuilt. Any day now, Watchers would return to guard the neighborhood.

Will hurried Honor all the way down to the danger zone fenced off near the shore. He lifted a piece of sagging barbed wire so that Honor could climb inside the barriers.

"We're going in *there*?" Honor asked, astonished. "But it's Not Allowed!"

"Come on," he said.

"We'll get hurt!" She pointed to the red DANGER signs posted.

"You know I'll keep you safe," Will told her. She hesitated. "You still trust me, don't you?"

She scrambled under the fence and he got down on his hands and knees and crawled after her.

Then she was terrified. She heard the sucking of the sea, the great dark mass of water and the crash of waves. She would have turned and run if her father hadn't held her. She thought she might be sick. She had sailed over the ocean to the island on a Corporation ship, but on the EMS *Serenity*, no one was allowed on deck. All the passengers had stayed safe inside. Before that trip she had traveled everywhere with her parents in little boats, but she had not known then what she knew now.

Honor's bare feet touched scratchy sand. Dry sea grass tickled like insects on her legs. The ocean swelled nearer and nearer. She almost screamed.

"No noise," Will said.

"I want to go home," she cried as Will half carried her to the water's edge.

"Not yet," her father said.

She closed her eyes and buried her head in his chest.

"Look," he told her. "I want you to look."

"No," she pleaded.

"I'm right here."

"But the waves," she said. She was trembling with fear. The water was going to swallow her up. Without realizing it, she began to pray. The words came rapidly as she had been taught in school. "Hail Mother, full of grace, the earth is with you, the sea is with you, the storms sink down before you . . . Teach us your ways, Mother, lead us and guide us . . ."

"Stop that!" Honor's father set her down and shook her hard by the shoulders.

Honor opened her eyes in shock.

"Never pray to her."

"Don't you believe in Earth Mother?" Honor asked.

"No, I don't," said Will.

"Don't you believe she's real?"

"Oh, she's real, all right," said Will. "But I don't worship her. I don't trust her."

Honor shrank back. "My teacher says Earth Mother is everywhere."

"Everywhere we allow her to be," said Will. "Don't you see? When you pray to her the Corporation controls you."

Honor did not see. She shook her head.

"Use your head, Honor. Use your eyes. Do you want Enclosure to Enclose *you*?"

"I want to be safe."

"Yes, Earth Mother's Corporation is counting on that. As long as you want to be safe, they win. They get to decide how many children families have and what those children will be called and where they go to school and what they think. They get to choose where people live and what people buy and wear. They control what people read. They try to control the weather. There are islands out there you can't see." Will pointed to the dark water. "Hundreds of islands like this one. Some are populated. Some are experimental islands for farming and for growing food. And some hold Weather Stations. Our regional Weather Station is on Island 364. The computers there run the clocks and the hourly broadcasts. They store all of our security information. Names, ages, job and school selection, possible criminal activities. The Corporation keeps data on all of us. Data on recycling patterns, food supply. The goal is to manage everyone."

"No—the goal is to manage storms." Honor was trying to get away from the water. She was pulling with all her might, but her father held her by the wrist.

"The world is big," he told her. "Weather is complicated. Do you really think the Corporation should control it all? Do you want regulated skies and filtered light? Do you want every day to be the same as the one before?" He pointed at the ocean. "Don't you see how lovely water is? The Corporation is an overlay like the seven stars and the moon," he whispered in Honor's ear. "Enclosure covers the Polar Seas, but she hasn't covered the Northern Islands yet. Not at all. Why do you think everyone is still living in the Colonies? Why do you think the Corporation retrieved us and brought us here? Because the Northern Islands aren't ready. They aren't safe. She's got these islands the way she wants them. She's got everyone living under her control, but she hasn't got the wild places. She hasn't even got the other side of this island. She hasn't got the whole world ceiled yet. Not the half of it."

Together they looked out at the water. The ocean was huge and black in the distance, but up close on the sand the rippling waves looked silvery and clear. The sea was calm. There were no big waves, just little ones.

Will bent down and trailed his hand in the foam. "Touch the water," he said.

"It's Unsafe."

"No," Will said. "It's beautiful." He scooped up wet sand and water and poured it over her hands.

She began to cry. Her father's ideas were dangerous. To call the wild ocean beautiful was crazy. To say don't pray to Earth Mother—people who spoke like that got taken. They disappeared and never came back.

"Is this water going to hurt you?" Will asked.

"Let me go home."

"Is this water going to hurt you?" he demanded.

The warm wet sand felt thick and sticky. She was afraid she couldn't get it off. She stumbled back toward the fence and stepped on something sharp. She thought it was a stone.

Her father picked up the sharp object as they walked home. He picked up another and another. "These are broken shells," he said. "You can dig with them, or you can just collect them and take them home."

They were hurrying back to their house now. With each step, Honor felt a little safer. Her heart began to calm.

"We can't take them home," Honor said. "Then people would know." She meant the Neighborhood Watch would know they had been to the shore.

"We'll hide them," said her father.

"But what if Mr. Pratt finds them?"

"Honor." Will pulled her to a stop and stood facing her in the artificial moonlight. "I have to tell you something important. Are you listening?"

"Yes."

"Don't ever be afraid. That's what they're hoping for."

• • •

In the evenings after school, only Pamela met Honor at the bus. Will was working extra hours because Pamela had no job. She talked about getting a letter from the Employment Bureau, but Honor knew her mother would not be chosen. How could she fit behind a desk? She was too big. When the two of them trudged home in the heat, Pamela had to stop to rest. Sometimes they took shelter in the shade of a ruined hotel called the Paradise Sands. The hotel was not submerged like the ones past the barriers on the beach, but it was marked with red tape for demolition. In front a smooth driveway and grand stone steps rose gracefully to shattered glass doors. The steps were shaded by a broken metal trellis covered with sweet-smelling vines. Pamela and Honor often rested on those steps, and Pamela played number games with Honor to pass the time. She taught Honor how to count by threes and nines and twelves. And then she taught Honor other ways to count.

"You don't have to count from one to ten the regular way," said Pamela. "There are other ways of counting. For example, you could count like this: zero, one, ten, eleven, one hundred . . ."

"Why would you want to do that?" Honor asked.

"Why not?" asked Pamela. "It's just notation. It's just another way to count. You've learned arithmetic in base ten, but there are other bases you can try. Base two, base seven. It's like a secret code. It's fun."

Honor liked the idea of a secret code. She learned how to count in base two. She practiced until she could count quickly, higher and higher: "Zero, one, ten, eleven, one hundred, one hundred one, one hundred ten, one hundred eleven, one thousand, one thousand one, one thousand ten." Once she knew the pattern, it was easy, but she knew better than to mention base two at school.

One day, Honor and Pamela were sitting on the hotel steps when a cat walked past. They often saw cats in the neighborhood. The cats were small and sleek and lived wild by the shore, crawling under chain-link fences, killing rats, and sunning themselves beside empty swimming pools. This one was black with two white paws in front, and he leaped down from the stairs into a shady spot filled with trash. He disappeared quickly, but Honor noticed something bright in the litter pile of smashed-up lounge chairs and broken glass. It was a blue bag with a blue strap.

"Don't touch that," warned Pamela, but Honor scrambled down anyway for a closer look. "You'll cut yourself," said Pamela.

"I'm being careful," Honor said. She reached as far as she could into the pile, snagged the strap of the bag, and brought it up to show her mother.

Instinctively, Pamela glanced in the direction of the watchtower, but they were sheltered by the trellis covered with thick vines. Pamela looked hard at the bag. She was straining to remember something. "It's a flight bag," she said at last.

"A flight bag? From when people could fly?" Honor's voice was hushed. When she was little her father had told her stories about the time when people flew in planes, but she'd never seen anything from back then. She'd imagined those days were so long ago that kings and queens still lived in castles. She'd pictured rockets and airplanes roaring through the sky like dragons in those once-upon-a-times when the atmosphere was not so delicate.

"See," said Pamela, pointing to the blue bag. "There's a picture of an airplane, and it says Blue Skies Kids. It must have been a child's flight bag."

"Open it," said Honor.

Pamela hesitated. Then she pulled open the zipper on top. The bag was floppy and nearly empty. Pamela pulled out some old candy wrappers. Honor was disappointed. Then Pamela pulled out a box half full of colored pencils and a small plastic pencil sharpener.

"There's something else," said Pamela. She drew out a floppy workbook. It was called *Learn to Draw, Step by Step*.

Pamela set the book down in front of them and they gazed at the book's yellow cover together. There was a drawing of a dog, half shaded, and the invitation, *Start with simple shapes and learn to draw!* They did not dare open the book because of Safety Measures. They both knew books were Not Approved for private use. Owning them was Not Allowed.

"Let's go," said Honor. The book was dangerous. She pulled at her mother and Pamela got up.

They started down the steps, but Pamela hesitated. She had a strange look on her face; her cheeks flushed pink. "I want it," she whispered to Honor.

"No!" Honor protested, but her mother didn't listen. She grabbed the book and stuffed it under her big shirt. "You can't!" Honor said.

Pamela just walked on. Honor scurried to keep up. "Please, Mommy," she begged.

"Shh," said Pamela.

The school year was long in those days. The Corporation did not recognize the old seasons, and so there was no summer vacation on Island 365. The children in Honor's class kept working. They harvested their vegetables and finished weaving their table runners. They sorted rocks and minerals and learned the properties of water.

One day in month seven they sat at their desks and copied Earth Mother's famous essay *The End of Winter.*

> *In days of old, snow covered half the earth for half the year. There was little food, little light, little hope. The world was asleep. In the first glorious year of Enclosure, winter in the North came to an end. We sheltered the North from storms and cold. We brightened the dark skies. . . .*

During copying Mrs. Whyte expected students to sit still. No talking or squirming was allowed. "Think of your penmanship," she said, but the essay was long. It went on for so many paragraphs that Honor's hand cramped. She snuck a look at the aquarium across the room, where new orange and purple fish swam back and forth. Only one more day and she would have a chance to feed them. She had been waiting for her turn. Fish monitor was her favorite job. *Warm weather came to the North and strayed,* copied Honor. Then she caught her mistake. She was supposed to have written *stayed*, not *strayed*. She sighed and took her white pen to blot out the error.

At that moment she saw Octavio move. He unfurled one long tentacle and then another. He seemed to be stretching. The suckers on his tentacles stuck to the glass as the octopus inched his way up the side of the tank. Why was he crawling up the glass? Was he sick? Was he trying to escape?

"Honor," Mrs. Whyte said sharply. "What are you looking at?"

Honor ducked her head and turned back to her work.

All that day Honor peeked at Octavio. She was sure he was trying to get out, but no one else noticed.

The next morning at chore time, Honor went to the supply cabinet. The other girls were busy taking out the broom and mop, the brush and pan and wool dusters. Honor took out the jar of fish food. She climbed the ladder to reach the top of the huge tank and opened the hatch in the aquarium lid. She stared down into the water. The colorful fish were swimming upward expectantly, but there was the octopus as well, almost at the surface. Children were not allowed to feed Octavio. Orderlies fed him slugs and snails. Honor wondered if he was hungry. His soft body, usually russet brown, had changed to pink. He waved two tentacles in a kind of greeting as Honor looked into the water. His dark eye opened. *He is looking at me again,* thought Honor, and then, *Wait till I tell Helix this.*

She sprinkled the fish food, and as the particles floated downward, the other fish gobbled up the flakes. The octopus ignored them. He spread out his body. Again, he seemed to be waving, unfolding his whole rubbery being. Honor leaned over the rectangular opening in the tank's lid and stared. Octavio shifted and she saw that he was staring back at her with his dark, bulbous eye. His tentacles beckoned just under the rippling water. All around Honor, the other students were going about their business, dusting and sweeping, spraying and wiping the desks. Mrs. Whyte was bending over Hedwig in the book corner, showing her something. Honor took a breath and dipped her fingers in the salty water.

In a flash, the octopus seized hold of her. Honor almost fell off the ladder, his grip was so strong. One tentacle wrapped around Honor's wrist, then another seized her arm. The animal was heavy, wet, and dexterous as he heaved himself out of the water and clung to Honor. For a moment, she had to squeeze her eyes shut so that she wouldn't scream. She clutched the side of the aquarium. Then, suddenly, Mrs. Whyte saw her with the octopus wrapped around her.

"Don't move," Mrs. Whyte cried. She snatched the broom from Hagar and hurried over. Mrs. Whyte's lips were tight; Honor had never seen her teacher look this way before. Not stern or angry, but scared. The other girls were shrieking. Mrs. Whyte brandished the broom in front of her.

Then Honor knew that Mrs. Whyte was going to kill the octopus. She knew it from the look on her teacher's face. Mrs. Whyte wasn't going to put the octopus back in the tank; she was going to pry him off with the broom and smash him to pulp. Octavio was wrapped around Honor's chest. He was not doing his job. He was going where he did not belong.

"No," Honor called. "Don't." She was five steps up on the

ladder. Her classmates were running to the other side of the room.

"Hold still." Mrs. Whyte was trying to control her voice.

Octavio seemed to hear Mrs. Whyte. His tentacles stopped moving and he clung to Honor's shoulder.

Honor felt faint. Her shirt was dripping wet. Her heart beat fast under the weight of the animal wrapped around her. She was afraid, but less frightened of the octopus than of her teacher.

"Honor," said Mrs. Whyte. "Do exactly as I say. Hold the broom handle and take one step down. Now take another."

Slowly, Honor descended the ladder. The classroom was still. The other girls were staring in silent horror.

As Honor crept down the ladder, she felt Mrs. Whyte grow bigger and bigger. Her teacher's blue eyes were fierce.

"Let go of the broom now," Mrs. Whyte said, but Honor held on to the broomstick. "I said let go," Mrs. Whyte told Honor in a low voice. Still, Honor held the broomstick, much as Octavio held on to her. "Now!" With one sharp pull, Mrs. Whyte yanked the broom from Honor's hands and Honor ran.

Octavio was heavy. Honor panted as she ran out the door with wet tentacles wrapped around her. She careened around the corner of the school building and ducked into the girls' bathroom with its white and gray tiles, its white sinks and silver stalls. The tiles were cool against her legs as she sank down in the corner. Water trickled from one of the sinks. For a moment she felt safe. Then the emergency bells began ringing. She heard the running steps of orderlies outside.

Octavio slipped off Honor's body and onto the floor. Gracefully, the creature began to scale the bathroom wall.

SEVEN

TWO ORDERLIES BURST THROUGH THE DOOR AND SCOOPED up Honor. They were immensely strong. Their faces were calm, not angry or fierce, but blank as always. The two lifted Honor right off the floor, one orderly under each elbow, and sped her away. She turned her head and saw two more orderlies following with sticks. She closed her eyes.

When the orderlies dropped her off, Honor saw that she was not back in her own classroom; she was in the nurse's office. The orderlies deposited her in a chair and the school nurse approached with a thermometer. "Are you all right?" the plump blond nurse asked.

Honor nodded.

"Where did the accident happen?" the nurse asked.

"I didn't have an accident," said Honor.

"Yes, but I have to fill out an accident report," the nurse said kindly, and she showed Honor her clipboard with the accident form printed on pink paper. "My name is Nurse Applebee."

Honor examined the nurse's dimpled hands. The name Applebee made her think of honey.

"Tell me exactly where the accident happened," said Nurse Applebee.

"In my classroom," said Honor.

"Yes?" said the nurse.

Honor remembered Mrs. Whyte's words: *We do not lie. Ever.*

"I fell into the aquarium," she said.

Fell into the aquarium, Nurse Applebee wrote slowly. Then she looked up and asked, "Why aren't you wet?"

"Look." Honor showed the nurse the front of her shirt.

"But shouldn't you be wet all over?"

Again, Honor remembered Mrs. Whyte. *Do you know what exaggeration is?* "Octavio pulled me out," said Honor.

"The class octopus?"

"Don't kill him," Honor pleaded. "He saved me."

"Why do you say that?" the nurse asked.

"Don't kill him," she begged. "Please, please . . ."

Nurse Applebee leaned forward. She spoke quickly and quietly. "Stop that. You aren't a baby, and you know as well as I do that if the orderlies got him, he's already dead."

When Honor returned to the classroom, she carried the pink accident report signed by Nurse Applebee and sealed in an envelope. She did not know what the report said, but Mrs.

Whyte frowned when she read it. "I'm disappointed," Mrs. Whyte said at last.

Honor bowed her head.

Mrs. Whyte spoke again, and each word fell like a blow. "I am very unhappy with you."

Honor stood silently before her teacher.

"What do you have to say for yourself?" Mrs. Whyte asked.

Honor couldn't speak.

"I'm waiting," Mrs. Whyte said.

Honor stared at the floor. No words came.

"Go to your loom and get to work," Mrs. Whyte snapped.

All that long afternoon, Honor kept her head down as she worked, avoiding the stares of the other children. She didn't dare look at Mrs. Whyte. She kept her eyes on her shuttle and the threads in her loom.

At the end of the day, when the students lined up for the bus, Honor didn't push to the front, but let the others go first. She felt beaten, even though no one had hit her; her body ached. When the doors finally opened for her stop, she trudged off the bus, dragging her book bag behind her.

Instead of her mother, her father was standing by the side of the road to meet her. "Hurry," he told her, taking her book bag. He seemed excited and nervous. "You can walk faster than that." He pulled her by the hand and they hurried to the City Center.

Thousands upon thousands of silvery bicycles flashed through the City. It was rush hour and the office workers were cycling home. The footbridges were packed, and as Honor and her father tried to walk across, there were so many workers crowded together that Honor could see nothing but their sweaty backs. Somehow, her father found an opening to push forward. Below them, the bicycles shimmered like a silver river in the afternoon sun.

Honor's father led her past the Safety Bureau, with its lavish waterless fountains casting colors through tall prisms. Will rushed Honor through the Corporation Plaza, with its flags flying. One hundred flags, and on each flag seven stars to represent the seven seas. They passed the windowless Central Store. They passed the Coupon Bank, the Island Bakery. They passed the bus depot, where a hundred silver buses waited to take the orderlies back to their Barracks on the other side of the island. At last they arrived at the hospital, surrounded by gardens and coral block walls.

Will showed his identification card to the usher and led Honor up the stairs to a room of beds. The room was painted clean white, but the paint was cracked. Several large windows were boarded up. The glass must have broken in the storm.

Honor's mother was sitting up against pillows in a white gown. Honor cried out and ran toward her.

"No, no, no." The nurse hustled Honor out of the room. "We cannot have children in the ward," the nurse scolded Will. "Take her downstairs, please."

"Can't she stay in the hall?" Will pleaded.

"Are you arguing with me?" the nurse asked.

Honor looked up at her father. His face was calm, but he was squeezing her hand so hard it hurt.

She almost fell trying to keep up with Will as he marched her down the stairs. "Stay here," her father told her when they came out to the hospital garden.

She waited for him on a green bench in the shade of a monkeypod tree. She watched two orderlies clipping hedges with sharp garden shears. She thought of Octavio. *You aren't a baby, and you know as well as I do that if the orderlies got him . . .*

Honor imagined the school orderlies clipping Octavio with garden shears. She thought of them slashing and puncturing his soft body. When she closed her eyes, she imagined Octavio looking up at her. She felt his delicate tentacle wrap her wrist.

"Honor."

She opened her eyes with a start. There was her father, walking toward her with a bundle of blankets in his arms. Honor's mother followed slowly. She had changed out of her nightgown and was dressed again in ordinary clothes.

Will and Pamela sat next to Honor on the bench. Then Honor saw that the bundle of blankets contained a baby.

"That's the baby?" Honor exclaimed. She'd had no idea he would be so little. She'd never seen a baby before.

"Honor," said her father, "this is Quintilian."

PART TWO

ONE

ALL THE CHILDREN IN THE NEIGHBORHOOD FELT SORRY FOR Honor. No one had ever heard of keeping a second child. Where would such children live when they grew up? The Corporation had not yet built cities in the Northern Islands, and there was no room in the Colonies for extra children. The Tranquil Sea was vast, but the islands left in it were small.

Every once in a while a family had a second baby by mistake, but in such cases, parents gave the infant to the Corporation for redistribution to those people who could not have children. This was called Giving Back to the Community. To keep an extra baby was shocking.

The neighborhood children hushed and stared when Honor approached. They would not play basketball with her anymore. Their parents had warned them. Honor's parents had committed a Selfish Act. Even though Corporation Counselors came to talk to them, Will and Pamela would not give up Quintilian.

Now every afternoon on day seven, Will was required to volunteer for digging ditches. He dug ditches to pay his debt to society. Pamela wheeled the recycling bins to the curb for the whole row of town houses. This was how she paid her debt. The bins were heavy, but none of the neighbors helped Pamela. No one wanted to be seen with the Greenspoons, because a family with two children was Not Approved.

There were no gifts or baby showers for second children, no balloons or celebrations. There were no openings for second children in the Colony day-care system, and so Pamela couldn't work like the other mothers; she had to stay home with Quintilian. Pamela did not complain. Even though she looked tired, she never said she was sorry for what she'd done. She loved Quintilian. At first Honor didn't think she could share her mother's feelings, because the baby had caused so much trouble, but gradually she changed her mind.

Quintilian was cheerful. His dark eyes were perfectly round, and when he learned to sit up, he clapped as if he were applauding himself. He made Honor laugh. She liked to squeeze his fat legs and watch him learn to stand and babble. She loved to rest her hand on his huge fuzzy head.

On Errand Day, when the family slept in late, Honor would carry Quintilian into their parents' room. Then she'd bring in the Errand Day Leaflet from the front door, and Will and Pamela would sit up against their pillows and fold paper gliders from the leaflet's stiff pages, announcing the new week's Goals and Initiatives. *Waste Not, Want Not: Save and Reuse Boxes, Bags, Bottles, Shoes. Anti-roach Week: Invest in Traps TODAY.* Families were meant to post the Goals and

Initiatives on the wall right next to their picture of Earth Mother. Sometimes the Greenspoons did, especially after Mr. Pratt or his wife, Mrs. Pratt, came calling. Most weeks they forgot.

Whoosh! Will and Pamela launched those paper gliders over to Quintilian, where he stood holding on to the foot of the bed. He'd laugh and laugh. Sometimes he laughed so hard he lost his balance. Then, with a surprised look on his face, he'd find himself sitting down. When Quintilian picked up the gliders, they went straight into his mouth.

For breakfast on Errand Day, Will made pancakes. He fried them on his griddle. "A big one for Daddy, a middle-size one for Honor, and a wee little tiny one for baby," he said.

"Aren't you forgetting someone?" Pamela asked.

"Patience, patience, don't be in such a rush," teased Will.

"I'm hungry, you know," said Pamela.

"Do you think we should feed her?" Will asked Honor and Quintilian. "Well, all right. A great big enormous one for Mommy." He scraped up all the leftover batter and poured an extra-big pancake for Pamela at the end.

Then, when breakfast was over, the family would go off shopping or wheel their dirty clothes to the neighborhood washing machines. They'd pile up their laundry in Quintilian's stroller and he'd ride on top.

But the best times of all were afternoons at Peaceful Park. The park was big and dusty, and hardly anybody played there. No one liked that scorching field without a single tree. No one except the Greenspoons. Peaceful Park was perfect for flying kites.

Will and Pamela built two kites, and they were amazing creations. Pamela cut the kites out of old red rain ponchos. Will rigged the fabric to the lightest, thinnest lengths of green bamboo and tied each kite to an extra-long roll of cord. Finally Pamela drew faces on the kites with black laundry marker. Great toothy smiles and crazy bloodshot eyes. On breezy days when the wind was not too light and not too strong, Will and Pamela and the children flew their homemade kites in Peaceful Park until they were specks in the blue sky. When the wind was just right, the kites felt so strong and safe up there that Honor imagined nothing could budge them.

"Ho hum," boasted Will, "I could stand here all day and this kite would hold. It's like fishing."

"Fishing in reverse," said Pamela. "Sky fishing."

"What do you fish for in the air?" asked Honor.

Pamela and Will started laughing. "Oh, planets," said Will. "The occasional comet. An asteroid or two."

Honor held one kite string, and Will held the other. Pamela held Quintilian. On those afternoons, four did not seem like the wrong number for a family. Four seemed just right.

Other days were difficult. Will stayed out late and Quintilian cried and wouldn't go to sleep. Then Pamela stroked his back, and Honor tried to sing him lullabies. She sang him "Safe We Shall Abide," the hymn she'd learned at school. *"Safe we shall abide, from wind and rain and tide . . ."*

But Quintilian didn't like the song and screamed louder than ever.

Pamela walked up and down with him until he finally drifted

off. Then Honor couldn't sleep. She stayed up worrying, afraid the Neighborhood Watch would find Will after curfew. Mr. Pratt and Mrs. Pratt were always on the lookout. Pamela sat next to Honor on the bed and drew pictures. Fluidly, Pamela drew animals with a pencil. Cats and horses seemed to come alive on paper. She practiced for hours, filling every scrap she could find. But Honor kept glancing at the window. Where did her father go at night? "Why is he late?" Honor asked.

Pamela never answered that question.

When Honor was eleven, she got a new teacher, Miss MacLaren, and her class visited the school library once a week. Although owning books was Not Allowed, borrowing books from the library was Encouraged. Once a week Honor borrowed a school library book to bring home. She read about the Emerald City in *The Wizard of Oz*. She read *The Lion, the Witch, and the Wardrobe*, a book about four children who teamed up with a lion to save the world from winter. And she read *The Secret Garden*, about a little girl and boy who planted flowers that never died.

Honor loved the school library, but she was also afraid of it. The floors were polished wood, and they creaked. The bookcases were high and set close together. In the center of the room Miss Tuttle, the small, golden-eyed librarian, sat watching everyone like a cat. Miss Tuttle had long thick hair she stroked back now and then away from her face. She powdered her face white, and her small hands and cheeks were puffy. Whenever classes came in, Miss Tuttle was working at her desk marking books and cutting out paragraphs with scissors. No one talked, because Miss Tuttle needed to concentrate. She bent over her work and every once in a while lifted up a page to admire the cutouts she had made—so many small and large rectangles in some places that the paper looked like lace. Then she swept the cuttings into her white recycling bin.

Every week, all the children in year *H*, both boys' and girls' classes, filed into the library, and each child picked out a book from the low shelves close to Miss Tuttle's desk. Honor and Helix often looked at the medium and higher shelves, but they knew better than to touch books up there. Once, when Miss Tuttle was bent down over her cutting work, Helix whispered, "I dare you."

Honor hesitated. Then she reached out and touched the edge of a dark blue book on the upper shelf. Instantly, Miss Tuttle said, "No, no, not for you. Those are for older children."

"How did she see me?" Honor whispered to Helix.

"She sees everything," he said. "If you ever try to hide a book from her, she'll find it. And if you . . ."

"Silence is golden," said Miss Tuttle.

That same day, two boys, Hawthorn and Hector, began pushing and shoving in the back of the library. Hector was an orphan. His parents had been taken, and so he slept at school with the other orphans in the Boarders' Houses. Everyone was supposed to treat orphans kindly, but they were scheming children. They always had a hungry, jealous look about their eyes. The girls in Honor's class called this look orphanish.

The truth was, orphans always wanted whatever anyone else had. Hector was fighting with Hawthorn because he wanted Hawthorn's book.

"Class, please come to the front," said Miss Tuttle, but the boys were too busy squabbling to listen. Miss Tuttle did not rise from her chair. She pushed a small red button with her finger. *Bing!* At once, as if by magic, a pair of doors opened at the back of the library. The doors opened wide to reveal a great dark cavern of a storage room. All the children stood transfixed. Hawthorn and Hector stopped fighting and stared in awe at the blackness. Then the doors swept closed again and Miss Tuttle beckoned the boys forward with the others. "There is no fighting," she said. "Fighters go in *there*. Any questions?" she asked the class assembled before her desk.

Bravely, Helix raised his hand. "Is it true that you're a Retriever?" he asked Miss Tuttle.

"Yes, I am a licensed Retriever," Miss Tuttle said. Coolly she opened her desk drawer and showed the children her tranquilizing darts. She held up a dart for them to see. The students stared in awe. The dart was slender and just the length of Miss Tuttle's finger. Honor could scarcely breathe. When she looked at the dart, its delicate point glinted silver. A memory was returning to her, a memory of long, long ago. She was almost sure that once she'd seen a dart like that. She was just on the edge of knowing. She closed her eyes. She saw the pebbled beach in the Northern Islands. She saw the glint of silver. She heard her mother scream.

Miss Tuttle shut her desk drawer with a snap. Honor opened her eyes. A little cry escaped.

"You had a question?" Miss Tuttle turned her gold eyes on Honor.

Mortified, Honor shook her head. The memory was gone.

Librarians had special powers in those days. They didn't just organize books; they were historians and record keepers. They were called Informational Safety Officers, and when families neglected to file forms, the librarians sent out notices marked *Overdue*.

After Honor's eleventh birthday her parents received three overdue notices in the mail. The first letter was stamped *Overdue* in black; the second letter was stamped *Overdue* in orange. The third letter was large and stiff and stamped *Final Notice* in bright red. After that letter came, Mr. Pratt sat down with Will and Pamela for a talk. Honor hid on the stairs and listened.

"You've missed all of your daughter's ten-year-old appointments," Mr. Pratt said.

"We're planning to—" Pamela began.

"Planning isn't good enough," said Mr. Pratt. "This is your last chance. If you fail to meet your obligations, you will suffer."

"Suffer?" said Will scornfully.

"Most people do suffer when they go to the Persuasion Booth," said Mr. Pratt. "Most people try to avoid twenty-four hours of Persuasive Reasoning and Positive Reinforcement. I'm telling you this for your own good. I've had some Positive Reinforcement myself. Ever notice my false teeth?"

After that visit, Honor's parents sent in all her forms.

Ten was an important number in those days—even more important than it is now. There were ten months in the year and ten hours in the day. There were ten days in the week: nine days of work and school and, of course, a tenth called Errand Day.

At ten, children could join the Young Engineers. Honor had begged her parents to let her join the neighborhood troop, but Will and Pamela had never taken her to a single meeting. Now, at last, at eleven, Honor got to wear a green neckerchief and pledge allegiance. "I pledge allegiance to the flag of the United Troops of Engineers and to the Corporation for which it stands, one planet, ceiled fast . . ."

"Just remember what you're saying is pure propaganda," Will told Honor when she practiced at home.

"What's propaganda?"

Pamela frowned and shook her head slightly, but Will answered, "Stories Mother tells us."

Honor glanced at the framed picture of Earth Mother on the living room wall. For a moment the smiling face looked sinister; the twinkling eyes looked small and hard. For just a split second Earth Mother looked like a witch. Honor looked away. "Oh, come on, Dad, don't you want me to have friends?"

Honor's troop was all neighborhood girls from year *H*, and they called themselves the Heliotropes. They met once a month at the Neighborhood Youth Center for fun and games and speeches by their troop leader, Hattie's mother. There were sleepovers in the Youth Center with its wonderful cooling units. There were spelling bees. There were cookouts—indoors, of course, because of the heat.

The Heliotropes worked to earn purple badges for their vests. They could only earn badges by working together. They were a team. Either all the Heliotropes earned a badge or none of them did. There were badges for recycling projects and badges for litter cleanup. There were badges for sewing and even badges for singing. "Let there always be sunshine," the Heliotropes sang. "Let there always be blue skies. Let there always be Mother. Let us always agree."

Even more important than the Young Engineers, in those days, ten-year-olds received official identity cards. Honor had been waiting and waiting for her card.

"Everybody else in my class has one!" She'd nagged her parents all year, but they always forgot, or they were busy with Quintilian. Will and Pamela were disorganized. They piled up papers in their closet and sometimes lost them altogether.

Now, at last, shamefully late, Pamela took Honor into the City on Errand Day and the two of them stood in line at the Identity Bureau. The line was long and snaked all the way around the edges of the tiled lobby.

Honor was so relieved and happy. She swung her hat by its strings.

"Stop that," said Pamela.

Honor was wearing her new school uniform: a khaki skirt and a white blouse with a window in the pocket for her iden- tity card, just like those on grown-up clothes. Honor craned her neck to see the front of the line, where ushers directed people into different offices.

"Stop fidgeting," snapped Pamela.

"Why are you angry?" Honor asked. She wasn't sure exactly

why her parents tried to keep her back the way they did. They didn't like her to go to the Young Engineers. They didn't want her to get her identity card with the privilege of her own little coupon book at the Central Store. She wasn't sure why all this made her parents so unhappy, except that they didn't want her to grow up.

"Next," said the usher, and the line edged forward. Nervously, Pamela smoothed Honor's bouncy hair.

They had been waiting an hour before Pamela signed a special permission slip and Honor was called into a small white room much cooler than the lobby. A registrar sat there on a stool. He didn't say hello. He looked tired and blotchy.

"Right thumb," said the registrar.

Honor pressed her thumb onto an ink pad and then onto special paper for a thumbprint. "Index finger," said the registrar.

She held out her finger and gasped in pain and surprise as he pricked her with a needle. Quickly, he smeared the drop of blood on a plastic card.

"Photo." The registrar sat her down in a straight-backed chair and disappeared behind a large camera on a tripod. "Keep still," he told her as he clicked the shutter. Then he pushed the buttons on what looked like a small adding machine. The machine spat out a slip of paper, which he gave her. "Here's your number," the registrar said. Her number was printed in gray ink: 571207. Head down, Honor left the room. She didn't feel excited anymore.

TWO

HONOR'S PARENTS DID NOT MISS ANY MORE IMPORTANT deadlines. She made sure of that. When she turned twelve, Honor got her own Storm Emergency Kit with flares and a bottle of water and packets of energy crackers. The kit included a booklet called *Youth Safety*, with directives for Safe disposal of dangerous litter. *"Dispose of needles in red biohazard bins. Dispose of shattered glass in blue glass bins. Dispose of leaflets immediately. Leaflets marked with the word* Forecaster *are dangerous to the community. Reading them is a crime. Keeping them is a crime. Fold them in half and then in half again. Drop them in the nearest white paper recycling bin."* When she turned thirteen, Honor went to the Corporation Health Office and received a pamphlet called *Earth Mother's Guide for Girls*, which had drawings of flowers with stamens and pistils and also cross sections of beehives, wasps' nests, termite mounds, and mole rat colonies. *We are here on earth to produce without stinting and reproduce within limits,* the book said. *We give what we can, do what we must, and take only what we need.*

The year Honor turned thirteen was important in the Greenspoon family because it was also the year Quintilian turned three. At three, Quintilian was finally eligible to start school. That meant Pamela could get a job.

Quintilian was a dreamy brown-eyed boy with short-cropped curls. He always had an imaginary story or game in his head and often bumped into things because he paid no attention to where he was going.

Will and Pamela worried Quintilian wouldn't get into the Old Colony School and that he would be sent to a special school for Special Children. Before Quintilian's interview, Will and Pamela and Honor all sat with him and told him what to say.

"Who cares for the earth?" Honor tested Quintilian.

"Earth Mother," Quintilian shouted.

"What are her watchwords?"

"Peas, dove, and toy," Quintilian answered.

"Stop it!" Honor said. "You know the answers."

But Quintilian just laughed at her. He thought he was funny.

Honor was worried when Miss Blessing came to the house for the interview. Quintilian did not know the Corporate Creed by heart. But Miss Blessing did not question a three-year-old so closely. She asked Quintilian to draw pictures instead. When he drew a picture of his family, he drew five round smiling faces with stick legs and arms.

"Who are all these people?" Miss Blessing asked him.

"Mommy, Daddy, Honor, Quintilian . . ."

"And who is this one?" Miss Blessing pointed to the largest face.

"Earth Mother," said Quintilian, looking at Miss Blessing with his dark, trusting eyes.

Miss Blessing smiled. "What a sweet child," she told Will and Pamela. "It's a pity you did not give him back to the community."

Honor looked at her parents, but they did not answer this. Tense, they sat across from Miss Blessing and waited for her verdict.

"We will do our best with him," Miss Blessing said at last.

On his first day of school, Quintilian was ready long before Honor. He didn't cry like other three-year-olds when the bus came. He had been waiting to ride the school bus his whole life.

"Pay attention to your teacher," Pamela reminded Quintilian as he climbed the bus stairs.

"Stay near Honor," said Will, as if it were perfectly normal for a family to send two children to school.

Quintilian sat next to the window and Honor sat on the aisle. She scrunched down and looked straight ahead when other students got on. She didn't want to hear them ask why a girl from H was sitting with a little kid from Q.

She'd been waiting for Quintilian to start school, but now that he was actually coming, she was embarrassed. As soon as the bus arrived at Old Colony, she took him by the hand and hurried him over to the teacher for year Q. She did not want to be seen with him.

"Class," said Mrs. Goldbetter that afternoon, "open your history books to page fifteen. Hildegard will recite today."

"North America was divided into three parts. . . ." recited Hildegard. "The Northern Lands were uninhabitable because of ice and snow. The Southern Lands were desert. The Midsection of the continent was more favorable, but the people there were Unpredictable. They built weapons; they practiced war; they committed so many Crimes against Nature that the climate overheated. Gas from factories, cars, and heating and cooling units damaged the earth's atmosphere. Heat built up until the polar ice caps melted. The tides rose; dams and levees broke. Houses, businesses, and streets filled with mud. After the Flood, North America was no more. With the ceiling of the Polar Seas, Earth Mother Stabilized and Secured the Northern Islands that remain. The Northern Islands now enjoy New Weather, but the Corporation has not yet numbered them for resettlement. Future Planners are now mapping new cities in the Northern Islands. This artist's drawing (facing page) shows a plan for a city called Security on an island in the Northeast. The Central Plaza displays the famous Arm, which broke from a larger idol known as the Statue of Liberty. The Arm holds a torch, which will light the plaza at night. . . ."

Even as Hildegard recited at the front of the class, Honor imagined the other girls were whispering about Quintilian. She sensed them passing notes.

At recess she was careful to stay far away from the small fenced playground where the littlest children ran and screamed.

"Look what I found," said Helix, running over.

"Let me see. Is it rare?"

"Hey, don't grab. Finders keepers." Helix's fist closed.

"Oh, come on, let me look," said Honor. "Did you find this with your magnet?"

"No. By hand. I think it's silver." Helix was trying to rub the mud off an ancient coin. He spat on it.

"That's disgusting," said Honor. "Take it to the water fountain."

They went to the water fountain near the swings and washed the coin until it shone. There was a face on one side and a statue on the other. They bent over the coin, and on the face side they read the words UNITED STATES OF AMERICA, LIBERTY, IN GOD WE TRUST, and QUARTER DOLLAR. On the statue side were the words NEW YORK 1788 GATEWAY TO FREEDOM, the old-style date 2001, and the ancient legend E PLURIBUS UNUM.

"Look, it still says *God* on it," Honor said.

"Where? Where?"

"It's in the small print."

"That's how you can tell it's from before the Flood," said Helix. He held the coin carefully between his thumb and index finger.

"What do you think you could buy with this?" Honor asked.

"I don't know, maybe a . . . book," said Helix. "A big coin

like this could buy a lot. That's why it says *e pluribus unum*. That means 'out of one, many.' One coin could buy many things. What would you buy if you could buy anything?"

Honor thought about this. "I would buy a . . . house on high ground."

"You can't buy houses," said Helix.

"You said if I could buy anything."

"Then I'd buy a telescope," Helix whispered.

"That's Not Allowed," Honor said automatically, but she wasn't really listening. She was gazing anxiously at the fenced area where the tiny boys were playing. Quintilian was there among them, but he looked like he was pushing another boy. Was he playing, or was he fighting? Where was the teacher? What if he got hurt? What if he got caught? Suddenly Honor sensed Helix watching her watching Quintilian. She turned away, embarrassed.

The teachers blew their whistles. Everyone ran to line up under the trees. The faster the children lined up, the faster they could reenter the air-conditioned classrooms.

"Here," Helix said, and he pressed the coin into Honor's hand.

She was confused. "What about finders keepers?"

But Helix had already run to get in line.

At the end of the day, Honor waited for Quintilian to get on the school bus. Everyone else boarded, but Honor didn't see Quintilian. The driver started up his engine and began closing the doors. He never waited more than a moment.

Honor jumped onto the steps and blocked the closing doors with her body.

"Wait! We're missing somebody."

"Sorry," said the driver, and he released the brake.

At that moment, a tearstained, disheveled Quintilian ran up the bus steps. Honor grabbed his arm and charged inside. *Swoosh.* The door swung shut behind them. The bus lurched forward, and Quintilian and Honor stumbled down the aisle to their seats.

"What happened to you?" Honor whispered, angry and dismayed.

Quintilian's clothes were ripped and muddy. He held out a red card from the office.

"You got a red card? Your first day?"

"Don't talk to me!" Quintilian squeezed his eyes closed and covered his ears with his hands.

"Why were you fighting? Don't you know better than that?"

"He called me a brother!" Quintilian said.

THREE

"MY MOM GOT A JOB," HONOR TOLD HELIX AS SOON AS SHE saw him at recess the next day. She'd been waiting all morning to tell him.

"But it's an Undesirable job," said Helix.

Honor was hurt. "How do you know?"

"My mother says you only get one chance to be an engineer. After that . . ."

"After that what?" Honor demanded, hands on her hips.

On Errand Day she found out. Will took Honor and Quintilian to see Pamela at the gift-wrapping department in the Central Store.

The Central Store was the size of a city block, and its doors were so tall they seemed to reach the sky. Inside the store there were whole rooms just for school uniforms. There were entire floors stocked with food. Will and the children walked through aisles of canned vegetables and aisles of frozen chicken parts.

There were shelves upon shelves of cereal boxes. However, all the vegetables were the same: green beans, corn, and sliced olives. All the chicken parts were breasts, giant breasts from the Central Chicken Factory on Island 221. All the cereal, thousands of boxes, was one kind of granola without raisins. In the Colonies, the selection of food for sale depended on what shipments had arrived that month. There was special food for high-ranking engineers and members of the Corporation, but everyone else had to buy what the Central Store offered.

Despite this, Will said, "Maybe we'll find something different this time." They were walking through an aisle of jelly. As far as Honor could see, as high as the ceiling were little jars of grape jelly. But Will was looking carefully. "Keep your eyes open," he told Honor. "You never know."

Quintilian was running around. He kept darting up the aisle and bumping into other customers.

"Stop him." Honor was embarrassed.

Will paid no attention. His eyes were fixed on a small jar on the bottom shelf. "Aha! Got one!" There it was, a tiny golden orange jar in the midst of all that purple. Will snatched it up. "Apricot preserves," he whispered to Honor. There must have been an inventory error in the Central Computer. Something so rare was never intended for the general public, but there was the jar with a regular price sticker: four points, just like the grape jelly. The orderlies at the cash registers would never look at what was in the jar, only the price. If you found something like that in the Central Store, you could keep it. "This will be for Mommy's birthday."

Will had a faraway look in his eyes. "I can't even remember the taste of apricots," he said.

To Honor the Central Store was like a palace. When they took the elevator up to the seventh floor, it was like going up to a beautiful fairground. There were booths with fresh popcorn popping and lollipops on sticks. There was a booth that sold little Corporation flags in green and blue, and there was a photo booth where you could get your picture taken and then framed—or even inserted into a glitter globe filled with water. You shook the globe and glitter swooshed up over your photo like confetti.

"Could we?" Honor begged, even though she knew they could not afford it.

At the back of the seventh floor was the gift-wrapping booth. Pamela stood behind such a high counter that Will had to lift Quintilian up to see, and Honor had to stand on tiptoe. Honor shuddered. Several of the workers with her mother were skilled orderlies.

Colorful sample boxes decorated the wall behind Pamela and the other workers. There were boxes wrapped with long curling ribbons and boxes wrapped for weddings in brown and silver, and some, for new babies, even had little toys or rattles tied onto the ribbons. Each sample had a number for customers to choose. Below, under the counter, were rolls of wrapping paper and ribbon.

"Oh, could I have a piece?" Honor whispered to her mother. Pamela was standing with her scissors just about to cut from a roll of luscious gold satin, and, almost without thinking, she snipped an extra piece for Honor, who pocketed it before anyone saw.

"I want one! I want one!" shouted Quintilian. Will set him down on the floor, but the supervisor came rushing over as Quintilian protested, "She got one."

"No free samples," the supervisor said. She was a scrunch-faced woman with silver-rimmed glasses. "Turn out your pockets," she told Honor.

Honor simply handed over the ribbon. The supervisor took the snip of ribbon and measured it against the long steel ruler embedded in the counter. "Two points," she told Will, and he had to take out his coupon book. Now he had two points less for everything else that week.

Now that Pamela and Will were both working, Honor and Quintilian walked home by themselves from the bus stop. They trudged home together in the heat, and when Quintilian got tired, Honor played I Spy with him. "I spy, with my little eye, something that begins with a *T*."

"Tower!" shouted Quintilian, pointing to the neighborhood watchtower.

"No, don't point," Honor whispered. "Never point at watch-towers. I meant *tree*. Now let's try another one. I spy, with my little eye . . ."

"I'm too tired," said Quintilian.

"Just a little farther," Honor said. She felt for the key to the town house in her skirt pocket.

By the time they got to the door, Quintilian was hopping,

suddenly remembering he had to use the bathroom. Honor turned the key in the lock. They were blinded at first, entering the dark house after the white sunshine outside, but they did not turn on the lights. The lights were off to save energy and keep the heat down.

Quintilian ran to the bathroom, and Honor checked the apartment as her father had taught her. She looked up and down. She glanced at the kitchen counters and the toy basket and then checked the trunks in the bedrooms to see if there had been a visit from the Neighborhood Watch.

"Just look to see if something is missing or out of place," her father had told her.

"What should I do if something *is* missing?" Honor asked.

"Nothing," her father said quickly. "Oh, you don't do anything."

"Shouldn't I call Safety Officers?" Honor asked.

"No, no," her mother told her then. "Don't call anyone."

"Why should I check the whole house if I'm not going to tell anyone when something is wrong?" Honor demanded.

"You'll tell *us*," her father said. He was so serious about it that Honor usually did check. But as far as she could tell, nothing in the house ever disappeared.

Honor poured two cups of milk, and she and Quintilian ate oatmeal cookies for their snack. The cookies contained a special chemical to prevent them from becoming soggy in the damp island air, and this chemical made them so hard they were difficult to bite or even break in half. In those days the oatmeal cookies had no raisins and little sugar because of Health Reasons, but the children were used to them.

After snack, Honor sat at the table and did her homework. She no longer had time to play outside with the neighborhood girls. She had to solve word problems and copy research papers. She had to take home a volume of *The Encyclopedia of Ancient Animals* and copy the entire article on penguins. *The emperor penguin was the size of a child. It was the largest penguin and lived in Antarctica. . . .*

While she worked at the table, Honor tried to keep Quintilian busy. She could not send him outside by himself. The one time she'd tried, he'd wandered off and the Neighborhood Watch had brought him back with a warning. His favorite game was cutting up the weekly newspaper with scissors and folding the pages to make hats and boats. No one could read the *Colony News* after he was done with it, but that didn't matter, because the news was nearly the same each week and always good. Generally, the headlines read: *New Five-Year Plan a Success* or *Litter: A Thing of the Past.* Then there was a color chart on the front page to show how litter disappeared or how New Weather was spreading over the world.

There were no weather reports in the newspaper. They were broadcast every hour from the tops of buildings in the City. Three short beeps, then a long one and a man's voice with the climate advisories. From inside the house, Honor couldn't make out every word, so the bulletins sounded something like: ". . . Colony Early Weather Warning . . . if this were an emergency . . . please . . . without delay . . . humidity will be . . . no chance of . . . otherwise unchanged . . ."

The two of them were sitting in this way in the living room when Honor heard a knock. She ran to the door immediately and opened it wide, as children were taught, and two Safety Officers stepped inside. They were wearing green jumpsuits and they carried drawstring sacks. They had no orderlies with them, but they were holding a grim-faced dog by the collar. Quintilian jumped up. He was afraid of dogs. He would have climbed on the table if Honor had let him.

"Lady of the house?" asked the first officer.

"Not home, sir," said Honor, holding Quintilian by the arm.

"Both parents at work?" asked the second officer.

"Yes, sir."

The dog was straining toward the kitchen. It was a brown search dog with vicious teeth, pointy ears, and yellow eyes.

"Mind if we take a look?" asked the first officer.

"Yes, sir," whispered Honor, because she did mind, very much. People got searched sometimes because of Safety Measures. Neighbors had been searched a year before; that didn't mean there was anything wrong. She kept telling herself this as she clutched Quintilian.

The dog broke away, lunging for the kitchen, and the Safety Officers rushed after him. Honor heard them opening the cabinets, the dog panting, pots and pans clamoring onto the floor. Glass shattered.

"Watch the pieces," one man warned the other. "Off. Get off," he ordered the dog. Honor heard the crunch of the broken glass beneath heavy boots.

The dog thundered up the stairs with the men behind. Honor could hear the scuffle and clatter of the dog's sharp-clawed feet. She knew better than to follow, and she held

Quintilian back. What were they looking for? Her heart raced as she thought of her mother's drawing book and pencils underneath the frayed carpet, the seashells hidden in the light fixture. But when the men came down, their bags looked empty. The dog was dragging the plaid winter blanket in his mouth. The men tried to rip it away, but the dog wouldn't let go until they threatened him with a stick. Even then, he circled and snarled at the old blanket until one Safety Officer dragged him outside. The other stood and filled out his paperwork. He looked hard at Honor.

"They're coming home when?" he asked her.

"My parents?"

"You'll expect them when."

"Hour six," she said.

He wrote this down. Then he said, "It's well past six now. Good night."

After the men left, Honor and Quintilian stood, frozen. Honor imagined the men striding down the walk, tramping down the cement steps past other houses, through the empty asphalt lot in front of the buildings. She pictured them jumping into their Safety Vehicle and speeding off. Only then did she let go of Quintilian. The two of them raced upstairs.

Sheets had been ripped from the beds. The closets and trunks were empty and all the clothes heaped on the floor. The dog had worried the frayed carpet and gnawed the ends, but when Honor felt for it, she could touch her mother's book. In the hallway, the light fixture was undisturbed. She sank down on the floor and rested her head on her knees. She strained to hear her father walking to the door with his keys jingling in his pocket, but she couldn't hear anything. She prayed for her mother to come. How could they leave her and Quintilian all alone? If it was already past six, where were they? *Don't ever be afraid,* she thought. *That's what they're hoping for.*

"I want Mommy and Daddy," whimpered Quintilian.

"They'll be back soon," said Honor.

"*Now.*"

"You'll have to wait," said Honor.

"What can I do?" Quintilian begged.

She scrambled to her feet. "We'll clean up." The children stuffed the clothes back into the closets. They made the beds. Finally, they tried to clean the kitchen. "Oh, the jam!" said Honor. The broken glass on the floor was the special jar of apricot preserves. "Don't come in!" she warned Quintilian. "You'll cut yourself."

She crouched down and tried to scoop up the apricots, but the jam was too runny. She mopped it all up instead.

They cleaned as best they could and ate bread and butter for dinner. The clock on the oven was broken, but she could tell time by the color of the sky. Like the stars and moon, sunset came from a projection booth in the City. With its powerful beam, the projection booth sent sky colors overhead. In hour six the sky was palest orange, in hour seven pink. A green flash signaled evening curfew at hour eight. Hour eight was lavender, also called Twilight. After that, night colors filled the sky: purple and indigo. Honor knew from the deep purple in the window that it was now past eight. "Let's go to bed," she told Quintilian.

"No!"

She began to drag him up the stairs, but he broke away. He cried himself to sleep on the couch and Honor lay down next to him.

Late, late that night, the key turned in the lock. Honor started up as Will and Pamela slipped inside. She thought, at first, that she was dreaming. Was that really her father walking in the door with his shirt so rumpled and sweaty? Was that her mother with her hair loose and the strap of her purse broken? She ran to them. "Where have you been? What took you so long?"

"We were held up," said Will.

"Who did that?" Honor pointed to her mother's purse.

"Shh," she said. "You'll wake Quintilian."

"We got robbed on the way home," Will whispered.

"And our house got searched while you were gone! What did you do?"

"We've done nothing wrong," Pamela said quietly.

"You're lying," Honor cried. "You do everything wrong. You wear the wrong clothes. You live in the wrong place. You say the wrong things." She turned on her father. "You buy the wrong jam." Tears welled in her eyes. "You break curfew! You're Unpredictable."

"That's enough," said Pamela. She picked up Quintilian and began carrying him upstairs. "Time for bed."

"I'm not going," said Honor. But her father took her by the hand and dragged her upstairs anyway. She said she wouldn't brush her teeth. She told her parents she wouldn't put on her pajamas, but in the end she did. She hung up her school uniform. She only had one other.

Her father bent down to kiss her good night.

Tears started again in Honor's eyes. "Why can't you just follow the rules?" she demanded.

Her father whispered, "The question is—*whose* rules?"

"What do you mean, whose rules? Her rules."

"Is she your parents?" Will asked Honor. "Does she tuck you in at night? You have a mother. You have a father. We're the ones who raise you; we're the ones who love you. Don't forget."

FOUR

GRADUALLY, HONOR BEGAN TO SLEEP BETTER, AND Quintilian's nightmares stopped. Safety Officers did not search the house again. When the children came home in the afternoon, they didn't jump at every little noise.

Life improved. Will was promoted at work, and at last the Greenspoons moved to a new house on higher ground. The house was an end unit with a little garden. The kitchen was big enough for a round table.

The previous tenants had disappeared and left their furniture. There was a green armchair and a couch with a pattern of palm leaves all over it. There were curtains at the picture window next to the front door.

"Don't catch the curtain in the door!" Pamela was always telling Honor when she came in or out. If the curtain got caught, it could get grease stains from the lock. Will laughed at Pamela for fussing, but she insisted, "Now that we have them, we're going to keep them nice; we've never had living room curtains before."

Honor and Quintilian got separate rooms. Quintilian got a tiny bedroom of his own, and Honor got to sleep in the study attached to the living room. The room had a built-in desk and a shelf, and sliding doors she could close at night to shut herself off from the living room when she wanted to sleep.

Honor was proud of her father's promotion and the new house. But when Honor looked at Will and Pamela, she felt helpless. They broke curfew more than once after moving. They went outside sometimes in the middle of the night. Honor asked them where they were going so late. "Stargazing," said Pamela.

"What's that supposed to mean?" Honor asked.

"When you look up at the stars, you can see patterns," Pamela said. "The Big Dipper and the Little Dipper, Orion's Belt. Gemini. You can learn hundreds of constellations."

"Your mother knows them all," Will said proudly.

"Well, not all of them," said Pamela, but she looked pleased.

"How can there be hundreds of constellations when there are seven stars in the sky at night?" Honor asked.

Pamela looked uncomfortable. "That's just the overlay," she said.

"Those stars are decorative," Will reminded Honor. "We look for the real ones."

"What real ones? Where can you see real ones?" Honor asked.

"Away from the City," said Will.

"And how is that Allowed?" asked Honor.

"No one ever said it's Not Allowed," her father told her.

"It's after curfew, so obviously it's Not Allowed! You can't just go off by yourselves in the dark."

"We aren't by ourselves. We go with the Thompsons," Pamela said.

Honor shook her head. Her parents were difficult. They laughed at weather drills and water regulations. They even complained aloud about their volunteer work. "Why do we have to *volunteer* for the anti-litter campaign?" Honor's father grumbled as he set off every evening on day three.

"Because everyone in the community has to combat litter," said Honor, accurately reciting what she'd learned in school.

"Yes, but why do they call it volunteering if I am required to go?"

Honor worried about her father constantly. He said all the wrong things and he didn't even care. She worried about her mother too. One day when Pamela was drawing, Honor saw a leaflet tucked inside her book.

Counter-Directives for a New World
1. *Cultivate your own fruit trees and eat fresh fruit each day.*
2. *Find dark places and study the night sky.*
3. *Try to remember something new each day.*
4. *You have nothing to fear but fear itself . . .*
—*The Forecaster*

"Where did this come from?" Honor demanded.

"I found it on the ground. In the City," her mother said.

"You're not allowed to collect these. You're not supposed to bring these home!"

"I need the paper," said Pamela. "I draw on the back."

Honor snatched Pamela's drawings and turned them over. "*Keep a diary. Write down your thoughts . . .*" On the back of each drawing, Honor saw the Forecaster's words. She began ripping the drawings, one after another.

"No, Honor!" Her mother snatched her artwork away.

"You can't keep those," Honor protested. It was a crime just to read the Forecaster's leaflets. If Safety Officers found them in the house, Honor didn't know what would happen.

"Please get rid of them," she begged her mother, but Pamela didn't listen.

Honor felt her family was heading toward disaster.

"I want to know where you go," she told her father.

"What are you really doing at night?" she asked her mother.

"Stargazing," her mother insisted.

"Tell that to Quintilian; don't tell that to me."

Her parents said nothing.

"Why can't you stay home?" Honor asked.

"We wouldn't go if it weren't important," said her mother.

"Tell me!"

Her parents turned away from her.

"What you don't know can't hurt you," her father murmured.

"At least give me some warning you'll be home late," Honor pleaded.

Her parents looked at each other. Then her father said, "Time for dinner." The discussion was over.

However, on Errand Day, when the four of them went to the Central Store, Will and Pamela stopped at the photo booth.

"We're getting our picture?" Quintilian exclaimed with delight.

"Honor," said Will, "you get to pick a glitter globe."

She couldn't believe her luck as she stood at the booth where a sign said: PICK YOUR OWN ENCLOSURE. She stood a long time gazing at the globes. They were the size of mangoes, perfect little worlds, each filled with water and glitter. She couldn't decide between the one with plastic palm trees, tiny pink flamingos, and the words *Safe and Secure* or the underwater scene with miniature fish and plastic coral. In the end she picked a different one altogether, a little red barn with a white picket fence, glitter green as grass, and the words *Welcome to Our Country*.

They paid twenty points and entered the photo booth one at a time for their portraits. Then they watched as their miniature full-length pictures emerged from the photo machine. In their photos, even Will and Pamela stood no more than half an inch high. A young woman in a white photo booth uniform cut out each image. She inserted the pictures in grooves in the black base of the globe and then took out a clear plastic Enclosure already filled with glitter, scenery, and water. She snapped the base and Enclosure together and gave the globe its first shake. There they were in miniature, the four of them smiling in their tiny farm. Quintilian grabbed the globe and shook it hard.

"Careful!" Will warned him.

"It's guaranteed watertight," the photo booth lady told them, "as long as no one drops it."

"Don't let him hold it," Honor begged her parents. "He'll drop it before we get out of the store."

Usually Pamela just told Honor not to complain about Quintilian, but this time she listened. She took the glitter globe and put it in her purse.

At home, Pamela kept the globe. Honor was disappointed. Since she'd chosen the scenery, she'd thought it was her special present.

"Why did you buy it if you're going to hide it?" she asked.

But the next afternoon, when she came home from school, Honor found the globe on her desk. Will and Pamela stayed out late that night, past curfew, past bedtime.

After Honor put Quintilian to sleep, she turned off the light in her room, lay down, and held the globe in her hand. She shook it and tried to make out the dim figures next to the little barn. Her eyes closed, and her fingers loosened. When she woke up in the morning, she was afraid she'd dropped the globe and broken it. Pamela came in and found Honor hunting under her bed.

"I put it away last night when I got back," Pamela said.

Then Honor understood that her parents had left the glitter globe out for her because they'd planned to be away. She sat back on her heels. Her parents had listened to her. They were giving her warnings about when they would be gone.

She began to see that she was quite different from her parents. She understood how to get along where they did not. At school she'd learned that if you played by the rules, you did well. Ms. Lynch was her teacher that year, and she said there was a time and a place for everything.

School wasn't hard, once you understood how to fit in. If you fit in, then you wouldn't need thinking time or accident forms. In fact, you would never get in trouble. Honor saw all this, but her parents didn't.

She decided that year she was going to fit in, even if they did not. She would be perfect. If she had a test, she would get all the answers right. If she had homework, she would earn the extra points for neatness.

Honor worked on her penmanship. Each letter was small and perfect on the page. Her printed words looked like ants marching along on the lines of her notebook paper. Gradually, she began to write even smaller. Now her words looked like aphids on the veins of a leaf. *The ancient civilizations waged war against each other,* Honor copied painstakingly. *Their weapons were loud and violent. Their guns shot missiles called bullets with tremendous force. Bullets lodged in the flesh of victims or even blew off parts of their bodies. Other weapons included bombs, which caused explosions and fires. There were no Watchers to guard against wrongdoing. There were no tasers or compost bins. The Rule of Self-order was unknown.* She got A's in all her classes because her work was Accurate. Ms. Lynch said so.

Know your place. Do your job. Live in peace. That was the Rule of Self-order. Honor lived by that rule now. She did not think about the Northern Islands. In fact, she could not remember them at all. She thought only about her life in the

Colonies and her work at school. She did not want to stick out anymore. She did not want to be unusual.

She decided she would change everything about herself that didn't fit. That meant she had to stop being friends with Helix. None of the other girls in her class was best friends with a boy. They talked about the boys and giggled about them, but they weren't friends with them; they were only friends with one another. So Honor decided she would tell Helix she couldn't play with him anymore at recess.

"We can't," she told him. They were at his parents' house sitting on the floor of his room, playing Truce. Quintilian was building with Gizmos on Helix's bed. Gizmos weren't just blocks. They had magnets inside so they clicked together. Some Gizmos were solid colored and some were clear so you could build cities and then build Enclosures all around them. They were Quintilian's favorite toy, and Helix had thousands of them from when he was little—whole boxes and bins of Gizmos. "We're too old for Archeology anyway," Honor said.

Helix got up and took down his coin collection from the shelf on his wall. He had a whole collection of coins now. Quarters, nickels, dimes. He even had an ancient penny. "Why are we too old?"

"Because," said Honor.

"Because what?"

"We're thirteen," said Honor. "When we spend all our time finding coins in the playground, we look odd."

"Why does it matter how we look?" asked Helix.

"Because!" Honor burst out, frustrated. She was having

trouble putting it into words. "You're supposed to be playing ball with the boys," she said. "My best friend is supposed to be a girl. We stick out."

"You never cared before," said Helix.

"If you stick out," said Honor, "then sooner or later, you're going to get in trouble."

"If you don't want to be friends anymore," said Helix, "then fine." He threw down his cards.

"Well, I do, but not . . ." Honor trailed off. "At school," she said at last in a small voice.

"You want to be like *them*," said Helix.

"No, I don't," said Honor, but that was exactly what she wanted. She wanted to be like the other girls.

"Hmm," said Helix. "You're stupider than I thought."

"No, you are."

"No, you."

"No more fighting," Quintilian said.

"Shut up," said Honor.

"I'm telling Mommy you said a bad word," said Quintilian, scrambling off the bed.

"Go ahead," said Honor.

"Mommy!" Quintilian raced down the hall.

"Coward." Helix glared at Honor as he scooped up the cards from the floor.

After that Honor and Helix didn't play together. When their parents made them come along to each other's houses, they wouldn't even look at each other. Honor stayed near her mother. But Helix got the best revenge. He made friends with

Quintilian. He taught Quintilian all the card games he and Honor used to enjoy and spent hours building Gizmo cities with him. Helix didn't just ignore Honor; he took Quintilian away from her.

Honor told herself she didn't care. She was busy all the time with homework and Heliotropes. And always at school she watched the other girls to learn how to be like them. She noticed how they combed their hair behind their ears and how they wore their sun hats far back on their heads. She copied the way they sat with their arms on their desks and the way they whispered about one another.

"Did you see Hortense had gum?" Honor told Helena as they cleared away their lunches.

Helena drew closer and Honor murmured, "She's got sticks of gum stuck up her socks."

"Eew!" Helena thought for a moment. Gum in school was forbidden. "Should we tell on her?"

Honor shrugged slightly. "You can if you want to."

"Tell her what?" asked Hester, hovering near.

"Well, I'm not going to tell you!" Honor said.

"Why not?" asked Hester, and Honor and Helena laughed. Making friends with the girls wasn't so hard once you knew what to do.

Honor became so busy she didn't even notice when her parents stopped going to Helix's house. One night after dinner she thought she saw her mother with tears in her eyes, but then she was sure she was imagining things and went back to studying geography.

That year the girls were allowed a walk once a week instead of recess. They were permitted to stroll around the school grounds for forty minutes. Of course students could not walk alone, only in pairs. Whenever Honor had a chance, she took Helena as her partner. Helena was blond and thin. She lived in a house high up the mountainside. Her mother was an architect, and her father was a famous engineer who had been posted to the island for Special Purposes. But Helena was not proud, despite her fancy house and her father's high position. She was quiet and good at whispering.

One day, Honor and Helena decided to take the path to the school's Model Forest. This was a steep trail and took almost half an hour to climb, but the forest was both interesting and educational. The Model Forest was the forest of the future, meant to demonstrate how the island would look when Enclosure was complete.

The Model Forest's trees were planted in neat rows. Vines hung down untangled, as if someone had combed them straight. Along the path, mountain apples and passion fruit grew abundantly. All the orchids were in bloom at once: white and pale green and golden yellow veined with red. In the Model Forest, orderlies set out dishes of fresh fruit to feed the butterflies and replaced dead or dying plants as soon as they began to decay.

Honor and Helena were breathing hard when they got to the lookout point that crowned the Model Forest. This was a spot where the trees had been cut away and students could look down over the school grounds and beyond—all the way down into the valley between the volcano's ridges. Honor could see the winding road the buses took to school, the green banana plantations below, and, far down, the island's only city clinging to the slope. Beyond that she saw the strip of empty beaches and the rough green ocean, big as the sky.

The wind whipped at the girls. "Hold on to your hat!" Helena called out, and Honor saved her hat just in time. The younger students had strings that tied under their chins, but older girls were meant to be responsible and keep their hats on without.

"Let's go back," said Helena as the wind whipped even harder. Their skirts blew out around their knees. "It's getting rough."

"I like it," Honor confessed. The lookout was the only outside place where she felt cool. The wind woke her up; its force thrilled her. "Don't you wish you could fly?" she asked Helena.

She saw Helena's horrified face and she was embarrassed.

"Let's go," Honor said.

They made their way back through the Model Forest and headed down toward the school buildings. Wisps of blond hair had escaped Helena's hat and blown about her face. Helena tucked them in. "I don't like it there," she said.

"I don't either," Honor lied.

Helena looked at her, confused. "You acted like you did."

"Well, I don't," Honor insisted. "It's too wild. It's scary!"

"I know," said Helena. "I was afraid of blowing away."

"Let's never go there again," Honor said.

"Watch your feet," Helena warned. The school grounds

were muddy after the rains, and students had to keep to a raised boardwalk.

The other girls were gathering now, walking in pairs down the other boardwalks to the classroom, but a couple of boys with wheelbarrows blocked the path in front of Honor and Helena. They were orphans wheeling fertilizer for the gardens.

Honor and Helena wrinkled their noses. The orphans all had jobs at the school in the gardens. They wore regular uniforms in class, but they had overalls for work.

"Hurry up or we'll be late," Helena told the boys worriedly.

One of them, a blond one, looked up and glared at the girls. "You could go around, you know."

Honor took Helena's arm and hurried her off the path and through the mud.

"My shoes!" cried Helena.

"That was Helix," Honor whispered.

"Stop pulling me."

"Helix isn't an orphan," said Honor.

Helena and Honor clambered back onto the walkway. "Yes, he is," Helena whispered back. "He's a new one."

"What do you mean?" Honor asked.

For a moment, Helena forgot her muddy shoes and flushed with pleasure at the chance to tell the news. "Didn't you hear? His parents were taken."

FIVE

LATENESS WAS NOT ALLOWED. HONOR HURRIED BACK INSIDE the classroom and sank into her chair. When had the Thompsons been taken? Why hadn't her parents told her? What had the Thompsons done?

No one ever knew how parents disappeared. They would go off to work as usual, and they'd never be heard from again. Or you could go to sleep at night, and in the morning your parents' bed was empty. It would happen without a sound. Who took them? Nobody knew. For what reason? None were ever given. No one talked about it. But of course parents were taken because they did wrong. Honor knew her criminal categories. She'd received a perfect score on that week's vocabulary test:

1. Dissembler
2. Objector
3. Rejector

4. Trespasser
5. Hijacker
6. Enemy of the community
7. Enemy of the Corporation
8. Enemy of Nature
9. Partisan

She had ranked those nine in order from least to most dangerous. She'd printed the worst last. Number ten: Reverse Engineer. Young children weren't even allowed to say those words.

Older students learned about RE's in climatology. Everyone remembered that lesson. Ms. Lynch had stood before the class and said, "We are going to talk about something very serious today."

Then the girls shuddered. They knew it was coming.

"What makes a Reverse Engineer the worst criminal?" asked Ms. Lynch.

"They're terrorists," said Hilary.

"Yes, but that's not all," said Ms. Lynch.

"They want to destroy the Corporation," said Hiroko.

"Yes. But there's something even worse."

"They want to crack the ceiling," Hagar said quietly.

The room was still.

"That's correct, Hagar," said Ms. Lynch. "Globe monitor?"

Hilary jumped to her feet and began wheeling the globe to the front of the room. The globe was beautiful and Accurate. Oceans were deep blue, and islands stood out in relief. Mountains on the larger islands pricked the surface of the globe. Above and below, over the arctic seas and lakes in the Far North and Far South, two clear plastic shells represented Enclosure.

Ms. Lynch pointed to the clear coverings over the poles. "Our engineers built these," she said. "When the Earth Mother designed our Enclosures, everyone knew they would protect us. But a few people did not understand. They did not accept the situation. What were these people called?"

"Objectors," said Hortense.

"That is correct. Almost every Objector was reeducated. However, a few would not join hands to protect the earth. These people refused to understand, and they did not learn their lesson. They wanted to stay in their old homes in the Northern Islands. They resisted Evacuation to the Colonies and went into hiding. They call themselves Partisans. The worst of the Partisans are called Reverse Engineers. Why are these Partisans the worst? Because they use their knowledge against us. Class, who is the leader of the Reverse Engineers?"

"The Forecaster," whispered Honor.

"And what is his goal?"

No one answered.

Ms. Lynch lowered her hand on the Northern Enclosure and pressed her palm hard and harder. Suddenly the clear plastic cracked. The delicate plastic shell snapped in two.

The girls gasped. Honor felt her chest tighten. She could hardly breathe.

"The Forecaster and his Reverse Engineers want to dismantle Earth's Enclosure." Ms. Lynch paused to let this sink in. "What will happen without a ceiling?" she asked.

Ice and snow, blizzards, whirlwinds, fires, earthquakes. They all knew, but they were afraid to say.

Honor raised her hand. "Why?" she asked. "Why would RE's do something like that?"

But Ms. Lynch was already looking at the clock. "Time for glassblowing," she said. "Please find your mitts and safety goggles."

What sort of criminals had Helix's parents been? And were they both equally bad? Why were parents taken in pairs or not at all? Honor could not stop thinking about these questions as she sat at her school desk. She could not stop wondering as she and Quintilian walked home through their pretty new neighborhood with its streets lined with lychee and pomegranate trees. The question that really scared her—the one she tried to blink away—was what would happen to her own parents? They were close to the Thompsons. They broke rules all the time. What if . . . ? What if her parents did more than break the little rules? What if they broke big ones too?

"What happened to the Thompsons?" she demanded that night at dinner.

"Not in front of Quintilian," said her mother.

"What do you mean not in front of Quintilian? Everybody knows," said Honor. "Everybody at school can see that Helix is wearing orphan's clothes."

"Well, if everybody knows, then why are you asking us?" asked her mother.

Honor's parents looked sad. They looked worn. Will and Pamela no longer laughed and made jokes or talked about the

island as an adventure. They had shadows under their eyes from lack of sleep.

"Are you going out tonight?" Honor asked.

Her parents didn't answer.

"Are you?" Honor asked again.

No answer.

Then she lost her temper. "Why are you keeping secrets if you know it's wrong?" she demanded. "Why do you stay out when you should be here taking care of us?" She pushed her chair away from the table and ran to her room.

Her mother came to her door. "You have not been excused," she told Honor.

"I don't care," said Honor from where she was lying on her bed.

Her mother opened Honor's sliding door and peeked inside.

"Go away," said Honor.

"You're frightened," her mother said.

"No, I'm not frightened," Honor snapped. "I'm angry at you."

"Be a little patient!" said her mother.

Honor buried her head under her pillow. "How can I be patient if I don't know what I'm waiting for?"

She woke up in the night and stared at her dark ceiling. She thought of the Thompsons. Even people with safe rooms weren't safe. The Thompsons had disappeared, and now she knew what would happen. She knew, even as day followed day. Her parents would be taken. She and Quintilian would wake up alone.

How could she keep her parents safe? How could she warn them? They wouldn't listen to her. There was nothing she could do or say. She saw that her parents had made their choices long ago. Two children, not one. Breaking curfew. Hiding books. Collecting leaflets. Had her father really taken her beyond the barriers at night and forced her to touch the ocean? Had he actually brought seashells into the house? What kind of dad was that? Honor looked back and she remembered her parents' old winter blankets and their songs. "Jingle Bells." What had they been thinking? Sometimes she looked at Will and Pamela and she had no idea who they were.

She decided she would have to change herself instead. She would protect them by doing everything right. In the morning she dressed in her uniform and examined herself in the mirror. She set her hat on her head just so and tied on her green neckerchief, the symbol of the Young Engineers. She looked like a proper schoolgirl from a predictable family. Her schoolwork was Accurate. She behaved appropriately. What else could she do? She looked into the mirror and stared into her own gray eyes, and she knew.

She told her parents, just as they left the house for work, "I want to change my name."

"Honor!" her mother exclaimed. "No!"

"We'll discuss this later," said her father.

"Honor isn't a real name," said Honor. "No one else in my class has a name like mine."

"It's the name we gave you," said Will.

"But it doesn't fit," said Honor. "I want to pick another name—a good one."

Her mother was rushing around, looking for her keys. "You may not pick another name. Your name was our decision."

"Was *my* name your decision?" Quintilian chimed in. "Was mine?"

"Here they are," said Will. He handed Pamela her key chain.

"You're lunatics," Honor whispered.

"How dare you use that kind of language in this house," said Pamela.

"Apologize. Now," Will ordered Honor.

"I'm sorry," Honor muttered.

"Say it like you mean it," said Will.

But Pamela shook her head. "If you wait for that, they'll miss their bus."

Honor had to run all the way to the bus stop. She dragged Quintilian by the hand, and they made it just in time.

At lunchtime she went up to the teacher's desk. "What can I do for you?" asked Ms. Lynch.

Honor hesitated. She felt a little sick. She had to force herself to talk. "It's about my name."

Ms. Lynch looked at her closely, but her eyes were kind and understanding.

"I want a new one," said Honor, "because mine doesn't have a proper *H*."

Then Ms. Lynch smiled. "That would be just fine," she said. "I will get you the list, and at recess you and the other girls can pick out a new one if you like. Once you've decided, all you have to do is go to Miss Blessing and she will register your new name in the school record books."

The whole class was excited at the idea of renaming Honor. Even the girls who liked her less gathered at recess at the green benches under the monkeypod tree. Together they pored over the list. "Ooh, ooh, what about Hecuba?"

"No! It sounds like geometry!"

"Hephzibah."

"Oh, that's so sweet. Could you be Hephzibah?" Haven asked.

Honor didn't answer. She felt funny. She'd been determined to go through with this, but now she felt as though she were falling.

"Hannah!" said Hildegard.

"Hypolita," said Harriet V.

Honor knew she had to pick a name fast, while she still had her nerve. She took the list and flipped the pages. She closed her eyes and set her finger down.

No one spoke. Honor opened her eyes and saw the name she'd picked. "Heloise," she said.

"Ooh, that's so cute," said Hortense. "I wish I could pick out my own name. You are so lucky."

"Heloise is *so* nice," said Helena, "and the beginning of your name will sound just like mine!"

Recess was over. Honor returned the list to Ms. Lynch and told her the name she'd chosen.

"That's very pretty," said Ms. Lynch. "You may see Miss Blessing while the rest of us are at archery."

• • •

All the school buildings had excellent cooling units, but Miss Blessing kept her office extra cold. As soon as she walked in, Honor wished she were at archery in the hot sun. She loved archery. She had a good eye and a strong arm. "You are extremely Accurate," Miss Teasdale, the archery teacher, had complimented Honor. Once Miss Teasdale even said, "If you practice, you could learn to shoot a taser when you grow up." Honor had been so pleased. She'd imagined herself high up in a watchtower. What a view she'd have! What cool breezes high in the air where she'd sit, guarding the community below.

"Sit down," Miss Blessing said now in her sweet voice. Her skin was smooth and white, her eyes watery blue. She was dressed in the same fashion as Earth Mother in the picture on the wall. Just like Earth Mother, Miss Blessing wore glasses dangling from a chain around her neck and a cardigan sweater draped over her shoulders. "I hear you have something important to tell me."

"I'm changing my name." Honor's voice trembled a little, but there was no turning back now.

Miss Blessing smiled and put on her glasses so that she could read the papers on her desk. "Ms. Lynch told me," she said. "I will record the new name in your file and I wish you great success with it." She turned to her papers and began writing.

Honor shifted in her chair. She wasn't sure whether or not she was excused to go. "Thank you," she whispered at last, hoping the principal would release her.

"There is something else I want to ask you about," said

Miss Blessing. "Please don't worry. You've done nothing wrong. I want to know if there is any trouble at home."

Honor tensed. Instinctively she held still. She tried not to move, but her heart was pounding. She did not know what Miss Blessing meant, but she sensed danger.

"Some trouble with Quintilian?" Miss Blessing asked.

Honor shook her head.

"Or with your mother and father?"

Honor swallowed.

"Was there some special reason you wished to change your name?"

"No," Honor said clearly. "I just wanted to have a name easier to pronounce."

"Of course you did," said Miss Blessing. "And your parents agreed."

She didn't ask it as a question, but she seemed to be waiting for Honor to answer.

"Yes," Honor lied. She couldn't breathe. She thought she'd suffocate for the long moment Miss Blessing examined her.

"Are you *sure*?" Now Miss Blessing's voice was chilly sweet.

Honor had two choices then. She could tell the truth or lie some more. If she told the truth, she'd be forgiven. She'd have Miss Blessing's sympathy. She would be perfect as she'd hoped, but she would also have to admit there was trouble at home, and then her parents would get in trouble. If she lied more . . . She remembered Mrs. Whyte's words her first day of school. *We do not lie. Do you know what happens to children who lie?* Honor had no idea what would happen.

She wanted to run away, but no one could run away from school. There was a watchtower right at the school gate. If she tried, the Watcher would sound the alarm, and Miss Tuttle would retrieve her.

"At first my parents didn't agree," Honor said. She was surprised at how clear her voice sounded. "But when I explained why, then they understood."

"Is that the truth?" Miss Blessing asked.

Half the truth, thought Honor, but she nodded solemnly. She might have looked too solemn, because Miss Blessing narrowed her eyes. "All right, Heloise," she said at last. "You may be excused."

Honor sat there a moment longer. Then she remembered *she* was Heloise and scrambled to her feet.

SIX

WILL AND PAMELA WOULD NOT CALL THEIR DAUGHTER
Heloise, no matter how Honor begged. They refused to believe
she had a new name.

"I need to go to the Identity Bureau," Honor pleaded on
Errand Day. "I have to get a new card."

"You will not go," said Will.

"We will not take you," said Pamela.

"I hate you!" Honor cried. She was desperate. She could not
get a new card without the signature of her parent or guardian.
She also knew she could not return to school after Errand Day
with her old card showing in her shirt pocket. That was all
the proof Miss Blessing would need that her parents had not
agreed to the change and that Honor had lied.

Errand Day passed, and a new week began. Honor came
to school on day one and hid in the crowd of girls in the
classroom doorway. She clutched her stack of books to her

chest. Ancient History, Intermediate Climatology, Algebra I. She hid in the crowd, but she had to walk to her desk, and she couldn't hold her books over her ID card forever. She had to put them down.

All that morning she bent self-consciously over her work. She felt her old name burning on her shirt. The other girls were so used to the old ID card they didn't notice. They kept calling her Honor and then catching themselves. "Oops! I mean Heloise." Ms. Lynch never made that mistake. She always called Honor by her new name. It was just a matter of time before Ms. Lynch noticed that Honor's ID card was wrong.

"Hiroko will recite today," Ms. Lynch announced in history. "Please open your books to chapter five."

"*When the Flood began,*" Hiroko recited, "*countries battled for fresh water.*"

"Let's hear your voice," said Ms. Lynch.

"*Armies fought for a safe food supply. When the Flood ended, ninety percent of Earth's population was no more. The old communication networks were broken. Fear and famine overcame Earth. At this time, the Earth Mother, our Provider, began to gather men and women from each country to form the New Consensus. She appointed seven Councilors to advise Her, and together they formed a new government. She called this new government the New Council for Cooperation, or the Corporation, for short. . . .*"

Ms. Lynch can't see my ID card, Honor thought as she bent over her open book. *Her eyes are bad.* For once she was grateful for the boring history recitation. Slowly, steadily, Hiroko kept talking.

"*Sadly, not all the survivors on Earth joined hands in Cooperation. Those who did not cooperate soon learned that Earth Mother could not provide food and water and housing for them. She cast them out. . . .*"

A sharp rap on the classroom door startled Honor. "Excuse me, Hiroko," said Ms. Lynch. She opened the door and there was Miss Blessing.

"We'd like to borrow Heloise," said Miss Blessing.

Now Honor wished she were invisible. She wished she could fly away, but she had to obey Miss Blessing.

"Go along, Heloise," said Ms. Lynch.

Honor set down her book and slipped through the classroom. She felt the other girls wondering about her as she walked past, but when she turned toward them, they looked down at their desks. "Shut the door behind you, please," Ms. Lynch said. Honor's hands trembled as she obeyed.

"We have a problem," Miss Blessing told Honor in the hall.

Distantly, Honor heard Hiroko picking up just where she'd left off. "*. . . into wild places. Those who did not cooperate could not survive. However, those who did join hands with Earth Mother soon formed a Safe and Secure society. They took refuge in the Colonies, the islands of the ancient South Pacific, now renamed the Tranquil Sea. . . .*"

"The problem is Quintilian," said Miss Blessing. "He is in the infirmary."

Honor's eyes widened. No mention of her card at all? And Quintilian sick? Or hurt? He was just three and a half and he came home with I's for Inaccuracies on his report card. He was known in year Q as Unruly. But he had never been in the infirmary before.

Nurse Applebee was sitting at her desk filling out a blue accident report. "We have left messages at your parents' places of work," she said to Honor. "Your little boy"—she politely avoided the term *brother*—"will have to spend the night here."

"But what did he do?" asked Honor.

"He fell out of the banyan tree in the playground," said Nurse Applebee.

"How did he—?"

"He didn't say," said the nurse. "He can't remember."

Honor followed Nurse Applebee and Miss Blessing into the clean white infirmary lined with beds. Quintilian lay small and pale, propped up with pillows. His head was bandaged, his eyes wide open.

"Quintilian," said the nurse gently, "can you hear me?"

"Yes," he said.

"Do you know what day it is?"

He hesitated.

"Do you know where you are?"

"In bed," he said.

"Where do you live?" asked the nurse.

"In the Colonies," he said.

"But what is your address?"

He didn't answer.

"And who owns the Colonies?"

"The Corporation," Quintilian said quickly. He seemed to be waking up. Honor sighed with relief.

"Good."

"And who is this?" Miss Blessing pointed to Honor.

He smiled at her even as he said the wrong name. "Honor."

"You see, he has a concussion," said Nurse Applebee.

But now Miss Blessing turned to Honor. "Where is your new identity card?"

"I don't know. I forgot it," Honor spluttered. Then she gave up. "I don't have one." She shuddered, tensing for the punishment she knew would come.

But Miss Blessing did not call her out into the hall. She did not threaten punishment. She just turned to leave, and as she did, her voice floated back into the room, so quiet and sweet and frightening. "You see now? Isn't it better to tell the truth?"

All that afternoon, Honor trembled to think what would happen. She could not concentrate on algebra and spoiled her bowl in ceramics class. She knew she would be punished for having the wrong identity card. The punishment would come, even if Miss Blessing chose not to mention it yet. Honor wished she were home. She wished she'd never thought of changing her name. If she'd listened to her parents, she wouldn't have gotten into this mess. All she'd wanted was to fit in, and now her card was Inaccurate. That was Not Allowed.

She rode the bus home without Quintilian. Alone, she

trudged up the hill to the house. Her book bag was heavy. The sun beat down on her shoulders and sweat trickled down her face. Once she got inside the cool house, she dumped her bag, pulled off her hat, and sank down on the tiled living room floor.

She missed Quintilian. Her afternoon was easy but also empty without him. A huge sadness welled up inside her as she wrote out her algebra equations. She wanted her parents—but once again they were late. She went to her bedroom, but they had not left the glitter globe out for her. This had happened once or twice before when they stayed out late. They always apologized in the morning.

Through the window she saw it was hour seven. In the pink light she ate oatmeal cookies and mangoes for dinner. She drank a glass of milk.

After the green flash, the sky shifted to lavender, then deep purple. No sign of her mother and father. Honor began pacing back and forth in the living room. Every few seconds she looked anxiously at the front door. Then a black mark on the curtain caught her eye. The curtain hanging near the front window had gotten caught in the door. She could see the grease stain from the lock. The stain her mother always warned about—"Don't catch the curtain!"

She looked back at the living room. Everything was as it should be, neat and orderly, maybe even neater than before. The coffee table was covered with Quintilian's toys, but they'd been arranged neatly, Evacuation in its box, playing cards stacked on top. She peeked into her bedroom, Quintilian's bedroom, the hall closet. The closet shelves were piled with folded sheets and towels. She stared for a long time at the two kites lying on the top shelf in a tangle of string and wrinkled wings.

She walked through the bedrooms. They were untouched, but the light was on in her parents' bathroom. The door stood ajar. She stood a long time before the door. She was afraid to open it. She didn't want to touch it, but she had to. She was beginning to shiver. She was so cold her teeth were chattering. She put her hand on the door and pushed. There on the tile floor lay the glitter globe, smashed in a little pool of sparkling water.

She doubled over, almost sick. She didn't know who'd broken it or how. Safety Officers? Search dogs? Had her mother tried to take the glitter globe with her? Or had her father smashed it to warn her? She didn't know. She would never find out. All she knew was that she and Quintilian were alone now. Their parents had been taken.

PART
THREE

ONE

AT FIRST, HONOR HOPED THERE WAS SOME MISTAKE. HER parents weren't missing, only late again or lost or robbed as they had been that time before. She hoped she was dreaming even when she saw the sunrise through the window. She was still wearing her school uniform, and she was curled up on the couch, wrapped in the old blue mohair blanket from the North.

The house was filled with light: pure canary yellow. The day's first weather bulletin was sounding. Honor shook off sleep. She raced into her parents' room, but their bed was smooth and blank, the white covers pulled up neatly. She didn't dare look again at the glitter globe on the floor of her parents' bathroom. Her uniform was wrinkled, and she had to catch the bus. What would she tell Quintilian? They couldn't be orphans. They just couldn't. They couldn't live with the boarders at school. There were no orphans in Honor's class of girls. Only Hector and Helix on the boys' side. The girls' class had a perfect twelve and Honor had been perfect too. Or she had tried to be.

She stared at herself in the bathroom mirror. The girl she'd been the day before was gone. Her hair was messy now, her uniform creased. Her face was pale and streaked with tears, even though she couldn't remember crying. The identity card in her pocket still said *Honor* and not *Heloise. You see now?* she heard Miss Blessing tell her. And she did see. She had brought this on her parents. She had exposed them just when she should have been protecting them. She'd changed her name against their wishes. She'd lied, and when at last she'd told the truth, everybody had known—Miss Blessing had known, and the Safety Officers had known. The whole Corporation knew that Honor's parents were unusual; their ideas were Inaccurate. They did not belong.

How could she have called her own parents lunatics? They might be going to the asylum now, the dusty glass houses on the moon. All the little children thought that was where the Disappeared ended up.

Honor was shivering again. What should she do? She began pulling out drawers in the kitchen. She looked inside all the cabinets. Wouldn't they have left a note? Some instructions for her, just in case? She searched under the beds. The sky changed from canary yellow to pale blue. She knew only one thing. She could not miss the bus to school.

There was no time for breakfast. She washed her face and brushed her teeth. Then she tore off her creased clothes and changed quickly into her other uniform. She brushed her hair and tried to smooth it down. She clapped her sun hat on her head and took her book bag and her key. She could not miss the bus; she had to catch it, or everyone would know.

Ms. Lynch did not treat Honor differently. She did not look at Honor specially or call her out of class. There was no message to go to Miss Blessing's office either, even though Honor sat on the edge of her chair expecting one. She concentrated on school. She thought only about her work. There would be no change in her. No one would ever know her parents were gone. She felt her life depended on it. When she took a math test, Honor checked her work twice, and she was grateful for the silence in the classroom and the slow-moving clock. She didn't want school to end.

Honor's heart jumped when the last bell rang, but she tried to stay calm. Head down, she gathered her books. She walked to the infirmary and got Quintilian, who was sitting up in bed and feeling much better. She didn't tell him anything but hurried him onto the bus as if it were an ordinary day.

They walked home from the bus stop and Quintilian dashed ahead, zooming and zipping and making noises like submarines—"Fooosh! Splashdown!"—for an imaginary story he was telling himself.

Honor didn't tell Quintilian anything. She unlocked the door as she always did and gave him New Directives to cut up while she did her homework. She half believed that somehow her parents would come home. When it got dark, Honor acted as though Will and Pamela were out late again, and she made toast for dinner. Quintilian liked toast with butter. But Honor saw when she opened the refrigerator that there was hardly any butter left. She hadn't cried all day, but when she saw only a sliver of butter, tears started in her eyes. How would they get enough food for dinner without their parents' coupon books? As a thirteen-year-old, Honor got only thirteen points a week, and Quintilian was only three, so he got none.

She gave Quintilian the butter and ate her own toast plain. Then she said, "Put on your pajamas and I'll tell you a story."

"Why?" asked Quintilian.

"Because it's time for bed."

"Where's Mommy and Daddy?"

"They must be late," Honor said. "Time to brush your teeth."

"No, I'm waiting," said Quintilian.

"It's your bedtime," said Honor, and started dragging him to his room.

Quintilian started screaming.

"Do you want the Neighborhood Watch to come?" Honor demanded, pulling hard on his arm.

"I don't care. I don't CARE!" Quintilian screamed even louder.

"Do you want them to come and give us a ticket? Those are thirty points! We won't have any food for a week! Quiet down. The Watch might be coming any minute."

Quintilian took a long shuddering breath and listened. "Do you hear them now?" he asked.

"No, not yet, but you'd better come." She had to get him to bed. She couldn't talk to him anymore. She didn't know what to say.

All that night she dreaded the morning, when Quintilian would come into their parents' room looking for them. She couldn't sleep. Then, after she finally drifted off, she almost overslept. Just as she heard Quintilian stirring, she rushed out in her nightgown and closed her parents' door and sat down in front of it for good measure.

"I want Mommy and Daddy," said Quintilian.

"You can't see them," said Honor.

"I want Mommy and Daddy. Open the door."

"Breakfast first," said Honor.

Quintilian looked at her. "Get up," he said.

"I will if you come with me."

"Get up," he said.

Slowly, she got to her feet.

He leaped for the door, but she blocked him.

"I want Mommy and Daddy!" he wailed. Kicking and biting, he threw himself at Honor.

She let him attack her, and then suddenly she thought there was no use holding him off. She couldn't pretend to him any longer. She opened the door and he rushed inside the empty bedroom. He searched everywhere. Then she sat down next to him in the hall and told him.

"But where are they?" Quintilian asked her.

"Nobody knows," said Honor.

"Where are Mommy and Daddy?" he asked.

"They're gone," she said.

"Gone where?"

"Gone."

"I want them!" He began to cry.

"I know. But it's late. We have to go to school."

"I don't want to go to school. I want Mommy and Daddy. They aren't taken; they're coming back."

"Please, please stop crying," Honor said.

"They are not gone," sobbed Quintilian. "They are not taken."

Honor tried stroking his hair; she tried promising him a treat. She tried everything until at last she lied, "You're right. They're coming back."

When he heard that, Quintilian stopped crying. "When are they coming? Tomorrow?"

Honor hesitated.

"The day after tomorrow?"

"Yes," she said. "But we have to do everything right. You are going to have to be very good."

TWO

THEY WERE CAREFUL, THE TWO OF THEM. THEY PRACTICALLY tiptoed around the house. Quintilian still looked for their parents. He looked in all the closets and under the beds, but Honor told him they wouldn't come if he screamed and cried. He played quietly while Honor washed the dishes and separated the recyclables into their ten bins. On Errand Day he helped Honor take the dirty clothes to the laundry machines. They washed Will's and Pamela's clothes as usual and set up the racks in the living room as usual to hang the clothes to dry.

They took the bus to the City, and Honor bought milk and bread and cans of fish with her coupons. Quintilian didn't say anything about candy because Honor had warned him. She'd told him what would happen if he made a fuss. "Do you want us to be orphans?" she'd asked him. "You have to listen to me, or they'll make us live at school."

Honor was afraid at first that Quintilian wouldn't listen to her, but as the days passed, he lost his stubbornness. He just looked tiny and scared and did exactly what she said. Every night he tried to wait up, but every night their parents didn't come, and he fell asleep holding Honor's old bear in his arms.

Honor did everything right. She got Quintilian to the bus on time. She did all her homework. She kept the house neat, although not as neat as it had been before. At night she pushed Quintilian's toys under the furniture. When mail arrived, Honor stacked it neatly in the closet. She never opened the envelopes.

At bedtime Honor told Quintilian his favorite bedtime story. It was a story from one of the books in the school library, the tale of Dorothy and how she fell asleep and dreamed of the land of Oz. Honor told that story every night. Eventually Quintilian drifted off, but Honor stayed awake for hours. Where were they? Where had they gone? How had she allowed this to happen? She asked those questions over and over again. But the questions that really frightened her were simpler than that. Why did no one ask about her parents? No one came looking for Will and Pamela from work. No one said anything at school. The mail came as usual. New Directives piled up. The Neighborhood Watch, which was supposed to notice everything, never came to call. It didn't feel as though her parents had been taken; it felt as though they'd never existed in the first place.

She became exhausted because she couldn't sleep at night. Honor couldn't keep her eyes open on the bus, and once she even drifted off in class. Ms. Lynch stood right over her and clapped in front of Honor's face.

"Heloise!"

Honor started back in surprise. The other girls covered their mouths with their hands.

Honor's classmates were quiet. They acted almost the same, and yet none of them, not even Helena, was quite as friendly to Honor as before. The girls did not come up to Honor and start conversations. She had to come over and talk to them. If she wanted Helena to be her walking partner, she had to ask first.

Quintilian was having trouble. He didn't listen; he had accidents. He brought home red cards again, and Honor forged their parents' signatures. She wrote the names as well as she could, but they looked nothing like Will's and Pamela's handwriting. Strangely, no one at school noticed. Eleven days passed.

The twelfth day was unusually hot, and Honor had archery practice. The heat was terrible on the field. Sweat trickled down her face, and she wanted desperately to take off her sun hat, but the students were not allowed to take off their hats outside. There were six targets set up, and the girls were shooting in pairs. Honor and Hedwig shot together. Hedwig was good, but Honor was better. She had been practicing at her Young Engineer meetings and had even won a school ribbon for Accuracy. When she lifted her bow, the other girls put theirs down to watch. Honor planted herself and stared at the target; she placed her arrow and pulled her bowstring taut all the way to her ear. She felt fierce and strong standing there with that weapon, and then she felt angry. She was furious. Her hands began to shake; her eyes filled with tears. She tried to steady herself, but when she released her first arrow, she shot straight into the grass. The other girls gasped. Honor wiped her tears on her sleeve and tried again, but she couldn't see, because she was crying too hard. Miss Teasdale, the archery teacher, hurried over and took her bow.

"Are you sick, dear?" asked Miss Teasdale. "Are you hurt?"

Honor didn't answer, but Miss Teasdale sent her straight to the infirmary anyway.

"Come in," called Nurse Applebee in her honey voice. "I've been waiting for you."

Honor froze. There in the room next to Nurse Applebee was Miss Blessing.

"Please tell me what's the matter." Nurse Applebee leaned forward with concern in her eyes.

"Nothing," said Honor.

"Please tell us the truth, Heloise," said Miss Blessing. "Something is wrong. What is it?"

Then Honor realized something. Everyone else knew exactly what had happened. Ms. Lynch knew. Nurse Applebee knew. Miss Blessing knew. They had known all along. They'd only been waiting for her to tell them herself. Honor began sobbing. All this time she'd tried to hide it, and now she had to tell them. They sat waiting; they would wait for as long as it took.

"My parents," she sobbed.

"It's better to tell the truth, isn't it?" said Miss Blessing. "It's a relief to be honest with one another. That's why we teach the Rule here: honesty is our policy. Your parents are no more. This is something you must Accept."

Honor bowed her head automatically when she heard the word *Accept.* Miss Blessing didn't seem to notice Honor's fists clenched in her lap. She smiled sadly. "I know. I know."

Nurse Applebee gave Honor a tissue for her nose. Miss Blessing held out a little blue booklet stamped *Nurse's Copy: Do Not Remove.* The title of the booklet was *What It Feels Like When Parents Disappear.*

"Open it," said Miss Blessing, "and please read it carefully to yourself."

Obediently, Honor opened the book. *You may feel that you are to blame,* she read. *Many children feel that way, but that is Inaccurate. You are not to blame. You may feel angry. Many children feel that way, and that is natural. Your parents may have behaved inappropriately. They may have hurt or disrespected others. They may have exaggerated or even lied. They may have committed crimes against Nature. It is only natural to feel angry at them. . . .*

Honor looked up. "Keep reading," said Miss Blessing.

"Where is Quintilian?" Honor asked.

"We'll be bringing him in at the end of the day," said Miss Blessing, and Honor saw a picture book on the nurse's desk. *Disappear Means No One Here: A First Experiences Book.*

"No," said Honor. "We have to catch the bus."

"You won't need to worry about the bus anymore," said Miss Blessing.

"We have to go home," said Honor desperately.

"You *are* home," said Miss Blessing.

THREE

QUINTILIAN PULLED BACK WHEN HONOR TOOK HIM TO THE Boarders' Houses that evening. He clung to her. He was afraid of the orphans' plain cinder-block buildings, half hidden by flowers and blooming trees.

"Come on." She dragged him by the hand.

There had been ten orphans at the school, and now, with Honor and Quintilian, there were twelve, six girls and six boys. The girls' and boys' houses were identical, long and narrow. Beds were lined up on one side and desks lined up against the wall opposite. Between the beds were nightstands. On each nightstand where family pictures might have been stood a framed picture of Earth Mother. On each nightstand there was also a copy of the little green book, placed in those days in all public buildings and offices, *Sayings of Earth Mother*. Every schoolchild knew the fifty sayings of Earth Mother:

"Cooperation makes it happen." That was one. *"We've got the whole world in our hands."* That was another. And, *"You get what you get, and you don't get upset."*

The only difference between the girls' house and the boys' house was that the girls had green blankets on their beds and the boys had blue. The girls had Mrs. Edwards to watch them and the boys had Mr. Edwards. Mrs. Edwards had wavy blond hair to her shoulders, but to Honor her hair looked dyed. Mr. Edwards had just a little gray hair and glasses. Both the Edwardses were short, but Mrs. Edwards looked much sturdier than her husband. The two had no child and lived in a tiny house of their own attached to the back of the Boarders' Houses. One door opened into the girls' house and one door opened into the boys' house so they could come in at any moment.

"Heloise," said Mr. Edwards. "Quintilian. Welcome to your new home. As you can see, our orphans come from all years, but everyone is equal here. Our work uniforms, for example, are all hand-me-downs." Mr. Edwards gave a pair of overalls to Quintilian and one to Honor too. "We share chores and we share food. We eat here every day." He pointed to a pair of picnic tables under a large green awning. "We hold a morning meeting, and then at night we have evening circle here as well."

"Why don't you go inside," said Mrs. Edwards, "and meet your new friends."

Quintilian and Honor stood together. Honor was holding her work uniform with one hand and Quintilian with the other. He was holding tight, and she didn't know what to do.

She really didn't know how Quintilian would sleep at night or how he would get along. He could barely dress himself. He often put his pants on backward. How many times had she reminded him that the zipper goes in front?

Mr. Edwards didn't seem concerned. He approached Quintilian with a smile and pulled him off Honor as fast as if he were ripping off a bandage. Quintilian yelped with surprise, but Mr. Edwards ushered him into the boys' house and left Honor to follow Mrs. Edwards.

The other girls were named Fanny, Gretel, Eva, Elspeth, and Eglantine. They were all big girls. Even though Honor was thirteen, she would be the youngest orphan. Gretel was fourteen and Fanny fifteen. Eva, Elspeth, and Eglantine were sixteen. They were sitting at their desks doing their homework. Honor shuddered as they all looked up at her. Together they had that look the girls in *H* had labeled orphanish. The look was a quick, hungry glance and then a ducking away, as though someone might hit them. Honor didn't want to go anywhere near those orphan girls. Wildly she thought, *This is a mistake; I don't belong here.*

Mrs. Edwards pushed Honor forward. "This is your bed, dear, and this is your desk. After homework there will be table setting and dinner, then table clearing, dish washing and kitchen cleaning, evening circle, and time for sleep."

Honor slumped down at her desk. She didn't even take out her books. What was the use? The worst had happened.

Eglantine was staring over at her from the next desk. She had a worried orphanish face, short brown hair, and round blue eyes.

Honor glared back. "Staring problems?" she demanded in her haughtiest voice.

Instantly, Eglantine turned back to the Advanced Climatology text in front of her. "You'd better do it," she whispered.

"Do what?" asked Honor.

"Your homework," said Eglantine. "They'll give you extra chores if you don't get it done."

Honor drew herself up. She sat in her chair and stared at the bare cinder-block wall in front of her. She did not take out her books. She was a prisoner. She knew that was what orphans really were. They were just prisoners who went to school. That was why no one talked to them.

An hour passed and Honor felt stiff sitting at her desk. Her mouth was parched and dry; her mind was numb. She did not know what to do. She had no ideas left, only the fear that she would not be able to protect Quintilian. At least Quintilian was with Helix in the boys' house. Quintilian loved Helix, and Honor knew Helix would look out for him.

"Heloise," said Mrs. Edwards when she came to check on the girls, "I am concerned that you have not completed your homework. Why is that the case?"

"Because I haven't started it," Honor whispered.

"Are you being facetious with me?" asked Mrs. Edwards.

"What does *facetious* mean?" asked Honor.

"You may look that word up in the dictionary," said Mrs. Edwards. "I will not punish you today," she added kindly. "But this will be your first and last warning. Every night your homework must be completed. Do you understand?"

"Yes," Honor whispered.

"And I have brought you something as well," Mrs. Edwards said cheerfully. She handed Honor a small envelope.

Honor felt the other girls staring. They were all trying to see what Mrs. Edwards was giving her.

"Aren't you going to open it?" Mrs. Edwards asked.

Honor opened the envelope and saw a brand-new identity card with her picture and her correct name, Heloise.

"There you are," said Mrs. Edwards softly. She touched Honor lightly on the shoulder and then took Honor's old identity card from her pocket. The card was stiff plastic, but Mrs. Edwards bent it one way and then another, and at last the card with Honor's old name broke in two. In place of the Inaccurate card, Mrs. Edwards slipped the new card into Honor's pocket. "Look at you now," said Mrs. Edwards. "You won't have to worry anymore."

Dinner was leftovers from the school lunch. The food was exactly the same: fried fish, rice, green salad, and stewed prunes. Two orphans wheeled the leftovers from the school kitchen to the Boarders' Houses.

The boys and girls ate together at one big table, and Honor sat next to Quintilian. "Eat the fish, at least," she whispered.

He looked at her as if he'd never seen her before. "No," he said.

"What's this I hear?" asked Mrs. Edwards, swooping down on Quintilian. "You don't eat fish?" She put her arm around him. "Are you allergic?"

Honor said, "He doesn't like the taste."

"Oh, is that all?" said Mrs. Edwards. And Mr. Edwards

took his tongs and placed a large helping of fried fish on Quintilian's plate along with a scoop of rice, a tangle of salad greens, and a spoonful of prunes.

"You'll need to eat everything on that plate," said Mrs. Edwards. "We don't have taste here."

After dinner and table clearing, the girls and boys sat in chairs under the awning for evening circle. Mr. and Mrs. Edwards led the children in "Safe We Shall Abide" and then the Corporate Creed. Nervously, Honor looked across the circle at Quintilian. There he was, sitting next to Helix. He was mouthing some of the Creed. He didn't know it well.

"We welcome Heloise and Quintilian to our circle," said Mrs. Edwards, "and we welcome them into our hearts as well." When Mrs. Edwards said "into our hearts," she touched her heart with her hand. Honor was startled to see Helix mocking Mrs. Edwards by putting his hand on his own heart.

"A moment of silence to reflect on the day," said Mrs. Edwards, and she closed her eyes.

The children bowed their heads and closed their eyes as well. Honor signaled anxiously to Quintilian to bow his head, but he wasn't paying attention.

After the moment of silence ended, Gretel spoke up. "Mrs. Edwards, Heloise wasn't closing her eyes."

"Is that true, Heloise?" asked Mrs. Edwards.

"How could she know my eyes were open if hers were closed?" Honor demanded. "Her eyes must have been open too!"

"Your eyes were open, then," Mrs. Edwards said sadly.

"I'm sorry to hear that," added Mr. Edwards. "There will be laundry duty tonight for you."

Eglantine was right. When orphans did anything wrong, they got more work. Extra chores were hard, because the orphans did so many to begin with. The orphans were part of what was called the Old Colony Work-Study Program.

After dinner, when the others were getting into their pajamas, Honor had to go to the laundry room. Eglantine showed her the way.

In the tiled room Honor separated white from colored laundry and Eglantine helped her. Together they loaded clothes into a giant washing machine. Honor struggled to lift and tip the enormous jug of detergent. When she poured it into the special hole in the top of the washing machine, she spilled, and clear detergent slid over the face of the washer and onto the floor.

"Here, mop it up with the dirty clothes," said Eglantine.

Honor grabbed a dirty pajama top from a bin and started mopping.

"Don't get it on your hands," Eglantine warned.

Honor nodded; she knew detergent was dangerous. Once Quintilian had gotten Planet Safe on his hands and rubbed some into his hair and face. For a day he was so memory-sick he couldn't even remember his own name.

Honor threw the pajama top back in the bin and washed her hands at the utility sink. She was tired and stiff, and she didn't want to talk. All she wanted to do was lie down and rest her head.

"I was just six," said Eglantine as they walked back to the Boarders' Houses. "I was a young orphan, so I've had more chance to get used to it. It's not so bad. The meetings are boring, and the work is hard, but you can earn prizes."

"What kind of prizes?" asked Honor.

"Chocolate, for one thing. And sometimes little toys."

"Aren't you too old for toys?" asked Honor.

Eglantine flushed. "Sometimes they're stuffed animals; sometimes they're miniature puzzles or games. Eva has Community. Gretel has travel Babble. We get three hours' recreation every Errand Day and then we can play."

"Could I ask you something?" Honor broke in. "Did you ever know any orphans who . . . Is there ever a mistake? And then the parents come back and get their kids?"

"Oh no, there's no mistake," said Eglantine. "But it's really not so bad. We have our own special birthday parties with almost any kind of cake. You can pick two friends to help you bake it in the Edwardses' kitchen. We get outings once a month."

"Where?" asked Honor.

"Usually the Central Store," said Eglantine. "Sometimes concerts." She paused and looked at Honor. "Well, I'm lucky," she admitted. "I was so little when I came that I don't miss my parents. I don't remember what they looked like anymore."

When Honor and Eglantine got back to the girls' house, Honor saw a pair of faded pajamas folded on top of her bed.

"Hurry," said Fanny, whose bed stood next to Honor's. Quickly, Honor took off her uniform and hung it from the hook above her nightstand. She pulled her pajamas on as fast as she could. Mrs. Edwards was already standing in the doorway when Honor climbed into bed. Honor pulled up the covers just in time.

"Peace, love, and joy," said Mrs. Edwards. "That's how we earn each day."

Earn? Honor thought. How could you earn a day? Each day came whether you wanted it or not.

"Lights out," said Mrs. Edwards, and the room went dark. Honor heard the door close and there was silence for several minutes. Then a shuffling whispering noise as girls sat up in bed to talk. Fanny scrambled right onto Honor's bed and sat cross-legged on it.

Honor was amazed. "But you can't get out of bed after lights-out. That's Not Allowed."

"Nothing fun is," Fanny pointed out.

"What if Mrs. Edwards comes back and turns on the lights?"

"The bulbs are Extra-Energy Savers," Fanny explained. "It takes over five minutes for the lights to come on—and by that time everyone's tucked in fast asleep again."

Honor almost laughed. "How long have you been . . . how long have you lived here?" she asked Fanny. She couldn't bring herself to say the word *orphan.*

"Only two years," said Fanny. "My parents disappeared two years ago on Errand Day. We went to the Central Store together. I was in the fitting room to try on my new uniform. I came out to show them how it looked and they were gone."

"What did you do?" asked Honor.

"Went to the Safety Officer on the floor, of course. I said I'd lost my parents. He took me to the store's Safety Office and we went to the supervisor. I told the supervisor my parents' names and asked if he could find them. He said he'd look them up in the store computer. There was a big computer on the desk. He looked them up and then he said, 'No, they're not lost. They've disappeared.'"

Honor held her pillow tight. She was trembling to hear this story, but Fanny's voice wasn't shaky at all. She sounded calm and even cheerful.

"The next day," said Fanny, "I came here."

"Who do you think took them?" Honor whispered.

"Don't know," said Fanny.

"What do you think they did?"

"No idea." Fanny yawned. "Something bad, I'm sure. I'm going back to bed."

"Wait," Honor said. "Were your parents strange? Were they unusual? Did you ever think they'd be taken?"

"Mmm. Maybe. They were disorganized," said Fanny. "They were messy. Our house was never clean. They never had enough coupons. They liked music too much."

"What do you mean?"

"They played instruments all the time—piano and violin. They played so much they forgot to go to their regular jobs. They'd sit and play their music and remember stuff. Like old people they used to know. And places filled with ancient paintings. And gardens. My mother could remember gardens where people danced. She said when she played she could remember women in long dresses and the hems of their dresses brushed the grass."

"Princesses?"

"I guess so," said Fanny. "There was one other thing they used to remember. Catching fish in mountain streams. In ancient times, people caught fish individually with hooks. When my father played his violin he always remembered that."

"That's so strange," said Honor.

"I know."

"Where do you think they were taken?"

"Where? Nowhere. They're dead, of course," said Fanny, amused.

"Not . . . on the moon?"

Fanny started giggling. "Oh, you believe all that about the asylum on the moon?"

"I'm not sure." Honor's voice trembled.

"Nobody lives on the moon, silly." Fanny slid off Honor's bed and jumped into her own.

The next morning Honor had to put on work overalls. The rough patched fabric scratched her skin; the baggy pants dragged on the ground. She felt like a criminal.

"Come on," said Eglantine, and she tried to take Honor by the hand. "I'll show you where the gardens are."

Honor shook her off. "Leave me alone."

Eglantine shot Honor an orphanish look, shy and patient. She waited for Honor in the doorway.

"I said leave me alone," Honor repeated.

"I have to wait for you," Eglantine explained. "We've been assigned together this week."

Then Honor followed Eglantine.

Every morning before school, the orphans worked for an hour in the vegetable gardens with farming and produce orderlies. Every evening after school, they took turns working in the kitchens or the recycling station or even cleaning classrooms with the school orderlies. The orphans would dust and shelve books while the orderlies vacuumed. Regular students didn't even look at orderlies, but the orphans worked alongside them.

After chores, the orphans hurried back to the Boarders' Houses and changed into their school uniforms. Honor couldn't wait to put on her skirt and blouse and sun hat and look normal again. She ran eagerly to class.

But when she arrived, the crowd of girls at the door parted for her. Helena and Hortense and the others stepped aside. When Honor glided to her desk, she felt like a ghost.

No one looked at Honor all that day. No one spoke to her unless it was absolutely necessary. "Thank you," Hiroko said dutifully when Honor passed the applesauce at lunchtime, but that was because saying "thank you" was the Rule.

When the girls lined up to go to the tennis courts, they were careful not to brush Honor in passing. Honor was door monitor and she held the door open for the class. Each girl made herself as small as possible as she passed through the doorway. Even Helena turned aside timidly from Honor at the door. Honor planted herself right in the center of the doorway. She made it impossible for the other girls to pass without looking at her or saying "excuse me." Honor's classmates squeezed past as best they could. However, Haven was a chubby girl and couldn't squeeze through. "Move," she whispered furiously.

Honor flushed and stepped aside.

"Did Miss Blessing show you that book about when your parents disappear?" Fanny asked as she and Honor and Elspeth walked back to the Boarders' Houses after class.

Honor nodded. Her classmates were hurrying off to catch the school bus and go home to their families. Hester and Hedwig raced past and held their noses. Honor stiffened and pretended she didn't notice. She would never look at those girls with hurt, envious eyes. They'd never catch her casting an orphanish glance.

"It's natural to feel anger," Fanny said in Miss Blessing's sweet voice. Elspeth doubled over laughing. "It's natural to feel hatred," said Fanny.

Honor couldn't help smiling at Fanny's perfect imitation of Miss Blessing.

"It's natural to want to KILL somebody," said Fanny. "But don't worry. We've killed your parents for you."

Elspeth's laughter trailed off. She and Honor looked at Fanny uncertainly.

"That wasn't funny," said Elspeth.

"I have a dark sense of humor," Fanny explained.

"What's that supposed to mean?" asked Honor.

"It means I'm funny once you get to know me," Fanny said.

• • •

At afternoon chore time, Honor helped Quintilian whenever she could. She helped him push his wheelbarrow and his laundry bins. Helix and the other big boys helped him too. She saw Helix weeding with Quintilian in the gardens. Even with help, Quintilian dragged behind. Honor went to Mrs. Edwards and said, "Quintilian is too little for chores."

Mrs. Edwards shook her head at Honor and told her, "Mr. Edwards and I have been guardians for over ten years. Even the youngest children do their share."

FOUR

WHEN HONOR CLOSED HER EYES TO SLEEP, SHE TRIED TO picture her mother and father. Sometimes she saw them clearly and sometimes only a piece of them: her mother's straight and shining hair sweeping over her shoulders, her father's smile. She wanted to practice remembering them, but strangely, when she closed her eyes and concentrated, her parents' faces didn't come to her. Only when she drifted off to sleep and almost forgot to look for them did her mother and father float back into her mind.

She asked Quintilian whenever she had a chance, "Do you remember what they looked like?" and he always said yes, but she didn't believe him. She quizzed, "What color was Mommy's hair? What color were Dad's eyes?" until he ran away from her. Then she got upset. She and Quintilian had no photographs, and she was afraid he would end up like Eglantine and forget what his parents looked like altogether.

She was tired all the time. She was no longer a perfect student. She didn't check her work when she did her math homework. What was the point? She'd tried being a perfect girl, and her parents had been taken anyway. She also knew that there was an O by her name in her permanent record. The O was for *orphan* and it meant the best she could qualify for when she finished school was a low-level job. Even if she got perfect scores on her exams, she would end up working alongside orderlies.

Eva, Eglantine, and Elspeth were all taking their exams soon, and they were worried.

"I'm afraid," Eglantine confessed one morning as the girls ate their early breakfast of granola and milk.

"Don't you think you'll pass?" asked Fanny.

"I think I'll pass," said Eglantine. She hesitated. "I'm afraid of leaving school."

Fanny scoffed at that. "Afraid of leaving school? I can't wait," she said. "I can't wait till I get out of here."

"But who will take care of you?" Eglantine asked.

"I'll be seventeen years old! I'll take care of myself," said Fanny. "I'm going to have my own little house and my own little garden and I'll grow grapes and dry them into raisins so when I have breakfast, I can put raisins on top!"

"Mmm, raisins," said Gretel.

The other girls hushed. They'd all heard of raisins, but they couldn't remember them. Because of Scarcity there had been no raisins in the Colonies for years.

"Can I come live with you?" Honor asked Fanny.

Fanny shook her head. "Don't you know orphans never get to stay together?"

"Why not?" Honor asked.

"Safety Measures, of course," said Fanny. "Since our parents were dangerous. There can't be too many of us in one place."

Eglantine explained, "Orphans are always reassigned."

"We'll just spread our love and caring throughout the world," said Fanny. She said this in such a funny voice that Elspeth and Gretel started giggling.

Honor didn't laugh. She put down her spoon.

That day she couldn't concentrate in history. Ms. Lynch was asking her a question, and Honor was thinking—*After I leave school, I won't see Quintilian anymore. I won't see . . .* She was thinking about Helix too, although he wasn't really her friend anymore.

"I don't want to ask you again," said Ms. Lynch. "What was the agenda of the First Global Conference?"

"War? Toxic waste?" Honor ventured.

"Are you asking me or telling me?" demanded Ms. Lynch.

"Telling you," said Honor.

"That's unfortunate," Ms. Lynch said. "Your answers are Inaccurate. Hester?"

"Famine, overpopulation, scarcity of resources, the end of the ozone . . ." Hester recited in perfect order.

"Excellent," said Ms. Lynch, and Hester smiled a little smile. Hester was excellent. She was Accurate. Honor hated her.

That very day, sitting alone in the lunch area of the classroom, Honor heard Hester and Helena whispering.

". . . How could she? They don't get their uniforms pressed . . . That's why she's . . . Ooh, I'd hate to look like that," said Hester.

"Did you see how she looked up at Ms. Lynch today? She looked so orphanish," said Helena. "I can't believe she used to be my friend."

Honor turned around and gazed straight at Hester and Helena where they sat cozily at their own table. Suddenly the girls stopped talking. Helena looked frightened.

Honor stood and took a step toward the girls. She kept her gaze on Helena. "Oh, I look orphanish now?" she asked. "My clothes are too wrinkled?"

"Leave her alone," said Hester, and she drew herself up, prim and neat, in her crisp uniform.

"How would you like it if your parents disappeared?" Honor demanded, her voice rising. She knew she must never touch another student. She knew the hands-off policy at school, but she stepped toward the girls anyway. She knew she shouldn't, but she reached out and pulled Hester's hat down over her eyes. Her hands seized Hester's starched white shirt and squeezed the fabric until it wrinkled and the pocket ripped. Hester was screaming. Helena was shrieking too. "What would you do if they never came back?" Honor cried out. "Then you'd be just like me. You'd be exactly like me."

Ms. Lynch came rushing over. She took Honor by the arm and said, "Heloise! What were you thinking? Go to Miss Blessing's office. Now."

She didn't have to tell Honor twice. All the children at school knew to take their consequences quickly or the punishment would be doubled. While Ms. Lynch comforted Helena, Honor took a red card from the box on her teacher's desk and marched to the principal's office.

When she got there, she was surprised to find the door closed. She had never seen Miss Blessing's door closed before. She knocked softly.

"Just a moment," Miss Blessing sang out.

But she did not come to the door for a long time. Honor stood out in the hall until her legs got tired. She stood on one foot and then on the other. Finally, she sat down on the floor and waited. Then, all at once, the door opened. Helix ambled out, carelessly, as if going to Miss Blessing's office were the easiest thing in the world. He didn't look at Honor, but she heard him whisper, "Have fun."

"Come in, Heloise," said Miss Blessing. She glanced at the red card in Honor's hand. "I am very sorry to see that."

Honor took her seat across from Miss Blessing's desk.

"What do you have to say for yourself?" Miss Blessing asked. Her voice was so strange. Her words chimed like silver bells.

"I'm sorry," said Honor.

"Is that the truth?" asked Miss Blessing.

"Of course it is," said Honor.

Then suddenly, Miss Blessing's eyes narrowed. She did not seem sweet at all. "Don't get orphanish with me, young lady," she said.

Honor was shocked. She had not known *orphanish* was a word that adults used.

"What do you say?" Miss Blessing demanded.

"I'm sorry," Honor said.

"There is a way orphans become that is sullen," Miss Blessing said. "When orphans become that way, they are Unhelpful and fall into bad mistakes. You may observe other orphans act that way. See that you don't. Now," Miss Blessing said, "tell me what you did."

"Hester and Helena were saying—"

"But I didn't ask what they were saying," said Miss Blessing. "I asked what you did."

"I wrinkled Hester's uniform," said Honor.

"And was that all?"

"The pocket ripped," admitted Honor.

"Was that all?"

"Yes."

"Then you will work in recycling for Mr. Sweeney three early mornings," said Miss Blessing. "You'll have an hour each day before your chores."

"But I start chores at sunrise," said Honor.

"Those who fight will lose some sleep," said Miss Blessing.

Honor did not know how she would wake up on time. She had no alarm clock. She couldn't sleep for fear she'd oversleep, and then when she did drift off, she'd wake with a start and stare at the clock on the wall, fearing it was now time. The colors of the night sky didn't help, because heavy shades covered all the windows. At last Honor gave up sleeping altogether and sat up in bed. When the wall clock showed almost hour four, she dressed and pulled on her work overalls and walked outside.

The air was cool before the sun began burning through the

atmosphere. The sky was still indigo. In two hours orderlies would begin the day shift, but now the school grounds were empty. Honor hurried to the recycling plant behind the gymnasium. The plant was built of cinder blocks. There were no proper windows, only places where the walls were built of glass bricks. Inside were separate sorting rooms for metal, glass, paper, and plastic. Ancient posters decorated the walls. They were printed with the legends DON'T BE A LITTERBUG! and REDUCE, RECYCLE, AND REUSE.

Honor heard a clanging, thumping sound inside the building. That was Mr. Sweeney smashing cans. He was an old white-haired man with bright blue eyes and gardening gloves. He stomped on the cans as though he liked his job.

"Let's get to work," said Mr. Sweeney when he saw Honor. "And you too," he called over his shoulder.

Honor saw Helix leaning against the wall.

"The two of you can start in the paper room and fill the wheelbarrows with white." He pushed a wheelbarrow toward Honor and one toward Helix and the two of them trundled the wheelbarrows to the door of the paper room. They left their wheelbarrows in the hall.

Honor stopped short in the doorway of the school's paper room. She'd never seen so much paper in her life. The room was stacked high, almost to the ceiling, with newspapers, broken-down boxes, folded brown paper bags. The floor was covered with white paper scraps. She and Helix could barely take a step; they were knee-deep in white paper. Some of the white paper was printed all over, some was blank, some pieces were large, and some snippets were as thin as Honor's finger.

"We have to collect all of this?" Honor asked. "How can we do this in an hour?"

"We can't," said Helix.

"But it won't get done," Honor said, almost despairing.

"Doesn't matter," said Helix. "It will never get done. Nothing ever does." His voice was hard and careless, as if to remind Honor that they weren't friends.

"I'll shovel, you push," said Helix. He took a great metal shovel and began filling the first wheelbarrow.

"I could shovel too," said Honor.

"I doubt it," said Helix. "You're not strong enough." He scooped a load of white scraps into the wheelbarrow. "And besides—there's just one shovel."

Honor tried to pick up piles of paper with her hands and carry them into the hall. The paper was heavy and slippery too. Her arms hurt. She tried to carry too much, and the paper slipped onto the floor. Stacking it up again, she cut her hand between her thumb and forefinger. The cut was small but painful. Tears started in her eyes.

Helix pretended not to notice. He said, "Wheel this down to the end of the hall and dump it in the bin while I fill the other one."

"My finger's bleeding," she said.

"It's just a paper cut."

She hesitated, but then she did as he said and wheeled the full load of paper down to the end of the hall. By the time she came back, Helix had the second wheelbarrow almost full of white paper. Honor watched him shoveling the white scraps. Suddenly a memory returned to her. "The paper is like snow."

"How do you know?"

"I've seen it."

Helix was shocked. Honor couldn't help grinning at his startled face.

"You have not," he said. "You have not seen snow."

"I have," she told him. "I saw it when I was little. We used to live in wild places."

"Was it as white as this?" Helix kicked the white scraps at his feet.

Honor nodded. "Yes."

"Was it like feathers?"

Honor tried to think.

"Was it soft like feathers? Or hard like crystals?"

Honor thought and thought, but she couldn't remember. All she could picture was her father shoveling. The snow itself had no substance in her memory, just the color, pure white.

"How come you never told me you saw snow?"

"I'd forgotten. Anyway, it's no longer Accurate," Honor added hastily. "Now snow is eradicated in the Far North—"

"What do you mean, eradicated?"

"The Polar Seas are ceiled in the North and in the South," said Honor. She was practically quoting from her climatology textbook. She'd copied the words so many times. "The North is Safe and Secure."

"No," said Helix.

"What do you mean?"

"The North isn't secure at all. Enclosure does not extend beyond the Polar Seas. Enclosure has just begun. They've barely started."

"How do you know?" Honor demanded.

"My father told me. Didn't your father tell you?"

Then, deep inside of her, Honor remembered when her father had taken her down to the shore. Dimly she remembered what he had told her that night and how the water shone silver and the sand felt like warm honey on her hands. But she also remembered how dangerous his ideas were. Her father had thought she was afraid of the sea, but that was only part of it. She had been afraid because even as he spoke, she knew that she would lose him.

She did not want to make her father's mistake and lose her life. Stubbornly, she shook her head at Helix. "If Enclosure were barely started, then none of us would be safe."

"We aren't safe," said Helix. "We never were safe. And we aren't going to be safe."

"Stop!" Honor cried out. Without even thinking, she lifted her hand and slapped Helix's face.

The two of them stood there stunned for a second. Helix's cheek was red where Honor had struck him. He rubbed the place with his hand.

"Look what you made me do," Honor said.

"What *I* made you do?" Helix asked.

"You're a liar," she accused him. "You're the one making up stories that aren't true."

"How do you know?"

She threw up her hands. "Because the Northern Islands are now Enclosed. They are almost ready. They are being numbered. Earth Mother is building cities for resettlement. It's in all the books."

Helix was staring down at the drifts of paper on the floor. "Do you want to see something?" he said. "This paper we're dumping—do you know where it's from?"

Honor shook her head.

"It's from books."

"What do you mean?"

"It's from libraries. It's from school libraries all over. These are the pages Miss Tuttle and the other librarians are cutting out." He glanced toward the door. Then he took a fistful of scraps. "Look," he said. He took a scrap and read, "*When the red red robin comes bob bob bobbin' along, along* . . . No, that's a bad example."

He took another scrap, a sliver printed: "*It was so easy to laugh in the springtime.*" Then another piece of paper, smashed so he had to unfold it: "*. . . The glassy peartree leaves and blooms, they brush / The descending blue . . .* Look at these, they're whole pages ripped from books. *Loveliest of trees, the cherry now . . .*" He rustled through the papers. "*To Autumn,*" he read. "Look, this is from an old calendar."

"Oh, a calendar? Does it have all the old months? Does it have July?" Honor was curious in spite of herself.

She puzzled over the words on the autumn page. "*Season of mists and mellow fruitfulness! / Close bosom-friend of the maturing sun; / Conspiring with him how to load and bless / With fruit the vines . . .* What does *that* mean?"

Helix shrugged.

"What's *thatch-eves*?" Honor asked, staring at the page.

"It's Old Weather," Helix said. "How should I know?"

"But—"

"Shh."

Mr. Sweeney's footsteps grew louder in the hall and then died away again.

"Don't you see?" Helix whispered to Honor. "They rip out everything about winter and cold and storms and even summer ending. Then they rewrite all the books."

"How do you know they rewrite them? How do you know these aren't just old books they're throwing away?"

"I have proof," Helix said. "But you have to swear you won't tell."

Honor nodded.

"Do you swear?"

"I swear," she said.

Solemnly he took out some folded pages from his overall pockets. "I found these here."

"Oh," Honor exclaimed as she looked at them.

"You've read that book, I bet," said Helix.

"The Wizard of Oz."

"How does Dorothy get to Oz?"

"She falls asleep and dreams she goes there," said Honor.

"Wrong!" said Helix. "Look at these pages they took out. There was a tornado and her house was swept away."

"No!" Honor grabbed the pages, devouring the words with her eyes. There it was in black and white. Dorothy's house was swept away by a tornado. "I can't believe it."

"See, they changed the book. They've changed all the books. They make the books up and they make the maps up too."

Honor didn't know what to say.

"Look where it says Dorothy's name," said Helix. "What's her name in the school library book?"

"Dorothy Dale," said Honor.

"But look what her name is here in the old version. Dorothy Gale."

"Why would they change her name?" Honor asked.

"Because gale is a storm," said Helix, and he pocketed the pages again.

"Don't take those," said Honor, horrified. "You'll get in trouble all over again. Do you want to come here every day of your life?"

"But I like it here," said Helix.

"Are you crazy? How can you like it here?"

"I like to read," he said. "I like finding things."

Honor looked down at the floor. She remembered how she and Helix had played Archeology when they were ten. "What happened to your coin collection?"

He shrugged. "It's gone, with everything else in my house."

"I kept the quarter for a long time," she told him.

"Why?" he asked her.

"I wanted to."

"Old coins aren't good for anything," said Helix. He kicked a pile of white pages at his feet. "These matter. Lies matter. Our parents—"

"What did they do?" Honor interrupted. "Why were they stargazing?"

"Shh. I hear him."

Mr. Sweeney opened the door to the paper room. "You're

a couple of lazy kids, I can see that," he said. "I'm separating you. Heloise, take the shovel and finish loading in here. Helix, into the metal room with me."

All that day as she sat in class, Honor thought about what Helix had said. She sat at her desk and suddenly the world, which had been so well organized, seemed wild and uncertain. She had come to believe there was something the matter with her parents, but Helix thought the rest of the world was all wrong.

How could Enclosure have barely begun? How could all the books and maps lie? She stared at a blue map of the world hanging on the classroom wall. There were the Seven Seas. Two Polar Seas, the Northern Sea, the Tranquil Sea, the Sea of Peace, the Sea of Light, the Sea of Reconciliation. There were the four hundred and one islands of the Colonies, each numbered carefully in black. And there were the numberless islands of the Northern Sea. On the map the Polar Seas were Secure, as were the numberless islands. Dotted lines showed where Enclosure was advancing next. The map was scientific. It even said Scientific Map Company on the bottom. What about the climatology textbook with its silky smooth paper and calm sentences? *"The steady march of Enclosure marks the progress of mankind."* What did that mean?

As soon as school was over, Honor hurried back to the Boarders' Houses for chores. She needed to talk to Helix, but she had no time with him alone. She was assigned laundry while he worked in the gardens.

Every day she tried to approach Helix, but it wasn't easy. Even if he was in her chore group, there were others around. She knew better than to pass him a note asking him to meet her somewhere. Passing notes was Not Allowed, and if Mr. and Mrs. Edwards didn't see, the other orphans would, and they would tease and laugh so much that the note was sure to reach some teacher in the end.

She watched and waited for him, and sometimes when she saw him coming around the corner or even glimpsed him from a distance, she thought of running up to him, but she couldn't. The others would see. She could not stop thinking about what he might know or might have figured out.

On day nine, she finally got her chance to work with him. Honor and Helix were assigned gardening, and as the weeding group was so big, the two of them were sent to the hot and humid greenhouses to pick tomatoes, cucumbers, and eggplants. No one wanted to work there, but when Helix headed over to the greenhouses, Honor put on thick gloves and followed eagerly.

The greenhouses were long and connected to each other, and they were planted so thickly that it was hard to make your way through them. Leaves pressed against the glass walls and even the sloping roofs of the greenhouses. The plants looked desperate, as if they were dying to escape.

Rapidly, Honor and Helix worked their way down the rows of tomatoes. Picking was easy. There was no need to bend over, because the plants were trained as vines along the greenhouse walls. The tricky part was picking enough before the misters went off. Misters sprayed the plants every hour with water and special Planet Safe fertilizer. Staying in a greenhouse during misting was dangerous. Even orderlies got sick. Once Fanny had seen an orderly malfunction in a greenhouse. She'd seen it through the glass. For some reason the orderly got jammed in a corner, and when the misters came on, he got sprayed. Mrs. Edwards called for help, but by the time a pair of orderlies dragged the jammed one out, he was completely disoriented, spinning like a top, and so memory-sick he had to be taken away for retraining.

Honor and Helix kept their eye on the greenhouse timer as they worked. Sweat trickled down their faces as they hurried to the next greenhouse, where they would gather eggplants.

"What did our parents do?" Honor asked. "Did your father tell you?"

"Just a little," Helix said.

"Well, what?" she demanded. "I have to know. No one's told me. My parents were taken before I had a chance to find out. They never warned me."

"How could they have warned you?" Helix asked. "If parents knew when it was going to happen, they'd never disappear."

"Yes, but I think mine always knew," said Honor. "Mine always knew they were in danger. I always knew it would happen to them."

Helix bent his head under hanging racks of eggplants. He seemed to be examining all the different kinds: the rich purple eggplants, the long skinny ones, the little white dwarf varieties.

"Of course they always knew. So did mine," said Helix.

"But they never knew the day; they never knew the exact minute. No one does."

"What were they working on?" asked Honor. "Were they really bad?"

"No, they're heroes," said Helix. "They are Objectors."

Even in the sticky greenhouse, Honor began to shiver. "Are you sure? Are you . . . What do you mean they *are* Objectors? Don't you know they're dead?"

"Who said they're dead?"

"Fanny," Honor told him. "Everyone."

"No," said Helix. "Our parents aren't dead. Haven't you figured that out yet? It's like the book they give the little kids: *Disappeared Means No One Here.* Not dead."

"What are you talking about?"

"Reduce, recycle, and reuse," said Helix.

"How can you reuse people?"

The timer was ticking above their heads. The yellow warning light began to flash, but Helix bent down for just a moment and whispered, "Look at the orderlies. Where do you think they come from?"

FIVE

NO ONE EVER LOOKED AT ORDERLIES. HONOR HADN'T LOOKED
at an orderly since that day on the playground when Mrs.
Whyte pulled her away. No one looked at them or spoke to
them except their managers, and those people had special
training. An orderly in the room was like furniture that moved.
An orderly glided silently along, vacuuming or scrubbing floors
or stocking shelves in the Central Store. Even if orderlies were
called for security, they ran silently in pairs and picked up
offenders gently. Orderlies did one job at a time. They jammed
when someone or something blocked them. Even little children
knew they must not block their way.

Honor had forgotten about orderlies. Everybody did. They
were everywhere, but they were silent. They all looked alike
with their bald heads and their smooth faces. Their eyes were
open and glassy bright. They stared straight ahead. Could
orderlies see like ordinary people? Could they hear? Could

they remember anything? All children wondered when they were young, but over time they grew out of these childish questions. Orderlies became part of the background, the clutter of daily life.

Now Honor thought about orderlies constantly. She tried not to stare, but she was watching them. She watched them wheeling recycling bins or hauling manure in the gardens. She watched the circular motion of the orderlies' arms as they washed the blackboards with wet rags. She watched the way they mowed and vacuumed one strip at a time, in straight and careful lines. When she could, she tried to look into the orderlies' wide-open eyes.

When Honor saw two orderlies together rolling trash barrels, she glanced quickly from one to the other to try to see if they were different, but the orderlies were so close in size, their faces so bland, and their movements so similar that it was hard to see them separately. If orderlies were all the same, then how would Honor recognize her parents among them? Standing on the boardwalk with the orderlies approaching two abreast, Honor could see no difference between them. She saw nothing distinctive, no matter how long she looked. A pair of orderlies in white uniforms looked like a matched pair of socks sorted and clean straight from the wash. The trash barrels rattled as the orderlies rolled them over the boardwalk. Honor stood still and waited. She should have moved aside to let the orderlies do their jobs, but she didn't move. She waited and waited. The pair of orderlies was almost on top of her. They were bearing down on her quickly and seemed to have no idea she was standing in their way.

Honor's heart beat fast. She was doing something dangerous. The trash barrels were huge and they could hit her, but she stood in the path of the orderlies like a girl on the tracks of an oncoming train. They were close. She should jump off the boardwalk and run away. She screamed instead. She shrieked and ran right between the trash barrels and stopped the orderlies with a hand on each of their arms.

She was shaking. Her fear of the orderlies was even stronger than her fear that someone had heard her cry out. She had never touched an orderly on purpose, and now she'd grabbed hold of two at once. She couldn't tell if they were men or women or if the pair was one of each, but they were alive; their arms felt strong and springy through the thin cloth of their jumpsuits. She held them for a moment, fiercely. They did not look at her, but she looked at them; she peered into their faces, first one, and then the other. *Who are you? Where did you come from?* she thought. *Were you somebody's parents once?* She'd stopped them, but neither orderly blinked. Glassy eyed, they remained fixed on the task in front of them. They were not exactly the same, and yet she couldn't figure out the difference between them. They were pushing against her with equal force. They were alike, except—she realized all in a rush—they were not alike at all up close. Their features were completely different once you stopped them to look. She hadn't realized. She had only known orderlies from a distance and in motion. Up close, they were different as two leaves or two potatoes. One had thick lips and the other thin; one had a long narrow face and the other a fat pink face; one had dark eyes and the other blue. She let them go.

· · ·

"Where did you get the idea that they used to be real people?" Honor asked Helix in the kitchen.

"When I had chores in the garden, I stuck one with a pin," said Helix. Heads down at the sinks, the two of them spoke so softly no one else could hear. "I stuck him right in the arm and made him bleed."

"That's nasty," said Honor.

"I wanted to see if he was alive," said Helix.

"What happened?"

"He yelled."

"He made a noise?"

"He said, 'OW!' Then he was quiet again."

"I didn't know they could make sounds," said Honor.

"Not just sounds. Ow is a word," said Helix. "It's a human word."

"I keep looking at them," Honor confessed as orderlies wheeled in racks of dirty dishes. She scraped and Helix rinsed. The orphans had to wash down the stainless steel counters and even the floors with spray hoses. There were drains in the polished cement floor for the dirty water. The work was hard and messy. No one liked to touch the filthy plates covered with smashed potatoes and peas, partly chewed chicken hanging off the bone, bread squeezed back into dough.

Mrs. Tannenbaum, the head cook, was strict. "Do it right," she told Gretel and Hector, who were washing the floors, "or do it again."

As soon as Mrs. Tannenbaum was out of earshot, Honor asked Helix, "How did you find out where orderlies come from? Have you told anyone else? Does anyone else know?"

"Everyone who knows anything knows," said Helix. "They just don't say."

"Did your parents tell you?"

"Of course."

"My parents didn't."

"Did you ever ask?"

"No," Honor admitted.

"You were too busy changing your name," said Helix.

Honor reached over and snatched Helix's spray hose from him. She shot a stream of water at him. He tried to duck aside, but she soaked his sleeve. "Take it back!"

"No!" Helix snatched the hose and shot water straight into Honor's face. Helix was laughing at Honor. She dove for the hose again and soaked Helix at close range. Suddenly they were both laughing. Water streamed from their eyes and ears and noses.

"Stop! Danger!" Mrs. Tannenbaum screamed. She came running toward them, scurrying on little feet. She was extremely fast, even though she was so fat her white cook's jacket strained at the buttons. "Roughhousing in the kitchen is Not Allowed."

Honor dropped the hose. She and Helix stood dripping before the cook.

"What happened here?" Mrs. Tannenbaum demanded.

Honor looked down at her wet sandals.

"You, Heloise. Tell me what happened here."

"I don't know," whispered Honor.

"Is that or is that not a lie?" asked Mrs. Tannenbaum.

"It is . . . not," Honor said.

"You, Helix. Wipe that smile off your face," said Mrs. Tannenbaum.

Helix wiped his hand across his mouth. When he dropped his hand again, he looked so deadly serious that now Honor couldn't help smiling. It was as if his smile had migrated to her.

Gretel and Hector stifled laughter. Mrs. Tannenbaum whipped around to look at them and the two began mopping again.

"You'll stay late," Mrs. Tannenbaum told Honor and Helix. "You'll clean the stoves. Get back to work."

The kitchens were dark now. The other orphans went to dinner and Mrs. Tannenbaum went home. Honor turned on the lights over the stove so that she and Helix could see. They scrubbed and scrubbed with steel wool and soapy water, but the stoves seemed as dirty as ever, black with charred food.

Honor rolled up her wet sleeves, and now her forearms were wet all over again, gray and slimy with soap and grease. "This is a job for orderlies," she said.

"That's why it's our punishment," said Helix.

"How do they turn people into orderlies?" Honor asked him.

"Why did you change your name?" Helix asked her almost at the same moment.

"I wanted to fit," said Honor. Then she felt ashamed. "My parents weren't like yours," she said. "They didn't explain; they just did everything wrong. They *tried* to stick out. They even gave me the wrong name. How would you like it if you had a silent *H*?"

"I *would* like it," Helix said rebelliously. "I'd be Elix. My name wouldn't be on any of the lists. People would think I'm three years older."

"Then you'd have to take exams," Honor pointed out.

"Then I'd be leaving school." Helix lowered his voice. "When I leave school, I'm going to find my parents."

"How?"

He hesitated. Then he said, "I'll go to the other side of the island where they keep the orderlies and I'll get into the Barracks and I'll find them and get my parents out."

"But you can't go there."

"Why not?"

"You know why." Everyone knew that the other side of the island was dangerous, entirely exposed and unprotected. The City Side had Watchers and Weather Stations, but the Windward Side was unregulated, completely wild.

"You'd never get over the mountains," Honor pointed out. "Even if you did, how would you know where to find them?"

Helix bent over the grill on the great stainless steel stove top. He was drawing something with his finger in the grease on the front rim of the stove. "Have you ever seen this? This," he said as he wrote, "is the slogan of the Objectors."

Honor looked down. He'd scrawled three words: *Knowledge is power.* "How do you know your knowledge is right?" she asked him. "How do you know the Objectors are right? How do you know Enclosure is barely started and we're not safe?"

"How do I know?" Helix said. "Because I know! Because my father told me."

"And how did he know? And why do you believe him?"

Honor asked. "Is it just because he's your dad? What proof do you have?"

"Didn't I show you the pieces they cut from books?" Helix retorted.

"But have you seen the Polar Seas? Have you really seen them for yourself?"

"No," he admitted. "But I've seen storms. I've seen the weather forecast fail and the sky colors run together when it rains. I've heard thunder. I've seen real clouds cover the overlay and turn the sunsets gray. Winds flatten houses. Waves crash over the seawall. Even here, in the City, with the projection booth, we aren't safe."

Honor listened in silence. She knew Helix was right, but the knowledge frightened her. When she glanced down at the words on the stove top, caution took over. She smeared the letters together, blotting the slogan with her scrubber.

SIX

WHENEVER THEY COULD, HONOR AND HELIX TALKED ABOUT the orderlies and which ones might be someone's parents. It became a private game to say, "I spotted one that looked just like Gretel by the recycling plant. He had Gretel's eyes—the same shade of green. I'm sure he was her father—or maybe mother." Or, "I saw an ugly one, just like Hector." They rarely talked about spotting their own parents, however. That was too painful. Even though they looked for their parents all the time, Honor and Helix never found them.

"Do you think they've been redistributed?" Honor whispered to Helix one morning early before breakfast.

"I think they're here," Helix insisted.

"Because you know they are or because you want them to be?" asked Honor.

"Because I know," said Helix.

"Really know? Or think you know?"

"I think I know," said Helix.

Honor sighed. "You read too many books."

"I found out what really happens at the end of *Bridge to Terabithia*," said Helix, but then he saw Mrs. Edwards coming.

"Move along," she told them. "It's time to hurry to class."

"The girl dies," Helix whispered to Honor as they picked up their book bags.

"No!"

"Yes." He nodded.

"But how?"

"Flood," he told Honor.

"I don't believe you."

"Well, I found the pages. A flash flood sweeps her away and she drowns!"

"She doesn't move away? Her parents aren't redistributed for three years and then transferred back?"

"Nope."

"That's terrible!" Honor shook her head. "I loved *Bridge to Terabithia*. Are you sure she dies?"

"Yup," said Helix.

"Well, then, I like the new version better," Honor said.

"Why?"

"Because if she drowns, that would be too sad!"

"I guess that's what Miss Tuttle thought," said Helix. "Haven't you noticed that there are hardly any sad books in the library?"

Honor had her fourteenth birthday in the Boarders' Houses.

She was lucky, because her birthday fell on Errand Day. Usually the birthday orphan got to bake a special cake with two friends, but because it was Errand Day, the celebration was combined with an outing to the Central Bakery.

The orphans set out in the morning with Mr. and Mrs. Edwards leading the way. They walked to the City in pairs. Helix walked with Quintilian. Honor walked with Fanny.

The orphans were giddy at the chance to leave school. Honor couldn't help staring at all the people. She'd only been an orphan half a year, but Honor could hardly remember coming to the City with her own family on Errand Day. She was no longer used to seeing strangers.

"Look at the Square!" Eglantine exclaimed. "It's so beautiful."

The Square shone silver in the sun. Bigger than the biggest field at school, it gleamed and sparkled, because it was tiled with millions and millions of tiny solar panels. There were solar panels on every building in the City, but the Central Square was the biggest Solar Collector on the island. In fact, the Square was the biggest Solar Collector in all the Colonies.

"And there's the New Weather Bureau," said Helix.

He pointed to a grand ancient building called the Paradise Theater, now used by the New Weather Bureau. On the front of the building a white sign emblazoned NOW SHOWING spelled out the weather and the hour in black letters. SUN WITH SCATTERED CLOUDS, HOUR TWO, AZURE BLUE. If the children craned their necks, they could see the beam of blue light streaming through the high window of the New Weather Bureau's projection booth. Pure bright azure blue so intense that Mrs. Edwards warned, "Look away. Never look directly at the light beam!"

The Central Bakery was tall and white, bigger than any school building. There were special entrances on the side for visitors. Each visitor wrote his or her name in a guest book in the vestibule. There were ten guest books open on ten tall tables, because the bakery was such a popular tourist destination. The Central Bakery was so famous in the islands that many couples chose to marry there. Honor saw a wedding party just inside the bakery doors. The bride wore brown and held *Sayings of Earth Mother* clasped in her hands. The groom wore a new tan suit with a white flower in his buttonhole.

The orphans signed the guest book, and then a Bakery Guide ushered them to a bank of elevators. Six went up with Mr. Edwards in one elevator, and six waited with Mrs. Edwards for another. Quintilian went up with the first group. Honor and Helix waited with the second.

Honor watched as the bride and groom and their friends made their way down the hall to the bakery's party room. Wedding parties were small in those days.

"Shift change, shift change. Move aside," announced one of the Bakery Guides. Honor and the other visitors backed up against the wall to make way for the new shift of orderlies arriving to take the freight elevator down to the bakery floor. There were at least fifty orderlies in the shift, all dressed in working white. They wore white caps on their bald heads and white aprons over their white jumpsuits. Their faces were pale; even their eyes seemed pale, as though they hardly ever saw the sun. The freight elevator doors opened and half the orderlies stepped inside. Those who were left stepped back five paces so that they stood well away from the elevator door as it closed. Honor wondered how the orderlies knew when to step and when to stop. How did they walk together so perfectly, in batches?

The bell rang for Visitor Elevator Four, and Mrs. Edwards hurried the orphans in front of the orderlies so they could squeeze inside. "Move along, move along," said Mrs. Edwards, but Honor turned to look at the orderlies' pale faces. Green eyes, brown eyes, black eyes. Wide eyes, pale blue. She caught her breath. Pale blue eyes and a faintly freckled nose. Smooth round cheeks, small ears with no hair to cover them. She was staring into her mother's face; she knew it.

"Oh," she said. Despite herself, the word escaped her, but fortunately no one heard. That was her mother. That was Pamela. She was a bakery orderly. Honor wanted to touch her mother; she wanted to rush forward, but she dared not. She only paused a moment.

Her mother made no noise; she made no sign. Honor was looking at her own mother, but Pamela stared straight ahead like all the other orderlies.

"Come along, Heloise," called Mrs. Edwards.

In that instant, the orderly with Pamela's eyes did something Honor had never seen an orderly do. She blinked.

"Doors are closing," said Mrs. Edwards, and Honor rushed into the elevator.

"We are going up to the bridge," said the Bakery Guide. "The bridge is where we welcome visitors to watch the activity on the bakery floor. Please stay together when the doors open."

The elevator was packed. Honor could scarcely breathe. She'd seen her mother, and it had happened so fast. Maybe she'd imagined the whole thing. Maybe she'd wanted to see her so much that her mind had tricked her into looking at those blue eyes.

Bing! The doors opened and Honor exhaled. She felt faint as she stepped into the glass bakery gallery. She felt she was dreaming, but she couldn't tell if it was a good dream or a nightmare. As in a dream, she couldn't feel her feet when she walked. As in a dream, she wanted to cry out, but she had no voice. She was moving slowly; her feet were heavy. For a moment she was a little child again, walking in marshy fields where the mud sucked her shoes. For just an instant her eyes closed and she was following her parents through tall grasses.

But she shook herself and opened her eyes and followed the Bakery Guide instead. She didn't stand out; she waited at the first viewing station and watched the orderlies below wheeling tubs of dough and bins of flour. Skilled orderlies by the dozen stood at stainless steel tables. They were cutting pieces of dough with curved metal knives and then weighing the cut pieces on scales. At the next table, orderlies were buttering coffee cans for baking Colony Loaves, the brown bread everybody ate in those days, bread in the shape of cylinders. At a second table, orderlies were spreading cinnamon onto dough, rolling up the dough, and then cutting it into cinnamon rolls. At yet another long table, orderlies kneaded dough with pieces of green olives.

"We make every kind of bread at the Central Bakery," announced the Guide. "Move along now, and we'll take a look at our specially built ovens."

The other orphans were talkative, practically dancing along. Honor followed the group, but she stayed close to the gallery's glass wall. She kept her eyes fixed on the orderlies. From above she couldn't see their faces, only their white caps, all alike. The group stared down at the ovens, which were lined with stone. They watched orderlies open the oven doors and shove long-handled wood paddles inside to remove loaves of bread.

"Once upon a time there were wood-fired ovens," said the Bakery Guide. "People cut down trees, chopped up the trunks and branches, and fed the wood into ovens, stoves, and fireplaces. Black smoke spread throughout the sky. Our ovens are clean and they run on gas made from . . . what?"

"Sunflower seeds," the orphans chorused together.

"That's right."

They marched down the long gallery to watch pie making, where orderlies worked in an assembly line at vast tables. The pie-filling table was ingenious. Vats of filling hung from metal cables in the ceiling. One by one, orderlies slid piecrusts below the proper vat and a skilled orderly pulled a cord to open a hole in the bottom of the vat so that just the right amount of filling poured into the crust. The skilled orderly worked so smoothly that not a drop of apple or cherry or blueberry filling spilled.

It was hard to follow the Bakery Guide's instructions to move along when there was pie filling to watch. The orphans dawdled and followed slowly, first to the cookie-baking viewing station and then to cake mixing. Honor was last of all. She held on to the metal guide rail as she trailed behind. Her forehead was damp with sweat.

"Come along, Heloise," said Mrs. Edwards. Then suddenly she put her hand to Honor's forehead. "Are you feeling well?"

"I'm fine," said Honor. But Helix was watching and he stood close to her at the next stop.

"What's wrong?" he asked in a low voice so no one else could hear.

"I saw her."

"Where?" Helix didn't need any further explanation. He knew exactly what Honor was talking about.

She kept her voice so quiet that she was breathing more than speaking. "Downstairs in the big batch coming for the new shift. I saw her."

They didn't look at each other when they spoke but kept their eyes fixed on the view below. Orderlies were pouring batter into flat sheet pans.

"She's down there," Honor said. Her voice must have sounded funny because Helix shot her a quick look.

"Don't cry," he warned. "Don't make any noise. They'll make you leave."

It was time for the last viewing station. "Watch your step," the Guide told them. "Fill in the front rows first." The last viewing station was the highlight of the tour. Stairs led down from the upper gallery into a glass viewing box with seats almost like a theater. There were at least thirty seats, enough for several tour groups to sit and watch all at the same time.

Mrs. Edwards said kindly to Honor, "Heloise, you are our birthday girl; please come sit in the front next to me."

"Lucky you," said Fanny.

Honor was afraid to look at Fanny. She didn't know what Fanny might see in her face.

Head down, Honor followed Mrs. Edwards to the front and sat between her and Eglantine as the Bakery Guide announced, "This is the end of our tour, and we have saved the best for last. The Central Bakery cake-decorating department finishes over one thousand special-occasion cakes each week. The process begins on your far left with orderlies spreading white icing on plain sheet cakes. Once the cakes are iced and smoothed, they move on to the decorating tables."

Honor leaned forward in her chair. She was quite close now. She could see every detail of work on the tables below. The orderlies were almost near enough to touch, almost, but a little too far down, and they worked with their backs toward the viewers in the gallery. They were trained to ignore visitors.

The cake decorators were highly skilled orderlies. Most orderlies could use one tool, but these used many beautifully. They put on a show with their brushes and sprinkles, their knives and spatulas and tubes of frosting in every color. Above the orderlies on a metal pot rack hung pink slips of paper with orders for special cakes. The orderlies glanced at each slip and then, in their hands, each plain cake became a painting and a little work of art. One cake became a garden. An orderly painted the cake in a wash of green for grass and then piped darker green stems for flowers. The blossoms were perfect roses and tulips and daisies in tints of lavender, pink, and pale yellow. The orderly left a blank space in the garden and scribed the cake's message in perfect script: *Happy Birthday, Laetitia.* Another cake turned into a mass of butterflies, some iced on the surface and some that seemed about to fly away on painted cookie wings. All the cakes were so beautiful and clever it was hard to believe these were orderlies at the tables. Lower-level orderlies stood ready to box the cakes, and a pair of regular supervisors checked the orderlies' work. *What if she's here?* Honor thought. She tried to recognize her mother from the back. She tried to make out some flower or some butterfly or even some word in her mother's handwriting. *If she's on the bakery floor, she will be here.*

Gardens and castles and spun sugar ribbons and bows. Circus cakes with sparkling acrobats and sports cakes with soccer balls. The cakes kept coming, one after another. *Happy Birthday, Abe; Happy Birthday, Irina.*

There was one orderly on the end who seemed to work faster than any other. From her position in the gallery, Honor watched as this orderly painted cakes with rainbows and balloons and fairy princesses. Each princess wore a tiny crown with sugar candy jewels. The orderly dusted each fairy princess gown with glittering sugar in lilac or in pink. The orderly drew a cat on her next cake and then three kittens playing. Honor tensed. This orderly drew with icing the way her mother drew animals on paper. She drew just the way she had learned from the drawing book. Honor wanted to tell Helix. She wanted to call out to him sitting two rows back. She gripped the sides of her chair with her hands instead. *I'm here,* she told her mother silently. *Turn around,* she begged her mother in her mind. *I'm right behind you in the gallery.*

Honor's mother slid the cat cake to the side. There was no message on that one. She took a large rectangular sheet cake and began painting it green. She took brown icing and painted bases and a pitcher's mound. She was creating a baseball diamond for a sports cake. She reached over to her supply boxes and pulled out tiny plastic baseball players. They were dressed in Colony uniforms of green, with blue numbers on their backs. She placed one on the pitcher's mound, one at bat, one on second base. Then she paused for a split second and switched the pitcher and second baseman. Honor could just barely make out that the figure on second base was number seven. The number was painted on the back of his shirt.

All along the table, other orderlies kept making their cakes. There was a cake with a yellow mother duck and seven little yellow ducklings waddling behind. There was a great cake with the earth on it and the words *Safe and Secure.* That one must have been for some official function. But Honor's mother hesitated. She seemed to be reading her order forms. Then she turned back to the baseball cake and began to write *Happy Birthday* just above the baseball diamond. She paused and Honor held her breath. Her mother was writing her name! *Happy Birthday, H-o-n . . .* Honor watched in shock as her mother scribed the first three letters. The world seemed to stop right there. The other orphans were pointing at the grand earth cake. The Bakery Guide was saying there were fewer than two errors a month in the cake-decorating department. But for Honor, time froze. Her mother was telling her happy birthday. She had remembered. Even now. Honor's mother was not just an orderly. She could blink.

What if Pamela got caught writing what she was not supposed to write! She would get caught and taken away again.
Honor was terrified. She could scarcely watch. And then the
world began spinning again. Honor's mother finished *H-o-n-*
with an *e-y.* She did not write *Honor.* She had written *Happy
Birthday, Honey.* Honor sank down in her chair, head on her
knees.

"Heloise? Heloise!" said Mrs. Edwards.

"I'm sorry," said Honor. Her voice was muffled. "I don't
feel well."

"Are you going to be sick?" Mrs. Edwards asked.

"No."

"Do I need to take you outside to rest?" Mrs. Edwards
asked less urgently.

"No," said Honor. She knew Mrs. Edwards didn't want to
miss the rest of the cake decorating.

"Then pull yourself together, please," said Mrs. Edwards.

"Ooh," Honor heard the visitors gasp around her.

"A rare error," announced the Bakery Guide.

Honor lifted her head and peeked. Her mother had been
trimming the baseball cake with a sharp knife and had somehow slashed the cake in two.

"You are all in luck," said the Guide. "We will be distribut-
ing the erroneous cake to visitors. You may pick up your own
piece as soon as you return to the lobby."

All the orphans cheered, and the other visitors applauded.
And of course Honor clapped as well, ducking her head to
wipe away her tears on her sleeves.

PART FOUR

ONE

"TELL ME!" WHISPERED HELIX AS HE AND HONOR CLEARED the orphans' table after dinner. "Did you get a good look at her?"

"Just one look at her face," Honor whispered back.

"Are you sure?" Helix asked.

She nodded and piled her stack of plates on the cart to return to the kitchen.

Suddenly she didn't want to talk about seeing her mother. She didn't want to tell Helix about seeing those blue eyes and those small ears. She was afraid if she spoke about it, she would forget. She would lose the feeling of seeing her mother's face.

But Helix was full of questions. He couldn't wait. "Did she make a sign? Did she recognize you? Did she try to tell you anything?"

"How could she tell me anything?" Honor whispered furiously. "They can't talk. You know that."

"But she could give you a signal. She could tell you without words."

"She didn't give me any signal. I got in the elevator. She went to the bakery floor and started decorating cakes. She did the fairy cake and the kittens and the baseball cake. . . ."

"The erroneous cake, the one we ate," said Helix. "Maybe that one was for you."

"She made it up," said Honor. "She started to write my name on it. Did you see?"

"Yes! She must have been trying to send a message."

But what message had Pamela sent? For days Helix and Honor thought about it. There was the baseball diamond. There was the message, *Happy Birthday, Honey.* Did *honey* mean something? Or was Pamela just disguising Honor's name? And how did she remember it was Honor's birthday? She must have some memory. But did orderlies have a sense of time?

"I heard Fanny say they get drops in their eyes every day," said Honor. "That's why they only see straight ahead. They get drugs in their food."

"They get trained to do just one thing as long as they're awake so they don't have time to think," said Helix. "I don't know how they'd keep track of days."

They were up early before the others and had begun weeding in the vegetable gardens. They were whispering with their heads down.

"There was a baseball diamond and a pitcher and a man on second base. Did she play baseball with you?" Helix asked.

Honor shook her head. "I don't think she knew anything about baseball. She knew how to draw."

"Something about drawing . . ." Helix tugged at the crabgrass sprouting between carrot tops. "Did she teach you to draw?"

"No."

"What did she do with you?"

"Number games," said Honor. "When we were walking home from the bus stop. She taught me how to count in different—" She stopped short.

"What is it?" asked Helix.

"In different bases," said Honor. "She taught me how to count in base two."

"The little plastic baseball player on second base," said Helix.

"And he had the number seven on his shirt. She moved number seven from pitcher to second base."

They stared at each other.

"It's a code," said Helix. "It's a secret number. What's seven in base two?"

"One hundred eleven," said Honor.

"That's it, then. She was sending you a secret code."

"One hundred eleven isn't a big enough number," Honor protested. "How could that be a code?"

"It is; it is." Helix was excited. "It must be."

That night Honor stayed awake in bed. She lay in the dark and waited until she heard quiet breathing all around her. Then she snuck outside into the night. Of course sneaking out at night was Not Allowed, but she wasn't frightened. She felt so calm she might have been dreaming. Ever since she'd seen her mother, she felt as though she were living in a dream.

She ran as softly as she could in her pajamas to the vegetable gardens, where Helix was waiting. He held a key to the potting shed and gestured for her to follow him.

Hour ten. Indigo. The night was warm. The artificial moon was almost but not quite full.

"Where did you get the key?" Honor asked.

"Shh."

Helix opened the potting shed door. It was dark inside, and the shed smelled of dirt and dry moss and the grass clippings that stuck to the lawn mowers orderlies pushed across the school grounds. There were no windows in the potting shed. Once Helix closed the door, it was safe to turn on a light. He pulled a string to a dim lightbulb. Then he dragged a huge bag of fertilizer to one side of a table and revealed an old utility sink full of rusty trowels, garden stakes, flowerpots. The sink was lined with yellowed newspapers. He lifted a stack of newspapers to reveal white pages underneath. These were pieces of books, cut scraps he'd saved from the recycling plant and even whole sections of books without their covers and their binding threads hanging out. There were torn-up red cards and folded papers. There were more keys, small ones like the key to the potting shed. There were tools, a pliers and a screwdriver, and there were paper packets of salt and pepper, the kind the school stocked in the kitchen. There were pictures. Colored photographs from magazines. Flooded cities. Bridges, boats, streets flowing with water.

"See," Helix whispered to Honor. "This is my collection."

She must have looked disappointed, because Helix turned on her with some indignation and said, "I have the end of *Bridge to Terabithia*, and I have the middle of *A Wizard of Earthsea*. I have an almanac of Old Weather."

"What's an almanac?" asked Honor.

"It gives you advice and tells you what the weather used to be and predicts what it will be like next."

"Is it an almanac for the Colonies?" Honor asked.

"Yes," said Helix, "but it's very ancient. "It's called *Poor Richard's*."

"This isn't going to help anything," said Honor, turning the torn pages of the almanac and staring for a moment at the calendar of the old month February with its little pictures of the phases of the moon. *"Waste not, want not,"* she read, and then she pointed out, "That's just a saying of Earth Mother." She handed the almanac back to Helix and folded her arms across her chest. "I thought you had something important."

"Look at this, then," said Helix, and he carefully unfolded a creased paper.

"What is it?" Honor asked, even though she saw what it was. "Where did you get that?" she whispered in awe.

Helix had unfolded the entire paper, and Honor was looking at something she had never seen before, in school or out, a detailed map of the entire island.

There was the island, like a short-tailed fish with a sharp nose and big fins. The volcanic mountains across the middle of the island looked like the fish's spine. The Capital City was colored pale green. The rest of the island, beyond city limits, was tinted yellow. On the City Side, the map showed neigh-borhoods rising up between the ridges of the volcano. There were the bus routes drawn in blue like veins leading from the City up to the highest houses. The other side of the island was easily twice the size of the City Side, but it was almost empty. There were no neighborhoods. There was only one road shown on the other side of the island. That road emerged from the mouth of a tunnel into a valley. In the valley was a square camp of buildings labeled Barracks. "The tunnel is gated and locked at both ends," said Helix. "You can't get into it. Only the bus drivers have the keys to the tunnel. They drive in a convoy and the first driver unlocks the tunnel and then the last bus driver locks up after them. But look. If you climb up through the Model Forest, you can get into the real forest. Then you hike over the mountains."

Honor was gazing at the drawings of the Barracks. The buildings were all rectangular. There were hundreds set up in a quadrangle with an open square between them. At the corners of the camp, the map showed small square buildings. "Those must be watchtowers," Honor said.

Outside the camp there were only two other buildings. One was labeled Maintenance and the other Transportation. "I think those are for the buses," said Helix.

Honor stared hard at the Barracks. "She's there," she whis-pered.

"All the taken parents are there," said Helix. "And I'm going to get mine."

"But how?"

"I'm waiting for a storm. A big one."

"And then what?"

"I don't know," he confessed, "but the last one was over two years ago. Remember?"

She nodded. Of course she remembered the night she and her parents had stayed with Helix and his parents in the safe room. She missed that night when they had all been safe together.

"Approximately every three years," Helix said, quoting the climatology textbook, "there has been a typhoon in the Colonies. When the storm comes and everyone runs to the shelter, I'll escape."

"But even if you could escape, how would you get to the other side?" Honor asked. "And how could you find them?"

"The map," said Helix, as if it were simple.

"They'd catch you," said Honor. "They'd . . . Wait," she said suddenly. "Why should you go? What about me?"

Helix bristled. "I could get them out."

"How do you know?"

"I stole this map from the library, didn't I?"

"And how did you get it?"

"I started a fire in the bathroom—just a little one. Then, when the alarm went off, I stole the map from Miss Tuttle's desk."

"But it was my mother who gave me the code," said Honor. "She's waiting for me. Even if you got to the other side, she might not recognize you. I have to go."

TWO

THEY MADE A PLAN. THEY MADE A HUNDRED PLANS TO leave school and rescue their parents. The plans were detailed, but they were detailed like the plans in dreams, full of little pieces of information, like how many steps it would take to get from the classrooms to the potting shed or how they would meet in the Model Forest at the lookout and start off from there. Their plans were missing the most important ideas, like how they would make their way across the steep volcanic mountains and what they would do once they got to the other side. Honor and Helix could not figure out answers to these questions, partly because they disagreed about what to do, and partly because they had so little sense of what the other side of the island would be like.

All their plans began with a storm. When everyone was hiding in the shelters, when the power went down and the world went black, that would be their chance. But where was bad weather? Where were the rain and surf? Where were the floods? Every day, Honor and Helix listened to the weather bulletins, but no storm was predicted. Every storm drill, Honor and Helix looked at the sky and hoped the sirens were sounding for the real thing. No such luck. Days passed and weeks, and not a drop of rain.

Honor had trouble concentrating in class. During geography tests, when she filled in blank maps with Corporation district numbers, she kept thinking of Helix's secret map of the island. She couldn't stop thinking about that map, folded in the potting shed. The map seemed to her to have magic powers, it was so strange and dangerous and Not Allowed. Every year in school she'd studied weather maps and oceanic maps, but she'd never seen a map of where she lived. She thought of the map and she thought of the escape plans and she did poorly on her algebra tests.

Quintilian was having trouble too. He had begun drawing on every scrap of paper he could find, even in the margins of his schoolbooks. The pictures were always the same, round smiling faces of the family and a big round face above them for Earth Mother. Sometimes he drew Earth Mother with lines radiating from her head like the sun.

He said his pencil couldn't help it. Drawings sprouted everywhere. One day, after three warnings, his teacher and Mr. Edwards met and decided Quintilian had to learn his lesson. He got a punishment of extra garden chores to do.

Quintilian's little hands were too small to weed the garden. He wasn't strong enough to push a wheelbarrow. All the orphans helped him when they thought Mr. and Mrs. Edwards weren't looking. After several days of weeding, Quintilian stopped drawing. He drooped sadly at his desk and ate hardly any dinner.

"How will you grow?" Honor asked him.

Quintilian shrugged.

"You can't grow if you don't eat," she said.

"I don't like food," he told her.

"But how do you know, if you don't even try?" she demanded. She didn't know what to do with him. Fanny had told her that orphans who didn't eat had to go to the infirmary and Nurse Applebee made them eat. She was afraid this would happen to Quintilian. He looked so listless and sad. He acted like a boy who thought nothing good would ever happen again.

"I'm going to tell him I saw our mother," she told Helix.

Helix was upset. "He's too little. He's only four. He can't keep a secret."

"Yes, he can," said Honor.

"Telling him is a mistake," Helix warned her.

"Why?"

"I don't want him to be disappointed," Helix said softly.

Honor was surprised at this. She put her hands on her hips. "Don't you think we'll be able to get them out?"

The next chance she got, she whispered in Quintilian's ear, "Promise if I tell you a secret, you'll eat."

"What's the secret?" Quintilian asked.

"Promise first."

"Promise."

"Mommy is alive."

He didn't ask how she knew, but he smiled at her. He said, "I'll eat bananas."

"No!" Honor protested. "Other things too."

"Bananas," Quintilian said.

There was an old saying of Earth Mother: *A watched pot never boils; a watched sky never rains.* Now that Honor and Helix were watching the sky, they could count day after day of sunny weather. Twenty-eight days of sunshine. Twenty-nine. The air was stifling; there was talk of drought. There had never been such heat. The teachers thought about canceling the school field day for fear that children would suffer heatstroke. Then they talked about holding field day inside. But there were no rooms big enough to hold so many footraces, three-legged races, wheelbarrow races, potato-sack races, egg-in-a-teaspoon races, relay races. The teachers decided to hold the field day first thing in the morning before the sun became unbearable.

That morning the sky was overcast, but the sun beat down anyway. The whole school gathered on the Upper Field, the same place Honor had come her first day at Old Colony. As on that day, teachers stood with banners for their classes, but now the littlest children lined up by a banner painted *R*. The littlest children had names like Rebecca and Rapunzel and Romulus. All the teachers shook their heads and said how time flies and how wonderful it was and was it possible. The youngest students had been born in the eighteenth glorious year of Enclosure.

Miss Blessing wore a white visor to keep the sun out of her eyes. She blew on a silver whistle. Other teachers held stopwatches in their hands, or lined up hundreds of plastic cups of water on the water tables, or arranged ribbons on the ribbon tables. The ribbon tables were covered with white cloths and then adorned with shining satin ribbons in orange and deep purple, sea blue and emerald green. The ribbons were printed in gold: 1st Place, 2nd Place, 3rd Place, 4th Place, and Participant. They were all beautiful, but the green first-place ribbons were the most beautiful of all, because they were adorned with a green satin rosette.

Quintilian competed in a hopping race and won a purple Participant ribbon. Helix ran in the three-legged race with Hector, and they won a red third-place ribbon. Honor stood in the special roped-off archery area and eyed her target. She was not the best at archery anymore and she knew it. True, her eyes were keen, her hand was steady, her arm was strong. She'd won many ribbons in the girls' archery competition when she was younger, but in the past year, other girls had improved at the sport. There was a group of younger girls, especially, who were now quite good. They practiced together during recreation time, while Honor had hardly touched a bow since the day she'd admitted her parents had been taken.

The younger archers all wore their sun hats at the same angle, and they clustered together and giggled. They had the superior look of girls with parents. They were from year *J,* and their names were Jessie, Jocasta, and Jill. Of course they wouldn't speak to Honor. She stood apart and didn't speak to them either.

A large crowd of students stood behind the ropes to watch.

All the children who had finished their races had come to see the competition, and they stood five and six deep with their satin ribbons fluttering in their hands.

Miss Teasdale said, "First three, take your places," and the three *J* girls stepped up to shoot. Honor watched with Fanny and Hagar from the waiting line, five yards behind the shooting marks.

Jessie, Jocasta, and Jill knocked back their arrows. Each arrow had a notch for the bowstring. The girls' arrows all had different feather crests, but the girls looked alike to Honor with their hats pulled back the same way and their smooth brushed hair and their flouncy way of standing, as if they owned the shooting line. When they let fly, each arrow hit its target.

Sweat streaked Honor's face as she waited and watched the younger girls. The best two out of three would advance to the next round, but the scores were close. It wasn't clear until the last moment which of the friends would move on. When Jocasta was eliminated, Jessie and Jill rushed to hug her and make her feel better while the audience applauded. The three girls reminded Honor of herself when she had decided to become perfect and make Helena her friend. They were sickeningly sweet.

She set her quiver down next to her mark and began testing the string of her bow.

"Oh no, Heloise, wait!" Miss Teasdale cried, alarmed, because the first-round shooters had not yet cleared away. "Back off! Back off! No shooters on the mark until I give the all-clear signal."

Honor did not back off. She stood and glared at the target

before her, while Miss Teasdale ushered the other girls away protectively. When Fanny and Hagar stepped up to shoot with Honor, Fanny whispered to Honor, "What's wrong with you? Do you want to get disqualified?"

Honor shrugged. She felt strange, as though she were standing outside herself. Why had she ever tried to act like those girls from J, sweet only to one another and mean to everybody else? What in the world had she been thinking? Why had she thought she could change her name and that would make her fit? How had she been so sure her parents were wrong about everything and her teachers were right? She could see herself standing there on the field, and she remembered the day she'd begun crying uncontrollably when she tried to shoot. She would not cry now. She would not shoot into the grass now. She would not behave like those girls from year J. She stared at the target. She stared so hard that the colored circles seemed to float before her eyes. Red, blue, black, white.

She scarcely heard Miss Teasdale give the signal. She knocked back her first arrow and let it fly, straight into the bull's-eye. "Ooh." The children watching drew a breath, but Honor didn't care. Fanny and Hagar were shooting next to her, but she didn't notice. She knocked back her second arrow and sent that close to the first, in the blue circle outside the bull's-eye. Then she took the third arrow from her quiver. She pulled her bowstring back and felt the muscles in her arm tense and ache. She felt a cold prickle on her shoulder, and for a split second she thought she might have hurt her arm pulling too hard. She let the arrow fly. "OOH." The crowd was louder this time. Bull's-eye, just to the right of the first.

The crowd grew louder. The onlookers had begun to scream. Honor realized it wasn't because of her shot. What she'd felt on her shoulder was cold rain. The sky was dark. Teachers were blowing their whistles and racing with the children for the shelters.

"Come on! Come on, Heloise!" screamed Fanny, but Honor held her bow, unable to move. The storm sirens were sounding; the wind was picking up. Honor knew what to do, but she had been waiting so long, she felt for a moment she couldn't do it. "Take my hand," Fanny shouted, and she began dragging Honor to the shelter. The girls were wet all over; they were already drenched. Honor slipped her hand from Fanny's and turned her head the other way. "No, Heloise!" screamed Fanny. "Come back! Come back! You'll get hurt. You'll get killed." Honor ducked her head, clutched her bow, slung her quiver over her shoulder, and began to run.

THREE

SHE SPRINTED OVER THE SLICK ARCHERY FIELD AND BEHIND the targets. She could hear the screaming and the sirens, but her heart was pounding louder. The quiver with her remaining arrows bounced against her back. The air was full of flying plastic cups and ribbons. The fields streamed with screaming children and teachers, shouting themselves hoarse. Faintly, far away, she heard Miss Blessing's silver whistle. Security orderlies wheeled around catching stray children, one in each hand. Everyone was racing to the shelters, but Honor ran the other way, up to the Model Forest.

Her feet slid out from under her. She tripped and fell flat, only to scramble up again. Her legs were streaked with mud, and her feet slid and sloshed in her wet sandals.

The rain weighed her down. Her drenched skirt slapped against her legs as she stumbled forward. The wind ripped off her sun hat, and her hair flew into her face. Trees shook above her. As she ran into the forest, branches slashed her face and body. Mud sucked her sandals. The sky was dark with the storm, and the trees made the way even darker and more difficult. She knew she shouldn't go to the lookout; it was too exposed. The wind would sweep her up into the sky. She couldn't go there. She was afraid Helix had tried, even though they'd agreed he would stay with Quintilian.

Her arms ached. She thought of casting off her tall bow and quiver, but she was afraid someone from school would find them. She knew she had to keep climbing as far as she could into the mountains. She was well past the Model Forest now. She stumbled between tree trunks wet and soft. Bark peeled off and stained her hands where she tried to hold on. Huge vines snaked upward into the tree branches, choking out the light. Philodendron leaves the size of open umbrellas shook water down on her. Spiky green shoots stabbed her legs. The forest thickened. She struggled against roots and branches as she pushed her way higher.

She didn't know how long she'd been running. She didn't know where she was, except that suddenly the ground grew steeper. The earth was red, and a path emerged between the trees, a muddy gully studded with rock but not impossible to climb. On hands and knees she clawed for a handhold here, a tree root there. Slowly, she made her way upward until— *whoosh*—a flood of water poured down from above. Honor tried to hold on, but the current was too strong and swept her under. The water tore her quiver from its strap and swept away her bow. Water gushed into Honor's eyes and mouth and ears. She reached out blindly, stretching for something solid to hold, but she felt nothing. She was choking. Her clothes dragged her down.

Like all children, she'd learned to fear water, not to swim. *I'm drowning,* she thought. She had to pull herself up; she had to breathe. She slammed into a huge fallen tree. The current tried to suck her under, but she held on to the tree's trailing branches. She clung to the tree and forced her head up. She was gasping for air as the water roared around her.

Honor held on, but every moment the current tried to pull her down into the tangle of branches and leaves below.

The water wasn't cold, but she was shaking, chilled from the inside. Her hands were bloodied where she held the tree branches. She knew she had to climb out or she would lose her grip. She slid one hand along the tree trunk, just an inch, and then the other. The water pulled at her with all its might; the current tangled her skirt around her knees. Still, she worked her way along the trunk, little by little. Her hands were raw, her body numb, and when she looked up, she almost despaired at how high and steep the bank was. Tree roots hung down, but she didn't know if they would hold her weight. She would have to thrust herself high up out of the water to grab hold of them. She was afraid to try for fear of falling, but she was also afraid to hang on where she was. She needed to catch her breath; she needed to wake from this nightmare and find herself in bed, but the water roared and pulled so hard she couldn't rest. She closed her eyes a moment and remembered her father and mother. Then she judged the distance to the roots and lunged for them.

She fell back, flailing. Desperately she reached out with both arms and snagged the fallen tree again. Here the tree roots on the bank were not so high. She gathered all her strength and jumped like a fish from the flowing stream. She seized the roots with one hand and then the other. Gasping, shivering, she dragged herself up the muddy bank. She was soaked to the bone, her body covered with bruises, her torn clothes caked with mud. She wedged herself between the roots of a young banyan tree and tucked her knees to her chest and tried to rest.

She slept fitfully. When she did drift off, she heard strange muddled voices. She dreamed of boats seeping with cold water. The thud and plink of raindrops into pots and pans and someone shaking her. Her mother shaking her awake. "We have to go. Wake up, we have to go now. They're coming."

She woke up sweating. Her heart was pounding, even though she saw no one coming. She was alone, and the storm was over. All the water in the gully below had sunk away, leaving a huge mud slick behind. Honor's white shirt and tan skirt were unrecognizable, nearly black with mud, but she had no way to clean herself. Her feet were bare. The flood had ripped away her sandals.

She was thirsty and her stomach hurt. When she stood, she felt sick with hunger. She needed to find food, but she was afraid she wasn't far enough from school. She could not hear the weather bulletins from the City, but she had no precise way to measure how far she'd come from the Model Forest. If she were anywhere near, then orderlies and search dogs would find her. She needed to climb farther, but there was no path in the wild rain forest, and she could scarcely find an opening.

Slowly, Honor moved upward from foothold to foothold, picking her way around sharp rocks, trying to avoid the hissing scorpions and the slimy lizards hidden under every leaf. She had been too tired before to fear the wild animals that lived in the mountains, but now she remembered everything she had learned in school, and she shuddered to think of the wild boars that might be hiding in the trees, just waiting to charge her and eat her. There were no snakes on the island, not a single one, but there were poisonous toads, and there were biting spiders. She knew the forest was a treacherous place.

Berries hung from vines, but she didn't know if they were safe to eat. She picked guavas hungrily, but they were green and made her feel sicker than before.

Some of the philodendron leaves had filled with fresh rainwater. With two hands, Honor tipped the leaves like great bowls. And so she made her way slowly up the mountain, sipping from one leaf and then another.

Night fell, and the dim forest grew dark. Mosquitoes clouded the air. Small animals scurried on the forest floor, rats or mongooses or something else. Moths the size of birds flew through the trees. False eyes glowed on their wings so that enemies couldn't tell whether they were coming or going. One moth flew at Honor and struck her arm. She cried out in fright because the moth was so big and heavy, more animal than insect. Bats hung in the trees, folding their brown leathern wings to feast on fruit. In the distance Honor could hear strange echoing sounds. "Oh-oh, oh-oh." And another sound like a question. "Twilleep? Ttttwilleep?" She had not heard birdcalls since she'd come to the island. In the City and at the shore there were no birds. Rats had destroyed all the nests long ago. The City was quiet. She had never thought about the silence before, but now she realized that without birdsong, the City streets were cold and dead.

She could not see the birds, but she felt that they could see her. What other animals were watching? If she still had her bow and arrows, she might have shot a charging boar, but she had no weapon to protect herself.

She looked uncertainly at trees crawling with ants and choked with creeping vines. Should she try to climb one?

It was then that she saw a white patch on a low tree branch. She thought at first the white was a cluster of toadstools, the kind so common in that damp place, but the bulge began to move, and she saw it was not toadstools or lichen, but the soft body of a creature—an octopus. As she drew closer, close enough to touch the animal, it opened its bulbous eye and looked at her.

"Octavio!" She recognized the animal immediately, or thought she did. Miss Blessing had said Octavio was a tree octopus, and this creature looked exactly like him. "They didn't get you," she whispered. "They didn't kill you." She touched Octavio's rubbery body, and he wrapped one tentacle delicately around her wrist.

Then Octavio drew back his tentacle and began to move. He sidled through vines and trees, and Honor followed him as best she could. She was slow, but she kept her eyes on Octavio's ghostly body, and she never lost sight of him. He was showing her an easier path, picking his way around the forest's thickest growth. When she stumbled or hesitated, he always waited for her.

She was so light-headed she might have been dreaming, but dreaming or not dreaming didn't seem so important anymore. She wasn't frightened, because she wasn't alone. Octavio was guiding her.

He took her to a stand of trees hung with passion fruit vines. The fruit was ripe and Honor ate greedily. Her tongue curled because it was so tart, but she gobbled up the juicy golden flesh, swallowing black seeds. Only when she stopped to pick more passion fruit did she realize that Octavio was gone. She looked for him, but he had slipped away.

She found a hidden place between the close-growing trees. It wasn't big enough to stretch out, but she could curl up safely, barricaded there by the young tree trunks, and sleep.

She dreamed of gold, an avalanche of gold leaves falling at her feet. She dreamed of Northern forests, massive beech trees and slender white birches, towering pines and oaks and scarlet maples. She dreamed she was with her mother picking black-berries. Their arms and hands were scratched by brambles, but the wild berries were so sweet, warmed by the unfiltered sun. She dreamed of ice. "Look, Honor." Her father showed her a cave jeweled with icicles. She dreamed of snow falling and falling from the white sky, no sun, no moon, no stars, only the snow falling, muffling every sound, softening every step, outlining every branch of every tree. "Will you remember the snow?" Honor's father asked her. "You won't forget?"

"No, I—"

She woke with a start. She was alone again. The trees were green around her, but she could still feel snow on her eyelashes and cheeks and hands. She felt faint. She realized her memory was playing tricks on her because she had no proper food to eat. If she closed her eyes even for a moment, the dream-snow returned to her: the whiteness and the crunch under her feet, drifts soft to the touch, melting at her fingertips like clouds.

She was near the crest of the mountain now, close to the clouds. The forest was just as thick, but the air was misty, and the sloping rock faces trickled with water, a hundred tiny waterfalls. She shook herself and rubbed the dreams from her eyes. Bending down, she drank and washed her face in the clear running water. Sometimes she couldn't tell which way a little waterfall was flowing, whether it was coming down from the mist or whether it was evaporating upward into the mysterious air. She imagined that no one from school could track her now. No straight-moving orderlies could follow her erratic trail.

She was alone, but she was fiercely glad. She had left everyone else behind. She had not been caught; she had not drowned. She did not worry anymore. Climbing up was so difficult it took all her strength, and she was glad. Climbing, she could scarcely think about anything else.

All that day she kept moving upward until, at last, the trees thinned and rock jutted from the mountainside. Then she wanted to creep out of the shadowy forest to look around her, but she waited. For all she knew, there was a watchtower on the mountain. Watchers might catch sight of her through their special viewfinders or even hear her somehow, creeping along the mountaintop. She had been taught in school that the Watchers who watch over us have every tool. *Every tool for every rule* went the saying of Earth Mother.

So she crouched down and rested. She had no sense of time, because she was too far away from the City's projection booth to count on sky color. How strange it was to lie and wait for pale orange hour six and then pink hour seven. Orange, pink, lavender, purple, indigo. She waited, but the familiar colors never came.

When the sun was weakening, she crept out onto the rock face. She kept her head down and crawled on her hands and knees. The wind was fierce, and she panicked for a moment, thinking that the storm wasn't really over and that the wind would blow her away. But the wind was nothing more than a passing breeze. She glanced up and winced. The sky stung, unfiltered blue, too clear, too bright. She shaded her eyes and looked down.

How strange the other side of the island was. The green slopes of the volcano were unscarred by roads or houses. Trees and other plants covered the mountains all the way down to vast valleys nestled between ridges, and those valleys were brimming with sunflowers, thousands and millions of them, a sea of gold faces upturned in the breeze. Honor had not expected this. She had seen no fields of gold on Helix's map. She sat back on her heels. She had known sunflowers were fuel, and she had diagrammed the parts of a sunflower in school, but she had never imagined they were so beautiful.

She saw the shadow before she heard the voice or saw the man. Dark shade fell across the rock. Rough arms seized her from behind, and a familiar voice said, "Well, well, look who we have here."

FOUR

HONOR TRIED TO FREE HERSELF, BUT SHE COULD NOT. THE
man pinned her arms back and tied them with rope. She
turned her head, and when she saw her captor, she sobbed
with despair. It was Mr. Pratt, the Neighborhood Watch from
her old house.

"I see you remember me," said Mr. Pratt. Then he said quietly, "Don't fight or try to run away. You'll just get hurt."

He slipped a blindfold over her eyes and tied it tight. Then
he took Honor's arm and led her back into the forest.

"Please," begged Honor, "let me see. I won't run away."

"Can't let you see," said Mr. Pratt.

"Please tell me where we're going."

"Can't do that either," said Mr. Pratt. She was frightened by
his calm, cheerful voice, as if tracking runaways was as easy as
taking trash to the recycling plant.

"Are we going back to school?" Honor's voice trembled.

"No more talking." Mr. Pratt's grip on her arm tightened.

Honor lowered her blindfolded head and stumbled along after him. Could she wrench herself away? Even if she could, how far could she get with her arms tied? There was no way she could get the blindfold off. She felt they were traveling down the mountain, but Mr. Pratt took so many turns she had no idea where they were heading. She could hear insects and the distant call of owls. She smelled the damp of rotting wood and the scent of cinnamon from the cinnamon trees. Her feet and legs were covered with little cuts from the sharp rocks in the path.

The moist warm air was slightly cooler on her skin. She knew that they were walking in the dark. Where did runaways end up? How would Miss Blessing punish her? She asked herself these questions even though she knew in her heart that Mr. Pratt was not taking her back to school. She knew that after what she'd done, she would end up in a much more dangerous place.

She tried to keep up, but her legs faltered. Her cut feet hurt too much. She was afraid to stop, but she could not go on. She fell to her knees and bowed her head, expecting Mr. Pratt to hit her. She was sure he would beat her with his hands, with sticks, with anything. Nothing happened. No blows came. She heard footsteps and she felt suddenly that Mr. Pratt was leaving her there, bound and blindfolded. Terrified, she called out to him, "Wait."

"No noise," snapped Mr. Pratt. He had returned dragging something, a container or bucket he lifted to her lips. "Drink this."

She took a sip. The drink was water.

"Now hold on to me," Mr. Pratt said, and he lifted Honor onto his back and carried her. "Almost there," he grunted, more to himself than to her. "Duck your head."

She ducked and tried to make herself as small as possible. Even then, her head brushed thick low-lying branches.

"Here we are," said Mr. Pratt, and he set Honor on the ground and untied her blindfold.

She trembled as Mr. Pratt untied her wrists. They were standing in a dark part of the forest, all night and shadow. Trees and vines grew so close together no moon or starlight could shine through. But Honor could make out a couple of rough shelters, tents covered with leaves and branches, and she saw someone who approached so eagerly that she shrank back, afraid.

"Do you remember me? I'm Mrs. Pratt."

"Do you remember me?" Out of the shadows stepped her father. In the next moment she was in his arms.

"You're bleeding." He kissed the cuts on her face. "How did you get out? Where is Quintilian?"

But she was telling her news at the same time. "I found her. I found her. She's in the bakery."

"Hold on. Take a minute. Catch your breath," said Mr. Pratt. "Let's start at the beginning."

And so they did. Honor and her father took turns. They began to tell each other everything.

"But aren't you in the Neighborhood Watch?" Honor interrupted herself to ask Mr. Pratt.

"No," said Mr. Pratt. "Not at all. I haven't worked in the

Neighborhood Watch for years. When your family moved to higher ground, Mrs. Pratt and I did too. We left our town house and moved up here."

"No one ever told us that," said Honor.

"Well, no, they wouldn't, would they? Officially, we've Disappeared."

"And that's when you became Partisans?"

"We were Partisans even when we lived in the City. I was a Partisan when you first met me. I helped your parents join our band when they first arrived."

Honor shook her head in disbelief. "How did you find me?"

"I found these first," said Mr. Pratt, and he held up Honor's bow and quiver. "Then these." He held up two arrows. "Then I started tracking you."

"Let's see those feet," said Mrs. Pratt. Honor sat on her father's lap while Mrs. Pratt washed her feet and cleaned the cuts with gauze dipped in stinging alcohol.

"How long have you been hiding here?" Honor asked.

"I've been here since the day I disappeared," her father told her. "Your mother and I were at a Partisan meeting."

"Where?" asked Honor.

"In our own house," Will said. "While you were at school."

"At home? In our own house in the middle of the day?" Honor couldn't help it. She was scandalized by her parents' recklessness.

"I thought I was safe because I had an excused absence from the office. Your mother had no work. The Central Store was closed for inventory day. But the Safety Officers found us anyway."

"How did you know?"

"We knew as soon as we heard the knock at the door. I was stupid. I panicked and tried barricading the door. Your mother ran upstairs while I was trying to block the way. They just kept knocking, louder and louder. Then they took an ax . . ."

"Who were they?"

"The Postal Service. We got taken by men driving a regular mail truck, a Corporation mail truck for packages. We scattered. I got out the back door, but they snatched your mother. They caught her by the arm and stuffed her into a canvas mail sack."

"And you ran here?"

Her father nodded. "We've built a boat. We have a sailboat hidden on the beach."

"What will you do with it?" Honor asked.

"Take the Weather Station."

"The one on Island 364? You can't pull it down. It's too big!"

"We're not going to take it down. We're going to take over. We're going to hack into the computers there and seize the network. Partisans on Island 323 have already seized theirs. Partisans in the North have taken a station there. If we can occupy this one, we can connect with them. We'll join their network. From there we can deregulate the clocks. We'll reprogram the projection booth in the City. Everyone will know we have begun."

"Begun what?" asked Honor.

"The revolution to take Her down."

"You're a Reverse Engineer," Honor whispered.

Will wrapped his arms around her and said, "Don't look at me like that."

"You're trying to crack the ceiling," Honor said.

"You've learned one thing in school," her father said. "You've learned it over and over again until it seems true. We can't crack the ceiling over the Polar Seas. There aren't enough of us yet. The Corporation is too powerful."

"Do you really want to go back to Old Weather?" Honor asked.

"Don't you see?" Will told her. "We've got Old Weather."

"But the Colonies are safe."

"No, sweetheart," said Will. "The Colonies are not safe. Earth Mother regulates the light and the night sky and the people in the cities. She covers the sky with her overlay. She conceals the real moon and stars—"

"To protect us!" Honor cut in. Even standing there in the tatters of her uniform, even after all she'd been through, it was hard to accept her father's ideas. In school, the world was strict and sometimes cruel but also neat and orderly. In school, she understood the rules. She could touch the islands on the classroom globe and chart the progress of Enclosure on the map. In school, Enclosure triumphed over danger. "She wants to protect us," Honor insisted.

"She wants to control us," said her father. "The sun still burns; the winds still blow. Overlays and projection booths are window dressing for what Earth Mother really wants: total cooperation. No questions, no complications. Everyone doing a job, no one sticking out."

"She saved us from Old Weather," Honor said.

"She organized us. She played on our fears."

"The weather stations and warning sirens keep us safe."

"They keep us indoors. Earth Mother wants us quiet and meek, like orderlies. She wants us to accept her ideas as our own. Forget our own identities, if possible."

Honor looked away, stung with shame. She saw herself through her father's eyes; she saw the girl she had been, copying passages from books, swearing allegiance with the Heliotropes, even changing her name.

"In the wild places," her father said, "the fruit is clean. There are no greenhouses with misters. There is no Planet Safe in the food or in the water. In the wild places memory is possible. Can't you feel the difference, here in the mountains?"

"Yes," Honor said, remembering her dreams.

"We want to crack the Corporation. We want to undermine Earth Mother's power. Someday, we want to take the Taker. But we're going to start with the Weather Station. The Corporation's Weather Station monitors the region. Weather Station computers provide the weather forecast every hour; they send out storm warnings. They control the projection booth in the City. Not just that. Those computers on the Weather Station store every piece of information on the City's inhabitants. Where we live and what we do. Who cooperates and who possibly objects. There's a file for each one of us. If we break into those computers we take back our lives."

"But the Weather Station's guarded. It's got Watchers," Honor spluttered. "How could a sailboat get there? How could you find it, so far out to sea? Only big ships can navigate there. You have no computers or radar."

"We'll navigate by the stars."

"For that," said Mrs. Pratt, "we need your mother."

Mr. Pratt explained, "We want to find her, either as she enters the buses or in the Barracks. The problem is that every building looks exactly the same, and every bunk is the same, and every orderly looks the same. Finding Pamela is like looking for a needle in a haystack. There are more than a thousand identical Barracks buildings on the other side of the island."

"She gave me a clue," Honor said. "Helix and I figured it out. She gave us a number in the bakery. Number seven in base two."

FIVE

ALL THAT NIGHT AND THE NEXT DAY WHILE THE PRATTS
and Will made their plans, Honor rested. She ate breadfruit and
mountain apples cut into slices and delicious lychees Mrs. Pratt
had gathered. She wore an old shirt while Mrs. Pratt washed
her ripped-up uniform. Mrs. Pratt did not have soap, only a
bucket of water and a washboard. She rinsed and scrubbed
Honor's shirt and skirt as best she could and got the worst of
the mud out. She hung them up to dry, but the air was so moist
that they were damp when Honor put them back on.

"You know what to do?" Honor's father asked her.

"Yes," she said.

"Do you think you can?"

She had no idea. "How will I know until I try?"

• • •

Will and Mr. Pratt took apart the tents and scattered
the leaves. They packed up clothes and tools. Each of them

strapped on a backpack and Mr. Pratt strapped a battered box to his back. Honor carried her bow and the two arrows Mr. Pratt had found, and the four of them set out into the forest. The climb was steep up the mountain and Honor's feet were sore, but this time her father was helping her. He lifted her over rocks and took her arm when they came to steep places. When Honor was tired, they all stopped to rest. Mrs. Pratt found ripe guavas to eat.

They came to the place they were searching for by afternoon. It was a lookout post from ancient times. The place was called a pillbox and it was made of cement. There was just one bare room with narrow slits for windows. From the pillbox they had a view down the slope of the volcano into the valley where the Barracks stood.

Mr. Pratt took out a pair of binoculars and let Honor look.

"That's the service road," said Mr. Pratt, pointing to a dark paved road curling below them. "And those are the buildings where they house the orderlies."

The buildings were strange. Their roofs were curved. They looked like long white cylinders half buried in the ground. The buildings were arranged in perfect rows.

"See over there." Mr. Pratt pointed to a white structure in the quad between the buildings. "That's the compost bin. And over there—that's the bus depot."

Honor gazed down at a parking lot. It was nearly empty.

"We've been observing them for a while now. In the evening, a hundred buses will drive in and unload the afternoon shift to sleep," said Mr. Pratt. "Then they'll load the night shift and drive back to the City. There are three shifts throughout the day. Morning, noon, and night."

"There's a special fuel station just for the orderlies' buses," said Mrs. Pratt.

"Look carefully at the watchtowers," said Mr. Pratt. "One on each corner."

"Are the Watchers orderlies?" Honor asked.

"No," said her father. "Orderlies do other jobs. They drive the buses day and night. But there is always the chance of escape or rebellion, and so armed Watchers guard them at all times."

"Where are the lights?"

Honor's father pointed. There were stadium lights on tall poles. There were floodlights as well on the roofs of the Barracks. The stadium lights were huge. The floodlights were small and hung in pairs over the doorways of each building.

"There are no numbers on the doors," said Honor's father.

"Then how do the orderlies know where to go?" asked Honor.

"They're trained to flock like birds," said her father. "They don't know anything *except* where to go."

"Are there numbers inside the buildings?" Honor asked.

"I don't know," said her father.

Honor gazed at the white Barracks below. She watched the afternoon shift of orderlies return and file off their buses. The orderlies did not make a sound. They walked in groups into different white buildings and as they walked, they faced forward, never turning aside, never distracted. They glided along in white and never touched one another.

The orderlies wore no chains and they had no Safety

Officers accompanying them. No dogs nipped at their heels. They didn't even have managers, as they sometimes did at work, to guide them. But high above the Barracks stood four towers, tall and slender, with ladders on the outside and little glass rooms on top. The orderlies never glanced at the watchtowers, but they never made a false move either.

All that day, Honor and her father and the Pratts watched the Barracks. They watched until they grew still with waiting. The sun began to set. No one spoke. Honor held her bow and arrows together in her fist. Her palms were sweating.

The sunset was gold and then deeper gold. The fierce blue of the sky began to soften and darken. The air was damp and smelled of earth. The real moon appeared, small as an eyelash. Together Mr. and Mrs. Pratt, Honor, and her father began to creep down the mountain. They left almost all their belongings behind in the pillbox so that they could move faster. Honor carried only her bow and arrows. The others carried flashlights and big knives and machetes to cut away the thick branches blocking their path. Honor could not see the Barracks through all the leaves, but her heart beat fast because she knew they were coming closer.

They dared not leave the forest when they reached the valley, but through the trees they could see the black paved service road and the barren ground on either side. There were no flowers or plants in this place. There was only asphalt and hard-packed reddish dirt. Everything was neat and clean and bare. If they looked down the service road, they could see one corner of the Barracks with its tall watchtower.

Darkness came. The night was hot. Termites rose up from the ground and from the trees, and millions of them filled the air with tiny flimsy wings. Honor brushed them away from her sweating face. Her heart was pounding now; it was agony to stand and wait.

"Soon," whispered her father.

In just minutes the stadium lights would switch on, illuminating the Barracks. The Pratts moved far to the left. Honor and her father moved to the right. They stood in two pairs at the edge of the forest. Honor held her bow and knocked back an arrow. Honor's father took a box of matches from his pocket. It was a box of kitchen matches. His hands trembled as he shook out a single match. They were all waiting for Mr. Pratt's signal.

Honor tried to calm her breathing, but her whole body was trembling. She could scarcely hold her arrow against the bowstring, but she forced herself to keep still. She forced herself to think about what she had to do.

The moment Mr. Pratt raised his arm, Honor's father struck the match. The tiny flame jumped in the darkness, and Will touched it to the alcohol-soaked, gauze-wrapped tip of Honor's arrow. He whispered just one word to Honor: "Run."

Honor sprinted forward onto the service road. She held her bow with the lit arrow and ran as fast as she could toward the nearest watchtower. Close as she dared, she stopped and aimed. She sent her flaming arrow right toward the wooden structure, but she was so nervous that her arrow didn't hit. The tip grazed the edge of the tower's ladder, where the flame caught and climbed. The fire alarm sounded, pulsing, ear-splitting.

Then Honor saw them—a squad of orderlies dragging a fire hose. The stadium lights switched on, and the road and the Barracks and even the flaming watchtower were flooded with white light. The Watcher inside was standing, screaming, as flames licked up the sides of the tower. Was the Watcher going to jump? The drop was too far. Honor hesitated for a moment, horrified. The white stadium lights were so strong and the flames so sudden that the orderlies stopped in their tracks, confused about which light to seek. Then the Watcher jumped. He dove into the orderlies' outstretched arms. Honor slung her bow and quiver across her back and ran.

She rushed to the door of the closest building and lifted the heavy metal bar securing it. There was no lock. The building was dark except for dim Energy Saver bulbs in the doorway. At first she could scarcely see into the triple bunks stacked against each wall. The beds were empty. She ran on. She knew her father was checking another quarter of buildings and Mr. Pratt was checking his quarter and Mrs. Pratt was checking her quarter. If she'd bought enough time with the fire, they could cover all the buildings.

Three Watchers were shooting their tasers, but the orderlies were busy fighting the fire on the fourth watchtower. A second group rushed out to help the first with the heavy fire hose. Honor dashed to the next building and got there even with the tasers lighting up the air around her.

She ran to the next building and the next. Each was empty.

The orderlies in these must have boarded buses for the night shift in the City. The fourth building she tried was full of orderlies sleeping on their backs, arms outstretched on top of their thin bedcovers. They were not wearing their long-sleeved jumpsuits, but short-sleeved nightshirts. There was no way to tell the orderlies apart and no clue anywhere in the Barracks. No numbers on the bunks. Nothing. A new siren was sounding, a wailing alarm. Honor heard the running steps of more orderlies outside.

How could she find her mother among all these inert bodies? She'd need to climb the ladder on each bunk to look at the orderlies in the highest beds, and she had no time. No time at all. She ran through the building into an anteroom stocked with sheets and hats and jumpsuits. The orderlies' footsteps were coming closer. Hundreds and hundreds of them were running in the open space between the Barracks. She crept to the doorway and peeked out. This squadron had no fire hose. They were running together in a thick pack from one building to the next in mute patrol. They were looking for interlopers, coming to find her. But what could they see? Honor pulled a white jumpsuit off a stack of freshly laundered uniforms. She struggled with the stiff material, trying to pull the suit over her clothes. There were no buttons and there was no zipper. The suit hooked in the front and hung too big on her. The orderlies were bursting through the door.

They charged for her. They saw that she did not belong. How could they tell? She almost screamed at the mass swarming her; she was surrounded by those pale, blank faces. Frantically she reached behind her and grabbed a white worker's hat. She covered her head with it. The orderlies shrank back again. The uniform was now complete, and they recognized her as one of them.

The new wail of the siren keened above the pulsing fire alarm. She forgot which building she should enter next. She followed the orderlies out of the room and ran with them across the quad. She tried to match the orderlies' steps. Desperately she tried to look like one of the pack, but her camouflage did not work. Far above, the Watchers could see that she was smaller and quicker than the others. They singled her out and shot at her again and again. A flash stunned an orderly at Honor's side. He fell, writhing in pain on the ground. For a moment Honor stopped in shock, but the other orderlies kept running, tripping over the fallen one. Another orderly fell over the first and, in a flash, the Watchers shot him as well. Two stunned orderlies on the ground. There was no blood; their wounds were invisible, but the orderlies were dying, both of them. They had the crazed look of the rat Honor had seen the Watcher shoot in her old neighborhood. Their eyes bulged and their limbs stiffened, even as they crawled away to the Barracks' huge compost bin and, one after the other, climbed inside.

Honor stumbled forward, trying to keep up with the squad. A stench of smoke and sweat filled the air. Her eyes smarted, and when she ran into the next building, she couldn't see at first after the bright lights outside.

These orderlies were sleeping, even in all this commotion. Their upturned faces were pale as death, and only the slight roll of a head or the gentle rise and fall of their chests showed that they were breathing. Honor raced down the aisles between the identical bunks. She was panting, tripping over herself; her legs could not move fast enough; her mind raced ahead of her body. Through the high, barred windows of the building the blue lights of the Watchers' tasers flashed. Dogs were barking outside now. That meant Safety Officers had arrived. All the while, the orderlies slept their deathly sleep. Were the Thompsons there among them? Were they sleeping near her mother?

Honor could not possibly examine them all. She had no time, and even if she'd had hours, she could not tell one sleeping face from another. She pressed on anyway. She ran down the last aisle toward the door. Should she make a break for it? Or wait? If she ran, the Watchers could shoot her. If she stayed, the dogs would track her. She could hear the animals barking and baying. She felt faint. The world dissolved for a second. She grabbed the frame of a bunk and steadied herself. Outside, the dogs were coming closer. New alarms were sounding, pulsing, screaming. Pierced by the sound, the orderlies did not awaken, but rolled and groaned, as if they were having nightmares.

A sleeping orderly's white arm jerked ever so slightly above the covers, and Honor saw something dark and shadowy. A bruise, she thought, but she looked more closely and found a number. The number TH239 was tattooed on the orderly's forearm. She whipped around to the next bunk and turned over that orderly's arm. GB240. There were no numbers on the buildings or the bunks, but the orderlies themselves were numbered, and they were sleeping in order. That was how they were organized.

Honor closed her eyes. She tried to shut out the sirens and smoke and her own fear. She had to think where the one hundreds might be if the two hundreds were here.

She dashed outside, and the smoke was so thick now that she could scarcely see. Clouds and billows of black smoke masked the stadium lights. The fire from the watchtower had spread to a Barracks building and licked the walls. Were the orderlies still inside? Was her mother burning there? Instinctively she rushed toward the burning building and almost fell over the mass of orderlies crawling out. Hundreds were creeping on their bellies into the quad. This was the standard procedure to escape from smoky buildings, but the sight was terrible, the mass of bodies writhing and wriggling forward. Hairless heads and bony limbs were coated with ash and dust so that the orderlies looked like figures formed of clay, or half-dead, half-born creatures emerging from the earth.

"Get back; get back!" Will shouted. Honor couldn't see her father. She could only hear his voice. She tried to get back or turn or run, but the creeping orderlies spread around her in every direction. Every move she made, she stepped on some head or back. She was mired in bodies, but even in the smoke, the Watchers would find her if she stopped. The dogs would hunt her down. She forced herself to step over and on top of the orderlies. She climbed over arms and legs and buttocks.

When at last she reached the edge of the crawling mass, she was disoriented and did not know which building she was entering or even if she had already looked inside. She checked the arms of the first sleeping orderlies she saw. Three hundreds. Outside again, she sprinted in the other direction. A black cloud of ash hung over the Barracks and another foul cloud thickened the air as well. Orderlies were spraying a new substance from their fire hoses: a yellowish gas that smelled like rotten eggs. Was that gas poison? Was it death to breathe? She ran from the thick part of the cloud and saw Mr. Pratt wrestling with a dog. Ears back, teeth bared, the dog was lunging, but Mr. Pratt had the animal by the throat.

"Check their arms. Their arms!" Honor screamed, but Mr. Pratt could not hear. They were all deafened by the sirens and half blind with smoke. And now another dog and then another raced around the corner and ran for Honor. She turned and sprinted for the nearest building with their hot breath on her heels. Just as she reached the door, the first dog lunged and grazed her leg. She was so frightened and she moved so fast that she felt the blood before she felt the pain. She ran inside and slammed the door. A long metal bar fell into place, securing the door against the animals.

She lifted the arm of the first orderly she found: SK430. She was in the four hundreds, and the dogs were scrabbling against the metal door outside.

Honor rushed down the long aisle toward the door at the other end of the building. Rolling carts of food were lined up here for the orderlies' meal. The carts were like the kitchen carts at school, with trays stacked one above the other, but there were no dishes. The food was white mush poured straight onto the trays. Honor pushed a heavy cart in front of her as she burst out the back door of the Barracks into the open. The blue light of tasers flashed, and sparks flew off the cart's metal frame as she pushed the cart like a battering ram before her and broke through the swarms of orderlies running, marching, crawling. Safety Officers were shouting through megaphones now, but the orderlies did not seem to understand. They could not learn new orders all at once. Those that marched kept marching; those that crawled kept crawling, until they piled up on the other side of the quad. And those in buildings as yet untouched by fire remained asleep.

Honor's ears were ringing, her face streaked with dirt and sweat. She crashed the food cart against the wall of the next building and left it there.

Was this building the right one? Was this one possible? She felt as though she were running in a dream, and, as in a dream, she lifted the arm of the nearest sleeping orderly. TJ106. At last. The hundreds. She looked into the next bunk. SK103. The numbers were going down. She ran to the other side. IS109. She climbed the ladder to check the bed just above. Trembling, trying to balance, she touched the orderly's slender arm. PG111. PG for Pamela Greenspoon. One hundred eleven.

She bent over her mother's sleeping face. "It's me. It's Honor. I found you."

But there was no answer.

"Wake up," she pleaded, but her mother did not wake up.

She shook her mother by the shoulders and tried to raise her head. Pamela's head was heavy and hard to lift. But as soon as Honor raised her head off the pillow, Pamela's eyes opened.

They opened wide, the way a doll's shut eyes flick open when it is raised upright. Now Pamela's blue eyes gazed at Honor. Her eyes were big and blank.

"Come with me," Honor said. "We have to run. We don't have time."

Her mother did not move. Her heavy head rested in Honor's hands.

"Come out," Honor said. "Now!" she told the orderly that was Pamela.

But it was no use. Honor was going to have to drag her. She took her mother's arms and, half lifting her, half falling under her, she pulled her down from the bunk. Sinking under her mother's weight, she struggled to carry her down the aisle between the rows of bunks. The door was far, and Honor strained under the body draped across her shoulders. *Come on, come on,* Honor thought. Her eyes devoured the distance to the door as she pushed forward, straining.

The building's security alarm sounded, piercing, screaming directly into Honor's ears. A red light above the door was pulsing. The orderlies lying on their bunks sat bolt upright. Their eyes opened and they jumped down from their beds. One hundred orderlies jumped down and filed to the door, blocking Honor and Pamela. They surrounded Honor and her mother and gazed at the two of them with glassy eyes. Pamela started up as well. She jumped off Honor's back and joined the others.

"Don't go!" Honor pleaded, and stretched her arms out to her mother. But the alarm was too loud and drowned out

Honor's voice. Her mother was disappearing into the crowd. The alarm was blaring and the red light pulsing, tinting every surface red, and Honor's mother stood with the other orderlies, blocking the exit. "Stay with me," Honor pleaded as she looked into her mother's eyes. She was afraid to look away. If she did, she'd lose her forever.

Remember me, she told her mother wordlessly. *Look at me. Remember me.* Then she unslung her bow and took the last remaining arrow from her quiver. The orderlies stared at Honor's weapon. They did not run away or even flinch, but stood inert before her. There was a kind of patience about them, as if they were waiting for her to decide which one of them to shoot. She measured her distance, knocked back her arrow, pulled the bowstring, and let fly.

Crashing glass. She'd shot out the alarm above the door. Glass tinkled from the red light and the building was dim again. The pulsing siren sighed into nothing. All the orderlies turned and marched back to their bunks. Like sleepwalkers in their white nightshirts, they glided serenely back to bed, and Honor, who had been the intruder, was invisible to them. Even when they bumped her as they passed, the orderlies took no notice.

But Honor was watching them, looking into their faces. As her mother passed, she lunged and seized Pamela by the shoulders, spun her around, and dragged her out the door—into the arms of the Pratts, who were waiting there.

"Are you sure she's the one?" asked Mr. Pratt.

"Where is my father?" Honor asked.

But they had no time. The valley had filled with smoke. More orderlies were massing to fight the fire that had spread from the watchtower. Fresh Safety Officers had arrived in trucks. Their dogs were already barking and straining at their leashes as Honor and the Pratts raced away with Pamela.

SIX

THEY RAN INTO THE FOREST, AND THEY DID NOT NEED TO carry Pamela. Once they set her in the right direction, she ran fearlessly, without even noticing the rocks or branches in her path. She seemed to feel no pain but kept rushing forward, even when branches snapped in her face or cut her arms. When they began to climb the mountain, she climbed capably, looking straight ahead. Honor was amazed at how agile her mother was and how strong.

Honor could hear dogs barking and Safety Officers crashing through the trees. She tried to climb faster, but she could hear the dogs panting louder. She could hear them panting, practically at her heels. She remembered the dog's teeth cutting her leg. She remembered the yellow eyes of the dogs that had come to search her house. It was too dark to see, and they were climbing blind, with only the dim glow of Mr. Pratt's flashlight to guide them. Honor was sweating and filthy, and her hands were numb from fighting vines and thorns. Her leg oozed and stung. Her body ached from pressing forward over the steep and slippery ground; she gasped for air, and when she slipped, she scrambled up again and climbed on, but the dogs were coming closer.

She stumbled. She reached for something, anything, to hold. Her mother and the Pratts were climbing ahead of her and didn't see. She wanted to call to them to wait, but she had no breath left. She was afraid the dogs would catch her and tear her apart. Her body screamed with exhaustion. She wanted to climb; she wanted to escape, but she couldn't run farther. She fell to the ground.

Even as she fell, she heard the dogs sink back. There was a confusion of barking, and then, like a tide drawn back, the animals yelped in pain and ran the other way.

The Pratts heard the change and turned back as well. Mrs. Pratt held Pamela by the hand to make her wait, and Mr. Pratt came to help Honor up again. The barking of the dogs was fading; the animals were racing down the mountain now. Honor was confused and dizzy.

"Don't stop," Mr. Pratt told her. "We're almost there. Take my hand." He pulled her into the pillbox, where they were safe.

"Pamela," Mr. Pratt said to Honor's mother, "can you hear me?"

Pamela was too confused to listen. She did not turn in the direction of his voice. Her face and bald head were covered with sweat, her nightshirt soaked through.

"Drink this," said Mrs. Pratt, and offered Pamela fresh-water.

The Pratts were taking care of her mother, but Honor couldn't help. She curled up on the floor of the pillbox and tucked her knees to her chest. She was shaking, freezing. She couldn't stop thinking of the Watcher screaming in the flaming tower. She kept thinking of the flames and the ground crawling with orderlies. As soon as she closed her eyes, she saw them writhing and creeping in the dust. She felt she would never be warm again.

In the morning, Honor found herself curled up at Pamela's side. She touched her mother and she was real. "It's me," she whispered. Pamela did not stir. Honor drew closer and whispered again in her mother's ear, "It's me."

"She's still sleeping. We have to be patient." Honor sat up now, wide awake. It was her father. He was standing with the Pratts, smiling down at her. His sleeve was torn and his arm bandaged, but there he was.

She sprang to her feet and rushed over to him. "How did you escape? How did you get here?" Her voice was muffled against his chest.

"I ran until I reached the north watchtower," he told her. "Then I climbed the ladder and knocked out the Watcher inside. I saw all of you running away and the Safety Officers and their dogs chasing you. I was afraid to shoot from up there and hit one of you, so I climbed down and followed at a distance."

"How many were they?"

"Two Safety Officers and two dogs. When they began closing in on you, I closed in on them. I ambushed them from behind and shot the dogs."

"How come the Safety Officers didn't capture you then?" Honor asked.

"They would have, but I had the taser and I had the Thompsons with me."

"They're alive!"

"They'd been waiting in the forest near the Barracks in case of emergency."

"But where have they been?"

"They ran away before I did."

"So they weren't taken to be orderlies."

"No, they'd escaped into the forest. After I ran away, I found them. At first we all camped together, but then we decided to split up. I stayed with the Pratts and they hid closer to the shore. We were hoping that if Retrievers found some of us they wouldn't find all. Mr. Pratt was the messenger between us because he knows the forest best."

"Now they've gone ahead," said Mr. Pratt. "We'll meet them tomorrow morning."

Will bent over Pamela and stroked her cheek.

"If you want her to open her eyes, lift her head, like a doll," Honor said.

Her father smiled. "That will wear off," he said. "You'll see."

All day they rested there while Pamela slept. Sometimes they talked, and sometimes they ate the fruit Mrs. Pratt had picked, and sometimes they just watched the white clouds in the bright sky.

When the sun began to set, Will told Honor, "Look at the colors. Tell me how many you can see."

"Gold," she said, "and yellow. Now the blue is changing to lavender."

"How many colors?"

"I can't count them all," she told him.

"But look again."

She'd only glanced away for a moment, but the whole sky had changed. The lavender was on fire, flaming red. Then the red was gone, and the clouds burned fiery orange. "Everything's changing," Honor said. "It's too fast."

"That's how natural sunsets are," her father reminded her. "And every night is different."

"We need to wake her and start hiking down," said Mr. Pratt.

They half lifted Pamela from the floor, but her eyes did not open. Honor spoke to her. Will spoke to her. Pamela did not respond. Her breathing was regular. Her arms hung loose and relaxed, not limp over the top of the blanket as they had in the Barracks. She was in a deep sleep.

"Pamela. It's time for us to go," Will said firmly. "Wake up now."

But she did not wake up.

Honor bent over her mother and sang softly, *"Over the river and through the wood to Grandmother's house we go . . ."*

Pamela rolled over on her side.

"*. . . the horse knows the way to carry the sleigh, o'er the white and drifting snow . . .*"

"*Over the river and through the wood,*" sang Will. "*Oh, how the wind does blow. It stings the toes and bites the nose as over the ground we go.*"

Pamela's eyes opened. She looked up at Will and blinked.

"Pamela," said Will.

She didn't answer. She just looked up at him.

Will cupped her face in his hands and kissed her lips. He whispered, "I'm here."

For a moment Honor saw a hint of recognition in her mother's eyes.

All night they hiked down the mountain. Mr. Pratt led the way with his flashlight. Will followed him, and then Honor and Pamela. Mrs. Pratt brought up the rear. Together they slipped and slid and clambered down through muddy gullies and overgrown gulches. Even Will had not traveled on this slope, but Mr. Pratt knew the ground, and he was confident they would not lose their way.

It was still dark when they came to the ragged seaside edge of the forest. The ground was sandy and covered with sea grapes—scraggly, succulent plants. The ocean was calm all around them, scarcely visible in the darkness except for silvery ripples on the shore. The sand was powder soft and, where it was wet, covered with tiny holes, the breathing holes of little white crabs so delicate Honor could almost see through them. Honor had never seen creatures so quick and fine as those white crabs skittering across the water-smoothed sand.

There was no one else at the shore. There were no drowned buildings or Danger signs or fences of barbed wire. The only noise was that of the water breathing softly in and out.

"We're here," said Will.

"We're here." That was Pamela's voice, echoing his. And those were the first words she spoke.

"Come into the water," Will told Pamela.

Honor was confused. She didn't understand, but Will led Pamela into the dark water, all the way up to her waist, and then he cupped his hands full of salt water and washed Pamela's eyes. Pamela cried out in pain when the salty water stung her. Water streamed down her face as she winced and blinked. Her eyes were no longer fixed and motionless. She looked everywhere. She recognized everyone.

Honor ran to the edge of the ocean. She only hesitated a moment. Then she waded into the warm water. The cut on her leg stung from the salt, but Honor ignored the pain and leaned against her mother. "Do you recognize me now? Did you know I'd find you?"

Pamela didn't answer at first. Then she wrapped her arms around Honor. She whispered, "I didn't know, but I was waiting. I waited so long I didn't even know I was waiting."

All the rest of that night they talked.

"Can you believe it?" Mrs. Pratt asked softly. "Did you ever think about escaping?"

"No," said Pamela. "I never thought of escaping on my own."

"I wished that they had taken me," Will murmured. "I wanted to trade places with you."

"But that's the strange part," Pamela told him. "I didn't want to trade with anyone. As soon as they put me in the sack I felt that I belonged there."

"Weren't you scared?" Honor asked.

"No," said Pamela. "The sack was coated inside with enough Planet Safe to tranquilize me. I curled up in the darkness and I felt calm, and as the drug began to work I felt relieved and even happy. I felt as though I were floating. One memory after another returned to me. . . ."

"But how? Weren't you memory-sick?" asked Will. "With that much Planet Safe you'd forget everything."

"I was forgetting the recent past," said Pamela, "but all the old times were coming back to me. I saw all the pieces of my life; it was like watching my life underwater. I saw you, Honor. And you," she said to Will. "Quintilian. I saw our kites up in the sky. I saw that little cat," she told Honor, "the one that jumped when we found the drawing book. I saw the Northern Islands and the light there in winter, the way the sun melted in the sky. I saw our wooden boat and felt the slosh of water in the bottom. I could see the chipped paint on our boat. Do you remember the color?"

Will shook his head.

"Blue. I remembered the name of our boat. Do you remember what we called her?"

"No," said Will.

Pamela laughed. "We called the boat *Shamela*. Wasn't that a funny name?"

"You remembered all those things?" asked Mrs. Pratt.

"Oh, it was lovely. Delicious. I remembered things I haven't thought about in years. All those times in the past came back to me, but they began rushing faster and faster. They began to blur. The boat and the water and the kites in the sky began to spin and I felt lighter and lighter. Soon the mail carriers were lifting me from the sack and setting me down on the ground."

"Were you in pain?" Will asked.

"No," said Pamela, "nothing hurt me, not even the needle tattooing the number on my arm."

"Didn't you want to run away?" asked Honor.

"Even if I'd wanted to, I had no control over my body. My legs wouldn't carry me," her mother said. "I grew lighter and lighter as the tranquilizer wore off. Then they fed me and gave me mineral water to drink."

"Orderlies consume much stronger food and drink than the rest of us," Mr. Pratt said. "Ordinary people only lose their long-term memories—of their childhoods, their parents, their first loves—but they keep their short-term memories. They're up-to-date within five years. I always thought orderlies lost their memories altogether."

"They lose the recent past and dream of long ago," said Pamela. "The longer orderlies work, the less they remember of themselves or where they were when they were taken. Eventually all they have is fragments of their early lives. They start dreaming all the time. It's like living in a trance."

"If you were in a trance, how did you remember me?" Honor asked.

Pamela thought for a moment. "You were always in my dream," she said. "You came back to me as you were in the

Northern Islands. In the bakery you didn't look the same as the little girl that I remembered, but I knew you must be Honor, because you looked directly at me."

"So your eyes worked," said Honor.

"Orderlies can see what's right in front of them. And they can see faces too," said Pamela. "But no one ever looks."

"What else did you remember?" Will asked Pamela.

She sifted the white sand through her fingers. "I remember the other beach," she said.

And for a moment Honor could remember too. She could remember the smooth pebbles on the beach in the Northern Islands and the gold light and the cold water. And she could almost remember something else. She could almost touch the memory; she wanted to, but she only felt the edge of it.

"Did you remember all the constellations?" Will asked Pamela. "Could you still find them when you looked at the stars?"

"No," Pamela said. "I never looked at the sky."

Mr. Pratt set his battered box on the sand. He opened the lid and unpacked something wrapped in scarves and soft cloth. It was a strange musical instrument of satiny smooth wood. The instrument had a body shaped like a teardrop, a long thin neck, and many strings. Honor counted fifteen. When Mr. Pratt plucked the strings, they rang softly. He turned pegs to tune each one, and as he tested the strings, Honor heard their sound amplified by the rounded body of the instrument.

"What is it?" she asked.

"This is a lute," Mr. Pratt told her. His left hand played on the instrument's neck as his right hand plucked. "Listen."

They lay on their backs in the sand and listened. Mr. Pratt played music that sounded like sweet rain falling and then like fairy tales. Like princesses running up and down secret staircases. He played music that sounded like dances and then like the memory of those dances, wistful recollections of times past.

"Why is the lute so sad?" Honor asked when Mr. Pratt finished playing.

Mr. Pratt smiled. "The lute isn't sad. The music was. I was playing a song in a minor key."

Honor was surprised. She went to music class three times a week, but she had never heard of a minor key. "We only learn happy songs," she said.

"Oh, you've been missing out," said Mr. Pratt as his fingers played on.

There was no other sound in the world like the sound of the lute mixed with the shushing waves. The music was wistful and quiet, ancient music with ancient patterns, sometimes expected and sometimes Unpredictable. Honor lay between her parents, and as they listened, they looked up at the stars. There were so many they seemed like silver dust. So many more stars than Honor remembered.

SEVEN

BEFORE DAWN, THEY BRUSHED THE SAND OFF AS BEST THEY could and walked back into the trees. They followed Mr. Pratt on a path skirting the shore to a cover where the Thompsons were waiting. They rushed to Pamela and to Honor. They wanted to touch Pamela and talk to her. She seemed almost like a dream to them. They had to know that she was real. And they had to ask Honor about Helix. If only there had been more time. The sky was brightening. Soon the sun would rise.

Mr. Thompson and Mr. Pratt and Honor's father walked back into the forest. When they returned, they dragged a boat through the sea grapes onto the sand. The boat was an outrigger canoe, and it was made of hollowed-out logs and rigged with the sinew of plants. In the hull of the canoe the Thompsons had hidden food and water. They also had new clothes for Pamela and Will. Mrs. Thompson gave Pamela a hat to protect her bald head from the sun.

Together they all pushed the boat into the shallow water. Mr. Pratt held it there, ready to sail.

"How will we all fit?" asked Honor.

"We aren't all going," said Mr. Pratt. "Just the Thompsons and your parents."

"But what about me?" asked Honor.

Her mother wrapped her arm around her.

"Why can't I go with you?" she pleaded.

"Who will watch Quintilian?" asked her mother.

Honor bowed her head, ashamed she had forgotten him. "But couldn't we take him too? And Helix? We could get them and—"

"You know it's not safe to get them," said her father. "And where we're going is not for children."

"We don't know if we'll succeed," her mother said.

"Other people have tried to take the Weather Station," Mr. Thompson told Honor.

"And what happened to them?" Honor demanded, holding on to her mother.

"No one knows," said Will.

"Then you can't go," Honor said. "I won't let you."

"We have to go. It's a day's sailing at least. Maybe two."

"How is it safe for me to stay here?" Honor demanded. "They'll send Retrievers after me. You know they will."

"We aren't going to let Retrievers find you," Will said. "You'll go back to school first."

"I can't go back there."

"You have to," said Will.

"We'll come for you, just like you came for me," Pamela promised.

"If we succeed, it won't be long," Will said. "Watch the sky and you'll know if we have the Weather Station."

"But you might not succeed," Honor said.

"We have to try," said Will. "We have to try, even if we might fail."

"And what will happen then?"

"Then you'll be at school," said Pamela. "You'll think about what to do next. You'll take care of your brother."

"We named you Honor for a reason," Will said.

EIGHT

"THIS IS WHERE I'LL LEAVE YOU," SAID MR. PRATT. HE HAD guided Honor back over the mountain to the edge of the Old Colony School's Model Forest. "You remember what your parents said."

Honor nodded.

"All right, then. Good-bye. No crying," Mr. Pratt added.

"I'm not."

Mr. Pratt looked hard at Honor and cleared his throat. Then he left her alone.

Garden orderlies were repairing damage from the storm, carting off debris and wheeling in new plants. Honor saw one orderly kneeling, planting new ferns, and another with a whole cart of potted orchids. He transplanted each into a special niche in a rock or on a tree. Honor hadn't understood before how tame the Model Forest was or how organized, with its pretty orchids hanging from every rock and tree. The real forest had no orderlies to keep it neat. The real forest was thick and dark and overgrown, not pretty; it was frightening—and also beautiful.

She came to a bench and lay down. She closed her eyes and dreamed of her parents and Helix's parents sailing out on the blue ocean. She imagined the clear warm night and her mother navigating by the stars.

Screams woke her. She started up to find Helena and Hortense shrieking in terror at the sight of her.

"Heloise!" Hortense exclaimed. "What happened to you?"

Helena didn't say a word. She ran as fast as she could to call for help.

Orderlies arrived in minutes to pick up Honor. A pair of them scooped her up and raced off with her down the path toward school. Familiar buildings flashed by, but they were all in ruins. Walls weren't just cracked; they'd crumbled. The vegetable gardens were soupy mud, the greenhouses piles of shattered glass. Monkeypod trees had been torn up by the roots, upended. Everywhere orderlies were digging, sweeping, raking, carting away more rubbish. Everywhere Honor heard the sound of hammers and saws. She smelled new lumber. Carpenters were erecting rough new wood buildings. The orderlies carried Honor into one of these. She saw a row of beds and a familiar desk. The orderlies had brought her straight to the infirmary.

"Heloise," gasped Nurse Applebee. "Look at you. Your uniform. Your hair!"

Honor looked down at herself. Her shirt was torn, her identity card missing. Her skirt was caked with mud.

Nurse Applebee looked almost as frightened as Hortense. "We almost gave you up for lost."

Honor was taken to the infirmary bathroom. Nurse Applebee gave Honor a bar of soap and a bottle of shampoo and a white towel and a fresh new uniform. Then she left Honor to wash herself.

When Honor emerged from the bathroom, she was pink and clean. Her fingers were wrinkled because she had enjoyed soaking so much. She had to sit on a low chair while Nurse Applebee combed the tangles out of her hair and searched for nits. The nurse was afraid that Honor was infested with lice.

There were no lice in Honor's hair, and so Nurse Applebee did not cut it off. She took Honor instead to rest in a clean infirmary bed and answer questions for an accident report.

"Did you leave the shelter during the storm?" the nurse asked.

"I don't know," Honor said.

"What happened to you?"

"I don't know," Honor said.

"Did you leave school grounds?"

"I don't know."

"Did you try to run away?"

"I don't know."

"Are you telling me the truth?"

"I think so," Honor murmured. The warm bath had made her so sleepy she could barely keep her eyes open. She wanted to say she was too tired to lie properly, but she knew better.

• • •

When she woke up, she had no idea how much time had passed. Nurse Applebee and Miss Blessing were sitting by her side.

"Welcome home," said Miss Blessing in her soft sweet voice. "We are thankful you are back with us."

Dazed and sleepy, Honor stared at Miss Blessing.

"What do you say?" Miss Blessing asked.

Honor wasn't sure. "I'm thankful," she said.

This seemed satisfactory, because Miss Blessing said, "We have a visitor for you."

Then Nurse Applebee opened the door and Quintilian rushed in and threw himself onto Honor's bed.

Honor dared not say anything in front of Nurse Applebee and Miss Blessing, but she smiled.

"Do you recognize this boy?" asked Nurse Applebee.

"Yes," said Honor.

"What is his name?"

"Quintilian," Honor said dutifully.

"And where are we now?"

"The infirmary," said Honor.

"And where have you been for the past four nights?"

"I don't know," said Honor.

"Where were you on the night of the storm?" Miss Blessing asked.

"What storm?" Honor asked, and she glanced at Quintilian.

"Would you like to tell about the storm?" Miss Blessing asked Quintilian.

"We had some rain," said Quintilian.

"Is that all?"

"Wind."

"Could you elaborate?"

"There was no power," Quintilian said. "No power whatsoever." He grinned. "It was a pretty good storm."

Miss Blessing's smile faded. "Tell Honor what happened to you."

"I got lost in the forest," Quintilian said.

"Did you get lost, or did you attempt to run away?"

"Actually," said Quintilian, "I got lost and then me and Helix both got lost, but searchers found us."

"That is Accurate," said Miss Blessing.

Honor lay still, afraid to react to what Quintilian said.

"Tell us why," Miss Blessing said gently.

"To find Mommy and Daddy," said Quintilian.

"And did you find them?" asked Miss Blessing.

"No," said Quintilian.

"And why is that?"

"Because they are no more," Quintilian said sweetly, and he bowed his head.

Only Honor, lying in bed, could see the little smile on Quintilian's downcast face. She knew he didn't believe for a second that his mommy and daddy were really gone.

"Now." Miss Blessing turned to Honor. "Surely you remember the storm?"

Honor shook her head. "I was asleep," she said. "There was no storm. I was asleep and I was dreaming."

"What did you dream, dear?" asked Nurse Applebee.

Honor pretended to search her memory. "I dreamed that I

traveled to a new country," she said. "With an Emerald City and—"

She sensed Quintilian about to laugh, and so she stopped.

"This is no joke," said Miss Blessing. "This is nothing to joke about." Her voice was cold enough to make Honor shiver. The sweetness in her voice drained away. She lifted her silver whistle to her lips and blew. "Take her," she told the two orderlies who appeared.

Then Honor knew this was the end. She knew she was gone, and it was so strange—just as her mother said, she could see herself disappearing. She could hear Quintilian's screams. She shut her eyes and allowed her body to relax. She drooped like a rag doll as the orderlies carried her aloft. She knew soon she would be packed into a sack. A truck would take her away. She'd feel cold tranquilizers in her veins.

She heard a tiny bell, and double doors opened before her into a cavernous space. The orderlies dropped her in a heap on the floor. The air was cool, the room big and dark. Honor saw bookcases and drawers, shadowy cabinets and storage containers. Miss Tuttle stood before her in the back room of the library.

"Yes," said Miss Tuttle. "Fighters go in here."

"I'm not a fighter," Honor blurted out.

"I beg to differ," said Miss Tuttle and she gazed at Honor with her golden eyes.

"What am I here for?" Honor asked.

"You know what you're here for," Miss Tuttle said. "You're here for Persuasive Reasoning and Positive Reinforcement."

Honor's heart was pounding. She remembered Mr. Pratt telling her parents to take care of their overdue notices or face

Positive Reinforcement. She remembered how he'd opened his mouth and said, *Ever notice my false teeth?* "Please don't hurt me," she begged.

Miss Tuttle smiled, but said nothing.

The silence in the room grew and grew until Honor could bear it no longer. "What do you want? What do you want me to do?"

"Sit in the chair," said Miss Tuttle, pointing to an old wooden chair with a desk attached to the arm.

Honor scrambled to her feet and sat in the chair.

"Now," said Miss Tuttle. "What would you like to say?"

"Nothing," said Honor.

"Nothing?" Miss Tuttle looked amused. "Nothing comes of nothing. Try again."

Honor ducked her head.

"Look at me," said Miss Tuttle. "What would you like to say?"

"I don't know," Honor whispered.

"The truth will set you free," said Miss Tuttle. "Why did you leave school?"

"I got lost," said Honor.

Miss Tuttle took a silver dart from the pocket of her cardigan sweater. She uncapped the dart and held it close to Honor's face. The tip was needle sharp. "I could numb you," she said, "but I'd rather not."

Honor took a breath. She knew she could not escape. She had no weapon. What could she do? Her parents were sailing for Island 364, and if Miss Tuttle heard about it first, she'd sound the alarm. She'd stop them.

"Tell me why you went into the woods," said Miss Tuttle in her odd way. "Tell me where you went and why you lived there."

"I don't know why I went," Honor protested.

"You know exactly why you went," said Miss Tuttle. "And so do I."

"If you know, then why are you asking me?" said Honor.

"I want to hear it in your own words," said the librarian. "Would you like to write it down? Take this pen." Honor flinched. Miss Tuttle threw a black pen just as she would throw a dart. In that moment the memory returned to her. The memory of Retrievers standing on a pebbled beach. The water cold in the Northern Islands. Her mother's scream. A silver dart sticking in Honor's bare thigh. She caught her breath.

"Here is paper." Miss Tuttle placed a small white piece of paper on the desk attached to Honor's chair. "Go on," she said, when she saw Honor hesitate.

"But this is a— "

"Turn it over and write on the back," said Miss Tuttle. "Reduce, recycle, and reuse."

Honor could not stop staring at the printed words before her.

1. *Cultivate your own fruit trees and eat fresh fruit each day.*
2. *Find dark places and study the night sky.*
3. *Try to remember something new each day . . .*

"This is a leaflet," Honor said.

"True," said Miss Tuttle.

"How do you have a leaflet in the library? How do you collect leaflets when they're Not Allowed?"

"I don't collect them," said Miss Tuttle. "I write them."

Honor was shivering. Miss Tuttle had frightened her before, but now Honor felt as though the world were coming to an end.

"Yes," said Miss Tuttle. "I am the Forecaster you may have heard about."

"You are not," whispered Honor. "You can't be."

"Why?" asked Miss Tuttle. "Because you've heard the Forecaster is a madman? Because you think the Forecaster is a man who runs through the City at night scattering leaflets on the streets? Because you think the Forecaster works for the Corporation to entrap Partisans? Is that it? Do you think I am in fact a committee in an office? Flattering, but no. I am the Forecaster. I am she."

Honor shook her head. If Miss Tuttle was the Forecaster, then there was no hope. If she wrote the leaflets, then there would be no revolution, only scraps of paper in the recycling plant. Poetry and pieces of books. "Not you," she said.

Miss Tuttle's eyes flashed with anger. "Who else might I be?"

"You aren't a prophet. You work for the Corporation like everybody else."

"The revolution starts within," said Miss Tuttle.

"You cut up books. . . ."

"I do my job," Miss Tuttle said.

"You hide maps."

"Lend them when they're needed," Miss Tuttle said. "How do you think your friend got his?"

"Helix stole it," Honor said.

"Yes, and how did he find that map? I left it on my desk for him."

For a moment, Honor couldn't speak. "You're Unpredictable," she said at last.

"Extremely," Miss Tuttle said.

"Why do you work here cutting everything sad out of the books? Why do you take out everything about the seasons?" pressed Honor. "Why are you holding a tranquilizing dart if you are the Forecaster?"

"Even prophets need a day job," Miss Tuttle said drily. "I'll continue to do mine until the revolution starts or I get taken. Whichever comes first. Tell me where your mother is now."

Honor shook her head.

"Tell me your parents have gone to take the Weather Station."

Again, Honor refused to speak.

"I was the one who instructed them to take it," Miss Tuttle said. "I was the one who told them to send you back to school. I was the one who promised to protect you."

"You saw them?" Honor asked. "You spoke to them?"

"No. I sent a letter with a messenger named Michael Pratt. I think you know him."

"Yes," said Honor.

"I think you know the Partisan song as well?"

Honor shook her head.

Again, Miss Tuttle smiled her small tight smile. "You knew it but you didn't know you knew it." She began to sing in a light, dry voice: "*Over the river and through the wood to grandmother's house we go . . .* I think you sang that with your parents once."

"It's just an old song," Honor said.

"Oh, there are no old songs anymore," said Miss Tuttle. "The old ones are long gone, except for those that we reuse."

"How do you reuse a song?"

"You understand it in a new way," said Miss Tuttle. "That old song is about the revolution. We sing it to remember that we'll travel through the forest and cross the river to Earth Mother's house and take Her."

"When will that happen?" Honor asked.

"It's beginning to happen now," Miss Tuttle said. "It will be a long battle, and we may well lose, but we've begun. Now, write your confession on that little piece of paper and I'll send you off to bed. Then we'll see what the world looks like in the morning."

Honor was shocked. "I'm not going to confess anything," she told Miss Tuttle. "How can you say that you'll protect me and then ask me to write my own confession?"

"Oh, I'll need to turn in my paperwork," said Miss Tuttle. "I'll need a confession for your file. Copy this paragraph here." She handed Honor a leaf ripped from an ancient book. "This section is about going into the forest. Where I Lived, and What I Lived For. Paragraph fifteen, please. Start here. *We must learn to reawaken and keep ourselves awake, not by mechanical aids, but by infinite expectation of the dawn . . .*"

Half an hour later, two orderlies brought Honor back to the infirmary. She kept her eyes closed as they tossed her onto her bed.

She tried to rest quietly that night as Miss Tuttle had instructed her. She tried to breathe deeply and pretend she was asleep, but her heart raced within her. All night she watched the gap between the infirmary's window shade and the window. She was waiting for the dawn.

She heard a scuffling, whispering noise outside the infirmary door.

"Is she here?"

"Shh. I told you to be quiet."

Honor sat up in bed. She could not open the door to her room because it was locked from the outside. She heard the key turn in the lock and for a moment she was frightened. She pulled the covers up to her chin.

"Who is it?" she whispered into the darkness.

"It's me." Quintilian ran toward her and scrambled up onto the bed. "Helix stole the key."

"Are you all right?" Helix asked Honor. "They said you went to see Miss Tuttle."

"Who's they?"

"Mrs. Edwards. What did Tuttle do to you?" He was straining to see her in the dark.

"I'm all right," said Honor. "She didn't hurt me."

"Where's Mommy and Daddy?" demanded Quintilian.

"I found them," said Honor. She turned to Helix. "And your parents too."

"How did you? What happened? Did you get to the Barracks?" Helix couldn't ask the questions fast enough.

"Shh. Listen, and I'll tell you," said Honor.

Helix and Quintilian sat at the foot of the bed while she told the story.

"You could have shot all four watchtowers at once," said Helix, "if you'd each had a bow and arrows."

"But we didn't," Honor said. "We only had mine."

"You could have set smoke bombs or thrown explosives to confuse the orderlies," Helix said. "A smoke bomb in each Barracks to make them run outside."

"We'd have been trampled," Honor said. "You don't know how many there were."

"I wish I'd been there with you," Helix whispered so only Honor could hear.

"You have to be brave," said Quintilian. "You have to be strong."

Honor smiled at this. She realized this was what Helix had told him while she was gone.

A screaming siren pierced the darkness. Terrified, Quintilian buried his head in Honor's lap. Helix jumped off the bed and opened the shade. Outside, security orderlies were racing to all the buildings. Was this a new storm? The deep colors of the night were gone. The overlay of moon and stars had vanished, but the pale clear colors of day had not replaced them. The sky was striped in a grid pattern with bars of color. *Watch the sky.* Honor's parents were sending their message.

"They got the Weather Station!" Honor shouted to Helix.

The emergency broadcast system announced, "We are experiencing technical difficulties. Please stand by." Over and over the fuzzy voice announced, "We are experiencing technical difficulties. Please stand by."

Honor and Helix laughed and laughed. Quintilian bounced on the bed, up and down.

Honor heard children shrieking. From the infirmary window she could see teachers rounding up students to take them to shelters. The others didn't know. They didn't yet know. And now Nurse Applebee burst through the door. "What are the . . . How did you . . . ?" she asked Helix and Quintilian. "Visiting the infirmary is not . . ."

Miss Blessing ran through the door with Honor's written statement in her hand.

"Heloise," Miss Blessing said, "what is the meaning of this? I have opened your file . . . I am . . . Helix? Quintilian? What are you doing here?" Miss Blessing's hair was mussed. She'd misbuttoned her cardigan sweater.

"Draw the shade! Draw the shade!" Nurse Applebee cried. For the stripes in the sky had faded, overwhelmed by an unfiltered dawn. The sun was fiery orange. Apricot. Clouds flamed gold all the way to the ground. Orderlies and children raced for shelter. They shielded their eyes with their hands.

Miss Blessing yanked down the shade, but the canvas glowed orange, lit from behind.

"You are part of this," Miss Blessing told Honor. "And you will take responsibility for what you have done."

"Come to the shelter," Nurse Applebee urged them in her breathy voice. "It's not safe; the light will blind us." She was already halfway out the door.

"You'll come with me," Miss Blessing told Honor, Helix,

and Quintilian. Nurse Applebee was running away, but Miss Blessing ignored her and blew her whistle. No orderlies arrived. The emergency sirens drowned out every other sound. Miss Blessing blew her whistle again. Nothing happened. "Come, Heloise," she said.

But Honor didn't move.

"Come along, Heloise."

"Who's Heloise?" Honor asked.

"*You* are Heloise," said Miss Blessing.

"I don't know anyone named Heloise," said Honor.

"You are Heloise," Miss Blessing repeated.

"I don't think so," said Honor.

"I know so," said Miss Blessing, and she took Honor by the arm. "Come to the shelter."

"No," said Honor.

"We don't have time for this. Come, Heloise." Miss Blessing's voice was tense.

"She's Honor," Quintilian said.

"He's right," said Helix.

"You see?" said Honor.

"Quiet!" Miss Blessing screamed.

Instinctively, Quintilian shrank back from Miss Blessing. Protectively, Helix moved closer to Honor. They had never heard Miss Blessing scream.

Miss Blessing took a breath. She steadied herself. "You will come with me," she said between her teeth. "You will tell me the truth. You'll tell me where you've been."

"I don't remember," Honor said.

"You'll tell me what you've done."

"I don't remember," Honor said.

"You will remember exactly who you are."

"I know who I am," Honor said.

Miss Blessing's blue eyes widened in alarm.

You are afraid of me, Honor thought. *You are afraid of what I might do. I am Unpredictable and the world is Unpredictable as well. The dawn is many colors, not just one.* But she did not say this. Instead she smiled and said sweetly to Miss Blessing, "My name is Honor. Who are you?"

I am grateful to the Radcliffe Institute for Advanced Study for the fellowship year in which I wrote this book.